"What cou
to

There was challenge in McHugh's voice,
Yet she knew she loved him, needed him as he
could never need her.

Even worse, she could not rid herself of the memory of
the sensations he'd evoked. Her thoughts kept returning
there, wanting more, *needing* more, and knowing
she could never submit to such intimacies again
if they did not come from him.

She lifted her chin in defiance, daring him to carry
out his threat, both dreading and needing the answer
to her question. *What did he mean to do?*

McHugh closed the remaining distance between
them and pulled her roughly against him. "Damn it!
You know what I want, Afton. You've always known,
and you've used it against me."

She sighed. "How could I when I wanted it, too?"

* * *

The Rake's Revenge
Harlequin Historical #731—December 2004

Praise for Gail Ranstrom

Saving Sarah
"Gail Ranstrom has written a unique story with
several twists that work within the confines of
Regency England…. If Ranstrom's first book
showed promise, then *Saving Sarah* is
when Ranstrom comes of age."
—*The Romance Reader*

A Wild Justice
"Gail Ranstrom certainly has both
writing talent and original ideas."
—*The Romance Reader*

THE RAKE'S REVENGE

GAIL RANSTROM

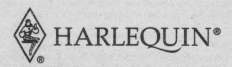

HARLEQUIN®

TORONTO • NEW YORK • LONDON
AMSTERDAM • PARIS • SYDNEY • HAMBURG
STOCKHOLM • ATHENS • TOKYO • MILAN • MADRID
PRAGUE • WARSAW • BUDAPEST • AUCKLAND

ISBN 0-373-29331-3

THE RAKE'S REVENGE

Copyright © 2004 by Gail Ranstrom

This edition published by arrangement with Harlequin Books S.A.

® and TM are trademarks of the publisher. Trademarks indicated with
® are registered in the United States Patent and Trademark Office, the
Canadian Trade Marks Office and in other countries.

www.eHarlequin.com

Printed in U.S.A.

Please address questions and book requests to:
Harlequin Reader Service
U.S.: 3010 Walden Ave., P.O. Box 1325, Buffalo, NY 14269
Canadian: P.O. Box 609, Fort Erie, Ont. L2A 5X3

For Natalie, Jay and Katie, the three best things that
ever happened to me. Thank you for being my best
friends and my biggest fans. I love you
more than words can ever say.

A grateful nod to the bridge ladies
of Missoula, Montana: Shari L., Linda K., Nancy G.,
Sherry S., Nancy N., Linda C. and Judy S.
Your strength, kindness and friendship have been
an inspiration. Thank you for being with me
through the darkest times and the brightest.

And, of course, the Wednesday League—
Margaret, Cynthia and Rosanne.

Prologue

London, December 3, 1818

"Dead? Madame Zoe is *dead?*"

Nodding, Afton Lovejoy paced her aunt Grace's parlor in wide circles and fought the lump in her throat. There was worse to come, but the Wednesday League, the group of five intrepid ladies who secretly obtained justice for wronged women, did not know that yet.

"When?" Annica Sinclair, Lady Auberville, blinked her deep green eyes and set her teacup aside.

"Yesterday morning. I cannot be certain how long she lay there, but 'twas then that I found her. She...she—" Afton paused to brace herself against the rising pain. She couldn't give way to it. If she did, she'd never stop crying.

"Sit down, dear," her aunt Grace said, waiting until Afton perched on the edge of a chair before continuing. "Madame Zoe was still alive when Afton arrived at her salon above La Meilleure Robe. She expired in Afton's arms. Afton went downstairs to Madame Marie, and Marie, knowing Afton is my niece, sent for me."

"How perfectly awful for you, Afton," Lady Sarah Travis gasped. "Had she been ill?"

"'Twas murder," Afton announced. "There were wounds on her temple and abdomen that had bled profusely, and bruises around her throat. Her assailant must have thought she was dead when he left."

Charity Wardlow's cup rattled in the saucer and she put it down before it could spill. "I always come over queer when there is a murder. Oh, dear—the gossip this will create! The ton's premier fortune-teller *dead* at the hand of a murderer."

"The ton must not find out, Charity. At least, not yet," Grace said.

"But the constabulary will report—"

Grace shook her head. "They will report nothing. We did not tell them. Everyone believed Madame Zoe was just another French émigré—a woman who lived on the fringe of society, a woman of little consequence. And that belief is preferable to the truth."

"What *is* the truth?" Lady Annica asked, leaning forward.

Grace hesitated only a moment before replying. "That Madame Zoe was, in fact, an English gentlewoman reduced to earning a living in the only way open to her, yet compelled to hide her identity to spare her family shame."

The heat of a blush stole up Afton's cheeks. How utterly humiliating it was to be the proverbial "poor relations." And how scandalous to admit your family's living was made by swindling the ton.

"You knew her? Personally?" Sarah asked.

"She was Henrietta Lovejoy," Grace admitted. "Afton's maiden aunt on her father's side."

There was a finality to hearing those words spoken aloud that Afton had been able to deny until this very minute. Auntie Hen was gone. Dead. Murdered. Buried secretly in a convent garden. Afton glanced up to see all eyes upon her. The desolation of loss spilled tears over her lashes and down her cheeks. She dashed them away with an impatient flick. Later. She'd deal with the pain later.

"How dreadful for you, Afton, and for you, Grace." Annica stood to give them each a warm hug. "But, if you did not call the authorities…" The question hung in the air.

"We waited until dark and then hired a dray to take Henrietta's b—remains to the nuns at St. Ann's. Under the guise of a nun, she was buried privately with due respect and consideration this morning," Grace explained. "Only Afton and I were present."

Charity leaned forward in her chair. "What of her friends and family? There will be questions."

"I fear not, Charity," Grace said with a little sigh. "Hen did not mix in London society, and she lost touch with her friends in Wiltshire long ago. She said that was the only way to maintain her anonymity as Madame Zoe. Five years as Madame Zoe, and only Madame Marie, Afton and I knew her true identity."

Lifting her chin with resolution, Afton said, "I have been thinking what I can do to make this right. How to…to—"

"Obtain justice for your aunt?" Annica guessed.

Afton nodded and braced herself for a storm of protest. Here, at last, was the crux of the matter. "The killer cannot be certain that Auntie Hen is dead, since she was still alive when I found her. I intend to pose as her and flush him out."

"What! No! You cannot!" The ladies spoke as one.

Annica and Sarah exchanged concerned glances. Afton knew they had both conducted investigations with near-dire consequences, barely escaping with their lives.

"Madame Zoe was the foremost fortune-teller in London. Why, anyone of consequence has been to her salon. How can you hope to deceive the entire ton?" Sarah asked.

Afton sighed. "Auntie Hen and I both learned to read tarot cards from a gypsy camped on the Lovejoy estate one rainy summer. I scoffed, but the crone told me that magic was real and that I would learn that someday,'' she said. '''Twas just a parlor game then, a lark, but 'twas great good fun, and I still remember what each of the cards mean. I intend to wear Auntie Hen's disguise of widow's weeds and veils, and speak in a low, damaged voice with a French accent. Sooner or later, the murderer will have to return.''

''To *kill* you,'' Charity said. '''Tis too dangerous. He will have the advantage because he knows that Zoe can identify him. But *you* will not know *him.* Oh, if we only knew more!''

Afton looked down at her closed fist. ''There *is* more. I found this on the floor beside her.'' She opened her hand to reveal a black onyx raven with a small diamond eye, mounted on a gold stickpin. The ladies leaned over her hand to study the object.

''Stunning,'' Annica declared. ''Quite valuable, unless I miss my guess. The murderer will be looking for Zoe, but he will also be looking for his lost pin.''

''I still cannot fathom how he gained entry,'' Charity ventured. ''I thought one was required to make an appointment with Madame Zoe through her factor. A man named Mr. Evans.''

''Auntie Hen had no appointments that night. The murderer either found her at her salon by chance, or stalked her until she was alone.'' Afton's voice tightened with anger.

Grace tucked a single stray strand of chestnut hair back into place and nodded. ''We hope the murderer will be so mystified by Zoe's survival that he will proceed with extreme caution. At the very least he will not be looking for Miss Afton Lovejoy from Little Upton, Wiltshire. But there will be undeniable danger when Afton is posing as Zoe in the salon above Madame Marie's dress shop. Perhaps one of us should hide in the little dressing room whenever Afton is there.''

"I know!" Charity exclaimed. "We shall ask Mr. Renquist to install a bell rope in Zoe's salon that rings in La Meilleure Robe's sewing room downstairs. Then Afton could ring for help if something should go awry."

Afton recalled that Mr. Renquist, Madame Marie's husband, was the Wednesday League's chief investigator and had a legion of Bow Street Runners at his disposal. She was comforted by the thought of having him within call. She might yet live through this affair.

Lady Annica leaned forward. "If you insist upon doing this, Afton, you will have our full support and assistance. I shall spread the story that Madame Zoe had an accident and cannot recall anything because of an injury to her head. Perhaps that will reassure the murderer that 'Madame Zoe' will not name him."

"Still, I am uneasy...." Grace began. "Very well, but only until the end of the month, Afton. After that, we shall have to inform the authorities. This sort of villainy cannot go unreported."

Afton took a deep breath. It was both more and less than she had hoped for—more help, less time. Thus, there was no time to lose. "I shall begin at once."

Chapter One

London, December 12, 1818

Could there be any greater contrast between these smells and sounds and the dank Moorish dungeon he had so recently escaped? Lord Robert McHugh, fourth earl of Glenross, shrugged out of his greatcoat and handed it to a waiting footman. The scent of evergreens mixed with spicy canapés and hot mulled wine wafted through the air. The soft strains of an orchestra and polite conversation carried from an adjacent room. Beside him, Lord Ethan Travis kept up a discourse on the many reasons Rob should reconsider attending this soiree tonight.

"You are not ready for this, McHugh. You are only a fortnight back in London. Give yourself more time before—"

"No time to spare, Travis," he said. "It ran out in Algiers."

"You need to reacquaint yourself with society. If you rush in where angels fear to tread—"

"Do you think society is not ready for me?" Rob could not help smiling at his friend's concern.

Ethan shot him an exasperated look. "I'd find a barber,

were I you. Your locks are beyond Byronic. And your emotions are as raw as a winter day. Diplomacy has never been your strong suit. Under the circumstances, no one could fault you, but why put yourself through the whispers, the pity...."

Pity? He'd have to squelch that. He'd rather be hated than pitied. "Why the concern, Ethan? The Foreign Office has kept me in isolation since my return. Two blasted weeks of picking my brains for any scrap of information I managed to gather during my...ah, residence at the Dey's palace. It is too early for you to have had complaints of me."

"That is what I am trying to forestall."

"Has anyone complained of my manners?" he asked.

"Your manners, when you choose, are impeccable, Rob. Not so your reputation. And you've done little to mend it. Your single-mindedness and complete lack of a conscience when pursuing a goal are legendary. But I still wouldn't be ready to toast debutantes and make polite conversation had I been through what you have the past few years, and worse these last six months."

Rob pushed the ache of memories back into the dark recesses of his mind. He couldn't allow his demons to divert him from his mission tonight. "Your concern is unnecessary, Ethan."

"I know you want to find this 'Madame Zoe' person and bring her down, but this is not the time for it, Rob."

"None better," he countered. "But have no fear. I shan't make a scene. To the contrary, I mean to keep my intentions secret. Bad hunting strategy to sound the horn and send the fox to ground."

Ethan cleared his throat. "Mrs. Forbush is my wife's close personal friend. She is introducing her niece, Miss Dianthe Lovejoy, to society tonight. She would be devastated if anything should go wrong."

"You regret obtaining the invitation for me?" he asked. "What could possibly go wrong?"

"Good God, McHugh. Can you be serious?"

Rob gave a grim laugh. "Did the Foreign Office ask you to watch me? You sound just like Lord Kilgrew. He urged me to take some time before resuming my...obligations." Rob tugged at the crisp curls at the back of his neck and permitted himself a small sigh. He supposed Ethan was right about one thing—he *should* have gotten a haircut.

But Ethan Travis needn't have worried. Rob's incarceration in Algiers had given him time to contain his cold fury at the forces that had set him on this path. Without that control, he'd be burning a path through London society in pursuit of the information he sought.

Ethan sprang a surprise of his own. "Your brother, now," he said in an obvious attempt to turn Rob's attention to a less volatile subject, "makes up for your social inadequacies. He's been making an impression on London society since arriving six weeks ago. Did you know he's staying at Limmer's?"

"Douglas is in London?" This *was* a surprise. The Foreign Office had permitted no news of the outside world during Rob's two-week interrogation.

Ethan nodded. "Your solicitor sent for him when the news reached us that the Dey had sentenced you to death, and that you...would not be coming back."

"Hope he's not squandering his inheritance." Rob grinned. "Does he know that I'm alive?"

"Not yet. But my note should be catching up to him within the hour. Be warned—he's got himself engaged."

"Has he now? In a month? That was quick work."

"You'll like her, Rob. 'Tis the Barlow girl. Do you recall Beatrice?"

Rob nodded as they entered the Forbush ballroom. If memory served, Beatrice "Bebe" Barlow was a pretty, petite blonde of about twenty-one years or so. She had engaged his attention for about two minutes before he realized she was quite ordinary—even a little flighty. That soft vagueness would appeal to Douglas, though, and Rob wished his brother well.

He noted the short hush that fell over the assembly, followed by looks of pity or common curiosity, as he entered. It would appear the news of the outcome of his mission and his escape had reached the ton even before he had. A lightning flash did not strike with the speed of London gossip. What a pity the Foreign Office could not harness that force for foreign intelligence-gathering.

He paused near the fireplace to reconnoiter. He could never enter a room without scanning it for potential hazards, enemies or traps, or identifying exits and escapes—a result of having been too long with the Foreign Office, and too long in a foreign prison. Ethan gave him a nod of support before going on alone to find his wife.

And there across the room, engaged in conversation with a stunning woman with reddish-blond hair in a pink gown, was his hostess, Mrs. Grace Forbush, a beautiful widow in her early thirties—and the very person to aid him in his quest. Mrs. Forbush, with her popular Friday afternoon salons, knew all that went on in the ton. All that mattered, that is. He assumed a pleasant smile and his best society manners, and went forward to do battle.

Grace lowered her voice to a whisper. "I am afraid for you, Afton. You have only a little more than two weeks. If you continue to pose as Madame Zoe after that, I fear that *we* might lose *you*."

"I cannot stop now, Aunt Grace. I've lost Mama and Papa, and Auntie Hen," Afton whispered back. Her heart caught in her throat as she thought of all that was at stake. "I cannot lose anyone else. I do not think I'd survive it."

She glanced to the dance floor, where her younger sister, Dianthe, waltzed by with an eligible young baron. Her blond hair shone in the candlelight and her pale blue gown was a perfect foil for her china-blue eyes. By any standard, Dianthe was an uncommon beauty. If she married well, Afton could count that one obligation met. One less task to claim her attention. One step closer to her final goal of meeting her promise to her dying father to keep the family safe and secure—a task his own incompetence had prevented *him* from accomplishing.

She was touched by Grace's concern but unswayed in her determination. "If the murderer meant to kill me, he has had ten days to attempt it. Lady Annica's rumor about Madame Zoe losing her memory must have eased his mind."

Grace stiffened as she glanced at a point beyond Afton's right shoulder. Judging from the expression on her face, her aunt was surprised and a little uncertain.

"Mrs. Forbush, thank you for inviting me this evening."

Something in the deep timbre and faint Scottish brogue of that voice sent a chill up Afton's spine. She turned to see the speaker bow over Grace's hand and lift it to his sensual lips. A shock of dark hair fell over his brow and light sparked in eyes the shade of moss. When he straightened, he was a full six feet and more. His shoulders were broad, his features were finely chiseled and, despite his beauty, he was intensely masculine. Or was it the hint of frozen danger hovering about him like a ghostly presence that made her shiver?

"Lord Glenross! Heavens! I did not expect you to come in view of—that is—I'm delighted, but I did not hope to see you."

Lord Glenross? The man the entire ton had been gossiping about for the past two hours? The man who had just escaped after six months in an Algerian prison under sentence of death? Ah, now she knew the reason for his detachment. And her unease. She could not even imagine what might be done to a British officer in an Algerian prison.

Lord Glenross smiled—at least Afton thought it was a smile, but it could have been a grimace—his attention still fastened on Grace. "I would not have dreamed of missing it."

"You flatter me, Lord Glenross. I was not altogether certain you would welcome an invitation under the circumstances. That is...I thought—"

Afton could not take her eyes off the man. He turned to her as Grace continued her apology. His glance traveled from her eyes, paused in study of her mouth, then dropped farther to linger a moment at her throat before dipping to the low décolletage of her pale pink gown. Her skin tingled in the wake of that heated gaze. When he returned his attention to her face, he gave her a devastating smile that made faint dimples appear in both cheeks, and Afton could not catch her breath. His appraisal, without the final smile, would have been insulting. She might have been flattered if there had not been something cynical in his study...as if there was really nothing personal in his assessment. As if he could appreciate, but never participate.

Lord Glenross returned his attention to Grace, as if remembering her suddenly. "Thank you, Mrs. Forbush, but I am quite all right," he said.

Grace gave him a doubtful smile. "I am glad to hear it. If there is anything I can do, my lord, you need only ask."

He paused long enough for Afton to realize he was measuring his reply—*managing* the impression he gave. That knowledge set her on her guard.

He lifted one shoulder in a negligent shrug. "I've had time to ponder the Fates, Mrs. Forbush, and wonder what forces set us on a path."

Fascinated by where he was headed with his conversation, Afton accepted a cup of rum punch from a passing footman's tray and fortified herself with a deep gulp while she awaited Lord Glenross's further explanation.

"Life is a great mystery, is it not? Any advantage one might gain would be of assistance, do you not agree?"

"Why, yes, I do," Grace said. "I have always believed that knowledge is a powerful thing."

"I knew you would think so, Mrs. Forbush, and that is why I have sought you out to ask how to contact a certain 'Madame Zoe.' Pray tell, how might I accomplish that?"

Surprise and shock made Afton choke, the punch halfway down her throat. Lord Glenross stepped forward, a concerned look on his face.

Grace intercepted him and thumped Afton on the back, glancing at her in silent desperation before answering. "Oh, Lord Glenross! How would I know such a thing?"

"You know everything worth knowing, Mrs. Forbush. And if you do not know, you know how to find out."

Afton finally caught her breath and Grace turned her attention back to Glenross. "Well, um, yes. I suppose I could make inquiries, but I must say that I am astonished, my lord. I would never have thought you to be the sort who would traffic with psychics."

"The collective ton says Madame Zoe is a phenomenon, Mrs. Forbush. Perhaps she will predict *my* future." His expression did not change, but the corner of his right eye twitched faintly. "Or perhaps I shall predict hers," he added.

Afton tried to gather her wits. *Madame Zoe?* Men like Lord Glenross did not consult fortune-tellers. He was playing some sort of deep game and, from what she'd seen of the man, no good could come from it. She glanced at Grace, wondering how she could possibly reply to such a request.

"That is very open-minded of you, my lord," Grace declared. "I shall have that information for you by Monday morning, latest. Shall I post the instructions to you at your hotel? Or shall I send 'round to your club?''

Afton contained her gasp of dismay even as Glenross smiled triumphantly. "Send to my hotel. I am staying at Pultney's in Piccadilly." That bit of business out of the way, he looked pointedly at Afton, and then back to Grace.

"Oh! I beg your pardon, my lord," she said. "May I present my niece, Miss Afton Lovejoy? Miss Lovejoy, please meet Robert McHugh, Lord Glenross."

"Lord Glenross," Afton managed to acknowledge. With some trepidation, she dropped a small curtsy and offered her hand. He accepted it and lifted it to his lips. The warmth of his fingers spread through her, and when those sensual lips brushed lightly across her knuckles, his breath warmed her blood.

"Miss *Afton* Lovejoy?" he asked, turning back to Grace. "I could have sworn the invitation stated that you were honoring a Miss *Dianthe* Lovejoy."

Grace indicated Dianthe with a wave as she waltzed by with yet another proud-looking partner. "Dianthe is Afton's sister."

Lord Glenross barely spared a glance for Dianthe before returning his attention to Afton. "Miss Lovejoy, I am charmed," he said. "Have you just now come to town?"

She wet lips gone dry with anxiety. "I've been in London six months, my lord. As Mrs. Forbush's companion."

Grace interceded once again. "Afton has shunned society since coming to town, my lord. She calls herself my companion, but she is my niece by marriage, as well as a very dear friend."

"I am pleased that you have joined society tonight, Miss Lovejoy. I would be honored if you would consent to dance the next waltz with me."

Her heartbeat tripped. If she danced with him, would he be able to recognize her through her disguise when he met her as Madame Zoe? She could not risk such a thing. "I have promised the next waltz, my lord," she lied.

His smile did not falter, nor did his expression change, but she felt a subtle change in him. *He knew she was lying!*

"I see," he murmured. "Another time, Miss Lovejoy?" Without waiting for an answer, he bowed and departed in the direction of the game room.

Afton was appalled at the odd mixture of excitement and dread that filled her at the thought of seeing Lord Glenross again. She turned to Grace and lamented, "If there were only some way to refuse him!"

Grace looked doubtful. "If you wish, I shall tell him I could not discover how to contact Madame Zoe."

A complete waste of time. If Glenross did not have the referral from Grace, he would acquire it elsewhere. Slowly, painfully, Afton's heartbeat steadied. She shook her head. "Send Glenross my factor's address, and I shall instruct Mr. Evans to grant an appointment as soon as possible. As Shakespeare said, 'If it were done when 'tis done, then…'"

"'…'twere well it were done quickly.'" Grace finished the quote with a nod of agreement. "An excellent idea. Mr. Evans shall handle it all. He is the very personification of discretion."

Afton steadied her nerves and gave her aunt a small smile. "I shall simply tell Lord Glenross a happy little fortune and be done with him."

Chapter Two

Someone was in his room…someone who didn't belong. Key in one hand, Rob paused with his other on the knob of his hotel room door. The fine hairs on the back of his neck stirred with an uneasy prickle.

It was unlikely that the Dey would have sent men after him. Unlikely, but not impossible. And he'd damn well die fighting before undergoing the Dey's ''hospitality'' again. Being locked cramped and naked for weeks on end in a box so small he could neither turn nor raise his hand to scratch an itch, being left to wallow in his own filth, freeze by night and swelter by day, had taken its toll. A good day had been when someone took pity and threw an urn of fetid water over the box, and a few drops had trickled between the slats and cooled his stinging flesh. Rob could not yet think of the bad days—days he had been manacled spread-eagled against a dank dungeon wall for whippings that tore flesh from his back, while demands for information were screamed in his ears.

But there had been worse. Much worse. Bile rose in his throat as a sweat broke out on his forehead. No. He'd deal with that later. He wasn't ready yet.

He braced himself and turned the knob. It gave without

a click. Unlocked. He distinctly recalled locking it before leaving for Mrs. Forbush's soiree.

He bent and slid his dagger from his boot. They wouldn't take him alive this time. A quick glance down the corridor confirmed that he was quite alone.

He gripped the dagger in his right hand and eased the door open. A faint glow from the banked fireplace barely afforded enough light to make out the form of furniture. A movement from the chair facing the fire drew his attention.

Every muscle controlled, he crept forward. He stilled his breathing as he approached the back of the chair, knowing that even the air stirred by his breath could alert a seasoned thief or a foreign assassin. Surprise was his greatest advantage.

He jerked the man's head back, his blade pressing against the interloper's throat before he could react. "Identify yourself," he snarled in the man's ear from behind.

"Gads, Robbie! It's Doogie! D'ye not remember me?"

Rob dropped his hand and released his brother, nearly weak with relief. "Douglas! What are you doing here?"

"I got Travis's note and I've been trailing your footsteps ever since, always a step behind. Thought I'd just come to your lodgings and wait. I got the maid to unlock for me."

Rob did not even want to know how his brother had bribed the maid. Douglas had a way with women, and never had trouble getting what he wanted of them. Rob slipped the dagger back in his boot as Douglas came around the chair to embrace him.

A moment later, embarrassed by his display of emotion, his brother released him and stepped back. "Damn me, Rob, say you won't be going abroad again. My heart canna take it."

"I willna," Rob promised, falling into the comfortable brogue of their youth. "I'm back to stay."

"That's good. I'd have made a poor laird." Douglas went

to the bureau and retrieved Rob's bottle of Scotch whiskey. He refilled his glass and poured one for Rob. "To the return of the McHugh!"

There'd been no whiskey in Algiers or in the government hospital where he'd been held since his return. Rob drank deep, eager for the fire and pleasant lethargy that would seep through him when the Scotch did its work. Maybe tonight he'd finally be able to sleep. "To Doogie McHugh and his lady fair."

"Ach. So you've heard?" Douglas grinned and sank back into his chair. "She's an angel, Rob. I don't deserve her."

"I met Miss Barlow last year. She is lovely, Douglas. She'll give you beautiful babes. Mind that the first one's a boy, for the title." Rob wondered how his brother could prefer bland Bebe Barlow when there were more tasty morsels about—like that appetizing little Miss Afton Lovejoy. Now *there* was something he could envy Douglas for. Aye, Miss Lovejoy was right to be wary of him. He'd swallow her in a single bite.

"I'll do my duty, and wear a smile doing it," Douglas vowed.

"I always said you were a brave lad," Rob teased. "You're fond of her, then? The match wasn't for expedience?"

"Bebe is my life, Rob. She's the reason I draw breath." Douglas's face sobered and he glanced down at his feet. "Sorry, Rob. I didn't mean to remind you. But, in time, you will marry again. You'll have the heir you always wanted."

"I'll leave that to you, Douglas. 'Twill be your son now who'll bear the Glenross title." Doogie hadn't known that Hamish hadn't been a McHugh by blood. No point in telling him now, Rob supposed. He had grown to love the boy and had learned to ignore Maeve's indiscretion.

"You say that now, Rob, but some pretty face will turn your head and you'll change your tune."

"I've not got the mettle for marriage." And he hadn't the heart to risk deceit again. Deceit and denigration.

"'Twas none of your fault, man. Maeve's the one who insisted she visit her sister in Venice. She was a determined woman and made her own decisions."

Douglas was wrong. Rob didn't blame Maeve for that particular decision. But he knew who was responsible—the damn charlatan who'd hinted that his wife's destiny awaited her in Venice. That she should go there to escape the man who would destroy her: him. Rob would hunt Madame Zoe until he could expose her for the imposter she was, and then he'd utterly destroy her—her confidence, her trade, her income and, sweetest of all, her reputation. By the time he was finished with her, no member of society would consult her.

Ah yes. He'd learned to be a very patient man lying alone in a cramped box while oozing infection from his wounds and planning his escape. All those months in the Dey's dungeon he'd been waiting, going slowly mad. And he'd planned. Madame Zoe would pay for destroying the McHughs.

Monday morning, in the well-appointed offices above a bank, Rob studied his fingernails in a pose of casual boredom as Mr. Evans, Madame Zoe's factor, leafed through her appointment book with a great show of accommodation. Indeed, Rob was anything but bored. It was December 14, and by his estimation, he should be finished with Madame Zoe no later than Christmas. He studied his surroundings, imagining the sort of woman who would employ Mr. Evans.

The office was estimable in every sense of the word. Comfortable chairs sat along one wall and the factor's desk was clean, polished and modest. Mr. Evans himself appeared to be an eminently respectable man in his middle years, and Rob wondered why he would represent a charlatan.

The London gossip mill held that Madame Zoe was a middle-aged French émigré, a fortune-teller to the French court who had foretold the rise and fall of Napoleon Bonaparte. She was a widow, 'twas told, and always wore black. Liberal use of veils prevented anyone from giving an accurate description. Some even speculated that she was a prominent member of the noble but impoverished French community in London and employed the veils to prevent recognition in that circle.

Charlatan or not, Madame Zoe was clever to have put such an elaborate process in place. Before she ever saw a new client, the person had been screened by her factor. Only then was the client given an appointment time and the address at which she could be found. What a sweet little setup.

Tired of waiting for what was essentially a simple task, Rob slouched in his chair and asked, "So you do all Madame Zoe's procuring?"

Mr. Evans flushed. "I make *appointments* for consultations with Madame Zoe. I am a factor, not a flesh peddler. She is extraordinarily busy, what with the ton in town for the season."

"I will take whatever appointment she has available."

The man cleared his throat. "Payment in advance."

"Payment in advance?" Rob repeated, just to be certain his displeasure was evident. What a lot of nerve—demanding to be paid in advance for a pack of lies!

"Yes, my lord. Without exception," the man confirmed.

"What if she has nothing to tell me?"

"There are no guarantees, my lord. And no refunds."

Rob watched the man steadily, knowing his attention was unnerving. It was a technique he frequently used when eliciting a confession. The enemy always feared his silence meant that he knew more than he actually did.

"Madame Zoe has had a cancellation," Mr. Evans said after flipping through a number of pages in the little leather-bound appointment book. "She can see you this afternoon at three o'clock," he said after an uneasy moment. "Shall I put you on the books, my lord?"

"Yes," Rob said, more harshly than he intended.

The factor dipped his pen in an inkwell and scratched a line of writing across a piece of paper. "Five pounds, please."

Five pounds! Though it galled him to pay even a ha'penny, Rob handed over the required sum in exchange for the address.

Afton climbed the steep stairway that rose from a hidden panel in La Meilleure Robe to open in the closet of Madame Zoe's second-floor flat. Should anyone follow her, it would appear as if she had gone to the shop for a fitting with Madame Marie. And when she left, it was through the same closet and out of Madame Marie's door.

At the top of the secret stairs, the abandoned servants' access from the time when the building had been a private residence, she listened carefully for a moment, her ear against the wooden panel. She was always a little afraid one of her patrons might have arrived early and entered by force, in an attempt to discover her true identity. Or worse—that the murderer had returned, broken into the flat, and lay in wait for her. That possibility had led Grace to insist that Afton carry a small, but very sharp, dagger. Reassured by the silence, she pushed the secret door open and slipped through into Zoe's salon.

Afton lifted the heavy tapestry curtain that separated the back room from the main room, and went to light the fire banked in the small fireplace. That done, she opened the cupboard containing the tools of her trade: a deck of tarot cards, a deck of ordinary playing cards, a crystal orb, a bowl

for water gazing, astrological charts, runes, candles, incense
and a host of other items that she had no idea how to use.
Guessing that Lord Glenross would not ask for anything
unusual, she retrieved a deck of cards and left it on the
round table in the center of the room.

Lord Glenross, Robert McHugh. Though foppish elegance and a slender frame were all the rage, Afton preferred
a more substantial man, and Glenross was certainly that. He
was almost too muscular for current styles. The narrowly
cut jackets strained over his shoulders and chest in a most
distracting manner. The prospect of being alone with him,
even in disguise, caused her no small amount of anxiety. To
her, he was larger than life. He filled a room, claiming it
with no more than a crooked smile. And his eyes! Those
cool ice-green eyes that looked right through her flesh to
her soul! Thank heavens for her veils!

A glance at the clock on the small dressing table inspired
her to hasten. She had slipped out of an impromptu tea and
lively discussion of Lord Byron's latest exploits, with barely
a nod in her aunt's direction, but the delay had caused her
to run late. She stripped and donned black crepe de chine
widow's garb that covered her from throat to toe. Above
that, a gray wig topped by black silk veils obscured her face.
Last, she pulled on a pair of white silk gloves to cover her
hands. Nothing, she knew, would betray her identity.

The clatter of horses' hooves and the jangle of harness
from the street below drew her to the window. A black town
coach drew up outside and the door opened. Instead of a
patron of Madame Marie, the occupant was none other than
her client. Early. Afton smiled, thinking he must be more
anxious for a reading than she'd thought, and watched
through the sheer lace panels as the top of his head disappeared though the doorway below. She wondered again at
the incongruity of a man like McHugh consulting a fortune-

teller as she decided not to pull the heavy velvet draperies over the lace curtains.

For good measure, Afton checked her appearance in the mirror above the fireplace. Yes, the veils obscured her features and made her virtually unrecognizable. She would be safe enough. Just as she lit white candles and sandalwood incense, a knock sounded at the door. She lifted the little brass disk that covered the peephole to see the Scot, quite alone. She paused with her hand on the latch, anxiety twisting her stomach in knots.

"He is just curious," she whispered to herself, though she was too well aware that any client—*this one?*—could be Auntie Hen's murderer. She glanced at the bell rope, touched the little dagger in her sewn-on pocket, squared her shoulders and lifted the latch.

The door opened slowly, revealing a smallish woman swathed in black. Even the heavy veils covering her face betrayed no hint of the features beneath. Though he itched to peel the layers back and expose the face, Rob schooled himself to patience. Madame Zoe's actual identity was only one part of his problem. He could discover that whenever he chose. He needed to know her weaknesses, to uncover her vulnerabilities and decide the perfect way to destroy her. He estimated he would need at least three visits.

"*Entrez, m'sieur.*" Soft, well-modulated tones greeted him as the veiled woman stepped aside to grant him entry. If that was a crone's voice, he was not Rob McHugh.

A quick glance around the small room revealed a dozen telling details. The meager supply of wood on the hearth indicated use of the room for only short periods of time. Personal items were at a minimum. This was a salon only, not a home for the fortune-teller. The furnishings were tasteful, though shabby and worn. A single window facing the street below was hung with an airy lace curtain, and small pots of greenery lined the sill. Blue velvet draperies could be pulled for additional privacy, and would darken the room for a mystical atmosphere. A curtained alcove in the far corner likely hid a chaise and washstand, perhaps a wardrobe or clothespress. The only concession to female vanity was the old mirror mounted above the fireplace.

But most interesting to Rob was the small dark stain on the threadbare rug beneath the central table. Tea? Wine? Blood? Very interesting. And then there was the discreet bell rope hung from a hook near the fireplace. Where would it ring?

"M'sieur?" the woman asked again.

"Madame Zoe? Am I late?"

"Mais non," she said. As he passed her going into the room, he caught the subtle scent of lilies of the valley. Sweet, warm, seductive. Also very interesting.

She swept her arm toward the table in the center of the room in an invitation to sit.

"Do you know who I am?" he asked, ignoring the chair.

Her voice was still soft and heavily accented, but now held a hint of humor. "I know all, *m'sieur.*"

He laughed, amused by her conceit. "Then who am I?"

"You are my three o'clock appointment, *m'sieur.*"

Clever thing. He shook his head. She was *not* going to make him like her. "Do you mock me?"

"Mais non, m'sieur." She gripped the back of the chair opposite the one she had indicated for him. "That would be very bad for the business, no?"

"My business, at any rate."

"So. You 'ave the curiosity to know what the future 'olds for you?"

"Yes, indeed." He nearly rubbed his hands together in anticipation.

"'Ow do you wish your fortune told, *m'sieur?* Cards? Tarot? Tea leaves? Crystal orb? Runes?"

Rob gestured at the deck of cards on the table. "Cards."

He smiled as she sat and made a graceful mystic gesture over the deck, as if invoking the fortune-telling god, before passing the deck to him. "You must shuffle the cards, *m'sieur*. They must carry your energy. Your…essence."

Without sitting, Rob shuffled the deck three times before sliding it back across the table to her. She then dealt a circular pattern of cards, faceup, on the table and placed one card facedown on top of each. In the center of the pattern, she turned a single card up. The king of spades.

Pointing to it, she said, "You, *m'sieur*."

"Are you quite certain?"

"*Oui*. Were this a tarot deck, you would be the king of swords. A good card. A strong card. A warrior."

Flattery? Somehow he thought not. "Swords, eh? What am I doing?"

She pointed to a queen of hearts. "*Doutant moi.*"

Another joke? "How do you know you are the queen of hearts?"

"She is presently close to you and 'as the gift of sight. Do you know such another?"

She had him there. "No," he admitted.

"*Voilà! C'est moi.*" There was a note of triumph in her voice, as if she had surprised even herself.

"Will my doubt prevent you from giving me a reading?"

Madame Zoe sat back, folded her hands in her lap. "*Mais non, m'sieur*. Do not concern yourself. The cards are what they are. But I feel the doubt in you. You do not think telling the future is possible, no?"

"Pray, do not allow my reservations to hinder you. This is my first time at a fortune-teller. You must allow me my little doubts." He took the chair across from her and folded his arms across his chest.

She appeared to be weighing her words, deciding what to say, or how much. "You are a warrior, *m'sieur*. You 'ave come 'ere with the…plan. The strategy. There is something you wish to know, but you will not speak it aloud.''

He raised an eyebrow. That was a clever ploy. While quite true of him, the same could be said of nearly everyone who visited a fortune-teller. ''Hmm. Must I speak it aloud, *madame*, for you to answer the question?''

''No. I confess it would be easier, but not needed.'' She pointed to the ten of spades. ''I think it 'as to do with the revenge. I do not see a 'appy outcome, *m'sieur*. Revenge is a two-edged sword. It draws blood on both sides, *n'est-ce pas?* One cannot be certain 'oo will be cut.''

A remarkably good guess, he thought. ''Sometimes the reason for revenge makes it worth the risk.''

She shook her head slowly. ''*Mais non, m'sieur.* There are only two reasons for revenge. Both silly.''

''And those reasons would be…''

''*L'amour ou l'argent, monsieur.*''

Of course. Love or money. One did not have to be a fortune-teller to know this. ''Which do you think is my motive?'' he asked, unable to keep the challenge from his voice.

Her own voice was steady and sure. ''Love. You are not a man to quibble over money.''

''You are very logical, *madame*. Very perceptive.'' Was it perception that passed for fortune-telling? Did she merely tell people what she guessed they wanted to hear? Was she little more than an intuitive observer?

''Not logical, *m'sieur*. I only speak what the cards say.''

''Balderdash!'' The word was out before he could stop it.

A small muffled laugh emerged from beneath the veils. ''I am sorry you think so. *Néanmoins,* you 'ave come for the reading, and I shall oblige.'' She bent over the spread cards once again in an attitude of rapt concentration, turning the facedown cards up in a precise pattern. ''You, and you alone, 'ave the power to determine your future. What I tell you now is only what *could* be…what *might* be. You must choose your course.

"You are now suffering from…'ow you say—*chagrin d'amour?*"

The corner of his mouth twitched. "You say, 'a broken 'eart.'" At last Madame Zoe was going astray. Maeve and Hamish's deaths had not broken his heart, they had hardened it.

"*Oui,* 'eartbreak. But you must not worry, *m'sieur.* You will love again. You will love deeper." She pointed to the queen of clubs. "She was not your *grande passion.* You will 'ave *la grande passion.* If…"

"If?"

She shrugged. "If you let go of your 'urt. If not, your quest for revenge will poison you and those around you."

Dangerously close! How could she garner that from a few common cards? "You misunderstand, *madame.* What you call revenge, I call justice. As for putting it aside—that's easy to say, impossible to do."

"*M'sieur,* I…" She trailed off in a sigh.

"If you have something to tell me, *madame,* do so," he said.

She leaned over the cards again and turned another three up, then another three, stopping to study the way the cards had fallen. "Danger. Clearly, danger. Spreading in a radius around the king—you, *m'sieur.* Alas, I cannot tell if the danger is *to* the king or *from* the king. It may be both. You must be very careful, *m'sieur.*" She fell silent, her head bent over the cards.

Damnation. Was she about to give him a warning from the cards? Had he just tipped his hand? He stirred uneasily as he waited for her to finish. "*Madame?* Have you fallen asleep?" he asked when the silence stretched out.

When she answered, her voice was subdued, and he felt

for the first time that she was hedging. "You must not worry, *m'sieur*. The matters that are troubling you will soon come clear."

"Is that what your cards tell you?"

She touched her forehead through her veil. "I…I 'ave suddenly come over with the malaise, *m'sieur*. I will instruct my factor to reimburse you."

"I do not want reimbursement, *madame*. I want a reading."

The hand on her forehead began to tremble, and Rob realized she was not feigning to get rid of him. She was actually in distress. He leaned toward her, surprising himself with a quick pang of concern. "Do you require assistance, *madame?*"

She waved one hand to prevent him from coming closer. "'Ow kind of you, *mais non*. I must 'ave quiet. I cannot see your future, *m'sieur*. There are clouds, barriers—"

"Ah." He nodded "The doubts you spoke of earlier."

"*Oui,*" she sighed.

"Then can you tell me the past?"

She studied the remaining cards after fanning them in an arc across the table. "Your past is filled with, ah, turbulence. And much pain, I think. There 'as been betrayal and injury. You 'ave learned not to trust. You…you are a man of strong passions, though you 'ide it well. You are intelligent, thoughtful, deliberate—relentless in pursuing your goal. Alas, *m'sieur,* you are not 'appy. You 'ave the deep 'urt. You must overcome these things if you are to live again. In the present, *m'sieur,* you do not allow for the—'ow you say—caprice of life. For the whim, the 'umor or the silly thought. You 'ave not learned that dreams, no matter 'ow impossible, make dreary lives worth living, and that when 'ope dies, the 'uman spirit dies. You 'ave not found within you the ability to laugh at life's absurdities. The world does not turn because you turn it, *m'sieur. Au contraire.* It turns of its own accord. Time is even more relentless than you."

He narrowed his eyes at the unvarnished rebuke. She had not falsely flattered him, nor couched her message in a veil of euphemisms. And her reckoning was dead-on. He hadn't a single whimsical bone in his body. That she knew so much about him made him uncomfortable. He began to think that, however misguided, she might be sincere in her delusions of "knowing all."

"You are loyal to your friends," she continued, "and will not 'esitate to protect them, even from themselves. You—"

"Enough!" he snapped. She was more than a fortune-teller—she was a witch! He stood so quickly the little wooden chair tipped backward and clattered on the floor. "That is enough for today. I will be back for my money's worth, *madame.* You may count on that." Feeling as if the walls were closing in on him, he turned on his heel and headed for the door. He could have sworn he heard a muffled curse on his way out.

In all, though, his visit had been a success. He had learned a great number of interesting things about the infamous Madame Zoe. Her soft youthful voice betrayed the fact that she could not be an ancient French émigré. Unless he missed his guess, she could not be above twenty and five. Her size was another clue. Despite the mourning weeds, he could tell that her figure was more willowy than that of an aging matron, her posture straight, not hunched. Her scent, lilies of the valley with the underlying hint of greens, was unaffected and free of the cloying heavy scents of musk and rose so popular today. It was a fragrance that had brought his blood up instantly.

But even more interesting, Madame Zoe was not French at all. No, when speaking the foreign words, her accent was flawless, but when speaking English, her affected French accent was appalling. Truly one of the worst he'd ever heard.

Best of all, now he had her address. He knew where to find her when he was ready to come for her. And that would be soon.

Oh, yes. Mr. Evans had been right. She'd been worth the five pounds. And Rob would gladly pay the price again for another visit.

Chapter Three

Afton glanced around the grand ballroom of the Argyle Rooms. The elegant setting, replete with crystal chandeliers and fresco-painted walls, was like something from a fairy tale. Everything was perfect and boded well for Dianthe's further success. It would never do to have other guests at the Lingate fete overhear their conversation and ruin it all.

She pulled her aunt toward a quiet corner. "I tell you, Aunt Grace, it was eerie," she whispered. "I know what each of the cards is supposed to mean, but I could not make out the meaning in the way they fell. I was in his fortune, and I was a danger to him—or he to me, I could not tell which. I tried to think, but I kept hearing the word *danger*, and I could not banish it from my mind. I vow, for a moment I thought it was Auntie Hen whispering to me."

Grace blanched. "You do not think—"

"No! Oh, no. Of course not," Afton assured her. "It wasn't real. The voice was in my head—more like a memory. But it distracted me, and Lord Glenross must think I'm quite mad. I had only started to tell his future when I... became mystified. He said he would be back."

Grace's clear brown eyes widened. "And so he is."

Afton turned in the direction of Grace's gaze. Lord Glenross, dressed in elegant eveningwear, was wending his way around groups and couples, progressing relentlessly toward them. Light-headed with anticipation, she said a quick prayer that she would do or say nothing that would betray her as Madame Zoe.

When he arrived before them, he gave a polite bow and straightened with a smile. Afton noted that he'd had a haircut since this afternoon. He now had the look of the haut monde, but there was something primitive in his bearing and his movements—as if someone had dressed a lion in a lamb disguise. She liked him better without his "civilized" veneer.

He gave a short bow. "Mrs. Forbush, I am in your debt."

Grace tilted her head to one side and returned his smile. "Whatever for, Lord Glenross?"

"Your assistance in contacting Madame Zoe. I hope it did not inconvenience you greatly."

"Not in the least, my lord. The information came easier than you might imagine. Were you successful?"

"Quite. I met with her this afternoon."

The knowledge that he did not know who she was intoxicated Afton and made her feel daring. She couldn't contain her curiosity. "Was your appointment satisfactory, my lord?"

He turned to her, looking surprised that she had addressed him. He smiled and nodded. "Miss Lovejoy, is it not? Yes, I was satisfied with the appointment. I found Madame Zoe to be quite…insightful."

"Is she as good as the *on dit* has it?"

"That remains to be seen."

Afton was about to reply when she noted Sir Martin Seymour coming their way. He was blond, tall, slender, handsome and perfectly groomed—a fair complement to Lord Glenross. He bowed to her and Grace before turning to Glenross.

"If it isn't the McHugh, my childhood chum," he said, grinning and embracing him. "I heard, but I dared not believe. Glad you made it back, old friend."

Glenross clapped the other man on the back and said, "Seymour, it is good to see you. Have you been well?"

"Tolerable. And you?"

Glenross's face clouded. "As you might expect."

"Sorry," Martin murmured. "I did not mean to awaken any loathsome memories."

"There are not many of the other kind." Glenross gave a short, self-deprecating laugh. "I do not usually indulge in self-pity. Bear with me, Seymour. I will regain my balance in another day or two."

Afton was touched by his obvious dismay. She was certain he did not often betray himself in such a blatant manner.

"No doubt," Martin said. He turned to her and Grace, then bent in a debonair bow. "Ladies, please excuse our lapse of good manners. The McHugh and I grew up not three miles apart, and I have not seen him since…before Algiers."

"How nice," Grace said. "It is always a pleasure to reacquaint oneself with old friends, is it not?"

"Without a doubt," Seymour said. "Are you ladies enjoying yourselves?"

"We have not been here long," Grace answered. "Mr. Julius Lingate claimed Dianthe for a waltz upon our arrival, and we have been awaiting her return to us. I believe she was claimed for another dance, but—"

"Ah, there she goes again." Martin laughed, gesturing at the waltzing couples. He nodded toward the dance floor and reached for Afton's hand. "We should join her, Miss Lovejoy. Since you are standing here, you cannot be spoken for."

Afton did not like being manipulated, but she could not disengage her hand without appearing rude. "Oh, Sir Martin, I am a poor partner. You can be nothing but disappointed. I had scant opportunity to practice waltzing in Little Upton.''

''Leave it to me, Miss Lovejoy. I have enough skill and practice for us both.'' He paused long enough to bow again in Grace's direction and call a farewell to Glenross as he led her toward the dance floor. ''Come 'round to my club later, Rob. We'll reacquaint you with some late entertainments.''

Afton felt heat creep into her cheeks when she wondered what sort of late entertainments that would be, and before she knew it, she was dancing her first waltz.

Her partner smiled. ''I say, Miss Lovejoy, you look quite fetching in violet. You ought to wear it more often.''

''Thank you, Sir Martin,'' she murmured as she scuffed the toe of his boot with her slipper. She liked the rhythm of the music, but she did not care to have Martin Seymour mere inches from her face. Nor did she quite understand what steps would be required of her next.

Her partner's hand on her waist gave her no guidance. Her foot landed squarely on top of his boot and he winced, trying, no doubt, to cover a look of annoyance.

''Oh, I am sorry. Perhaps I am not suited.''

''I shan't hold it against you, Miss Lovejoy. You will learn.''

She wondered if she would. She suspected she was more suited for country reels and quadrilles. Then a sudden thought occurred to her. *Sir Martin was eminently qualified to court Dianthe.* ''My sister is much in demand. Have you danced with her?''

''I have, indeed. She is light of foot, but she hasn't your fire.'' Sir Martin gave her a meaningful look.

''You like red hair, sir?''

''Your locks are more a reddish-blond, and I like it very much, indeed. My inquiries have revealed that you have been in town six entire months, Miss Lovejoy. How is it that you are yet unattached?''

"Luck?'' she ventured.

He grinned. "My *good* luck. I should have been distraught if you'd been spoken for before I had my chance.''

Afton blinked in surprise. Was he asking if his attentions were welcome? "I...I have not been much in society, sir. Did your inquiries reveal that I am my aunt's companion?''

Sir Martin affected a wounded look as he spun her in a tight circle. "Miss Lovejoy, say you do not think me so parsimonious as to be a fortune hunter.''

She laughed. "Sir, most women are judged as worthy as their fortunes, and I come with more liabilities than assets.''

"Noted. And yet I am undaunted.''

What *will* it take? Afton thought. Ashamed of herself, she smiled. "You are very kind, sir.''

"Not at all. Bloodlines are also important, would you not agree? You are of a good family, and your father was only once removed from a title, I think?''

"The Lovejoy pedigree stands up to scrutiny.''

The waltz ended. Sir Martin offered his arm as he escorted her back to Grace. He leaned close to her ear and whispered, "We shall waltz again, Miss Lovejoy.''

She put on a polite smile. "Do not forget Dianthe.''

The moment Sir Martin departed, Grace took Afton's hand and led her apart from the little group she'd been standing in. "Glenross said he'd be back to claim a dance. He was asking about you, Afton, and your circumstances.''

"What if he suspects I am...''

"I pray that is not possible. Though he seemed to study you overmuch, you betrayed nothing of your identity.''

"I am certain of it. I was swathed head to toe in Auntie Hen's disguise. Why, I even wore gloves to cover my hands. I lowered my voice and spoke with an accent. Still, he was behaving oddly.''

"Then he must be smitten with Afton Lovejoy."

"Also impossible, Aunt. From the *on dit*, Glenross is notorious for being blind to a pretty face. I've heard that from too many sources to doubt it. And he is still mourning his late wife, Lady Maeve."

"Did you see that in the cards?"

"Heavens!" Afton laughed. "You mustn't believe such silly stuff. Who would know better than I what balderdash that is? A parlor game, Aunt Grace. Put no more stock in it than that."

"Then perhaps you ought to tell your own fortune, Afton. But later. Here comes Glenross again."

"I think I am not meant to dance the waltz, Lord Glenross. I fear I have lamed poor Sir Martin for life."

He deflected her mild protest with an unarguable counter. "Allow me to worry over the state of my own feet, Miss Lovejoy. You cannot know just how sturdy I am."

She laughed, thinking it would be interesting to make a comparison between him and Sir Martin. She offered her hand.

"When you ran off last night, I thought I might have offended you in some way," he said when the music started.

"Not in the least, my lord." She placed her right hand across his left palm and was fascinated by how small it looked in his. As he settled his warm right hand at her waist, a quiver of excitement traveled up her spine. She was acutely aware of his size, his scent, his proximity and the odd gentleness of his touch despite his rough strength. No, he did not offend her in the slightest possible way.

"That is a relief," he said as he led her into the dance. "I am usually deliberate when I am giving offense, but I must allow for the occasional faux pas. You will correct me if I err, will you not?"

"With alacrity," she teased. "I thought you had been back long enough to have reclaimed your social graces."

He gave her a curious look, his cool eyes searching hers. "I have, Miss Lovejoy. What you see before you is the polished version of Rob McHugh."

"I suspected as much, my lord." Indeed, he was so polished that he left her breathless. His admission that she was looking at that side of him made her ashamed of teasing him. Thus far, as Afton, she had seen little of the cold, dangerous, fierce reputation that the ton gossiped about. Ah, but as Madame Zoe she had experienced a decided frost.

She took a deep breath and stiffened her spine. She had to be very careful not to betray the tiniest hint of Madame Zoe to Glenross. She suspected he would not take kindly to being deceived.

Seeking a change of subject, she realized she had not stepped on his toe once since the dance began. "I think this is going rather well," she ventured. "Better than my first waltz."

"Beginnings are always difficult, Miss Lovejoy. One cannot be proficient in…any task on one's fledgling tries. 'Firsts' can be disappointing." His voice lowered to that deep timbre that tickled her psyche. "But with a skilled and patient instructor, you may exceed your highest hopes."

Afton grappled with that statement for a moment. "A…a good instructor can accomplish much," she finally allowed.

Glenross tilted his head back in a hearty guffaw and led her into a quick turn. Miraculously, she did not even stumble. The strength and firmness of his hand had guided her unfalteringly through the maneuver. "I shall be pleased to devote myself to the task of teaching you to waltz, Miss Lovejoy. I cannot wait to see how much *you* might accomplish."

Even though she wished the dance could last forever, the whisper in her ear was back. *Danger. Danger.*

*   *   *

As Seymour prattled beside him at the tavern bar, Rob tossed back another whiskey. He'd meant to go back to his room and make an early evening of it, but when little Miss Lovejoy had challenged him, made him laugh, made him forget—just for a minute—he'd become rife with guilt. A guilt he was desperate to assuage. In any way possible. He didn't need the damn guilt to remind him that he'd failed— at being a father and a husband.

Failed so miserably that Maeve had been moved to tell him so. He was too intemperate, too fierce in his passions, she'd informed him. He unsettled her, she'd said. She'd feared he would consume her if she let him. She'd said she needed a finer emotion from him—something gentler, less intense. Safer. He was, according to his deceased wife, on a level scarcely above an animal. "McHugh the Destroyer," she'd called him, because he'd destroyed her only chance for happiness. Thus far, he'd been unable to find anything that would prove her wrong. He *had* wanted her each time he'd been with her, but he hadn't…what? Become soft and moon-eyed over her many vaunted attributes? Craved her? Thought of her constantly when they were apart? Been anxious for the next time he'd see her?

Loved her?

Sadly, he hadn't. Their marriage had been arranged by their families when they were still in the nursery. And that lack of love was the true source of his guilt. He was left to conclude that he simply did not possess the finer emotions. So, when Maeve had ripened with child at a time when he could not have been the sire, he'd remained silent and claimed Hamish as his own. That was the least he could do for a wife he had failed in every other way.

But, animal that he was, he'd obsessed over the identity of Hamish's sire, and about many interesting ways he could kill the damn poacher. Who had given Maeve what Rob had not been able to give her? God help him, it made no difference now, but that question still ate at him.

Tonight, he'd thought a trip to the gaming hells and brothels of London's squalid side would sate his animal needs. He'd thought he'd be able to overcome the humiliation of the atrocity his body had become. He'd hoped he'd find relief, release, repose, if only for the night. Instead, when Seymour had taken him to the most popular brothel in London, he'd chosen a saucy redhead with blue eyes and a teasing smile. When he realized he'd selected a pale copy of Miss Lovejoy, he'd given the prostitute a guilty pass. He damn well wasn't dead below the waist, but he also wasn't interested in simple ejaculation. Fool that he was, he craved possession. He craved contact on a deeper level than the physical. He craved meaning.

"McHugh?" Seymour asked.

A sideways glance revealed an ale-sodden gentleman staring into his tankard. "Aye?"

"Too bad about Maeve and Hamish."

Rob had no reply for that. He gestured to the publican for another glass of whiskey.

Seymour shook his head. "You shouldn't have let them go."

"I live with that every day, Seymour." He studied the wet circle left on the bar by his glass.

"Too late now, though."

He tossed his whiskey down in a single gulp and slammed the glass on the bar. "I'm gone, Seymour. My pillow is calling."

"But you haven't made the two-backed beast yet. 'Tisn't natural. You're on edge, McHugh. The least little thing could set you off. When was the last time you—"

Rob shook his head as he turned to the door. He wasn't about to tell Seymour he hadn't been with a woman in months—no, years. They'd all blurred together and been so exceedingly forgettable, the women *and* the years. And he'd grown accustomed to being on edge. Hell, he'd almost grown to like it.

Afton drew the warm velvet robe closer around her and went to curl up before the fire as she waited for Grace and Dianthe's return. Though she had more important things to think about, her mind kept wandering back to her dance with Lord Glenross and the feeling of his hand on her waist. She craved more of that feeling, and cringed with guilt every time she thought of it. She was taking his money, pretending to tell his fortune, and using knowledge she gathered as Afton Lovejoy to deceive him into thinking Madame Zoe was clairvoyant. For the first time, she *felt* like a common fraud.

To complicate matters, since her sister's arrival in London one week ago, Afton had purchased ball and riding gowns, shoes, riding boots, dancing slippers, gloves, bonnets, reticules, morning and afternoon gowns, calling cards—and the costs added up. She would not have the resources to give Dianthe a second season. In fact, if she gave up the income as Madame Zoe, she would not be able to see Dianthe through *this* season.

Gads! Five years of scrimping and saving, five years of mind-numbing drudgery in Wiltshire and now in London, and all her carefully laid plans were about to go awry because an unspeakable villain had murdered Aunt Henrietta!

Afton stood and began pacing. She had lost so much. Her mother, her father, Aunt Henrietta, the meager savings for her dowry—all gone. Lord, she was so tired! Dianthe found the uncertainty exciting, but Afton ached to feel safe for just a moment.

Near dawn, the clatter of hooves on cobblestones pulled her from her reverie, and she hurried to her bedroom window to watch as the Forbush coach pulled up to the front door. Dianthe, accompanied by Grace and Lord Ronald Barrington, one of Grace's many admirers, stepped out and hurried inside just as the tall grandfather clock struck the hour of four. Afton knew the routine. Lord Ronald would beg a bedtime sherry and then leave, still unrequited in his lust for Grace.

Turning away from the window, Afton went to wait, cross-legged, on her bed. By the time her door flew open and Dianthe danced in, she had a smile fixed firmly in place.

"Was it wonderful, Di? Did all the ton fall at your feet?"

Her sister untied the strings of her cape and let it slide to the floor. "It was extraordinary! I feel like a princess. I adore London! I revel in all my new gowns! Why, oh why, did you not send for me ere now?"

"I did not know how much you would like town," Afton replied with a laugh. "I have not experienced your success."

"I cannot imagine why not." Dianthe gazed at herself in the looking glass. "You are much prettier than I, Afton, and so petite. Men love that."

"I am not your competition, Di." Afton smiled.

"I know you would not want it so, but men are positively intrigued by redheads."

"I am past my prime."

"*Au contraire,*" Dianthe laughed. "Twenty and five is fully ripe. You are poised to fall from the tree."

Afton had a sudden image of herself as an apple clinging to the tree with her last scrap of strength as Robert McHugh stood below, his hand cupped and ready to catch her. She shivered and put the distracting thought away. "No, Dianthe, you will be the one to make a match before the season ends."

"Oh, I hope so. That is why I ordered a new ball gown when I was shopping with the Thayer twins this afternoon.

Hortense and Harriett said I shall need every advantage I can secure.''

A new gown? Afton winced. Between Dianthe's recent purchases and Auntie Hen's death, where would she find the resources?

Dianthe's eyes widened as she took in Afton's expression. ''Oh, dear. Should I have asked before I ordered the gown?''

She touched her sister's cheek tenderly. Dianthe would be crushed to think she had caused a problem. ''I wish I had gone with you. You know how I adore shopping.''

''Then you must come next time.'' Dianthe began pulling the pins from her silken blond hair, letting it fall around her shoulders. ''Why have you not entered society, Afton? Aunt Grace told me that she offered to pay your expenses and to sponsor you, but that you would not accept.''

Dianthe softened her voice. ''Have you refused Aunt Grace's offer because of Papa? You know you cannot go through life trying to make up for his shortcomings.''

''Shortcomings?'' She gave a gentle laugh. ''You are a master of understatement, Dianthe. Father was a pauper who borrowed from his friends and family until he had none left. People fled when they saw him coming. Do you not remember the humiliation? I will never impose in such a manner.''

''He did it for us, Binky,'' Dianthe said, using Afton's pet name.

''I'd rather have done without than live by charity,'' Afton murmured.

''Never mind,'' Dianthe soothed. ''With hard work and determination, we have reversed the family fortunes—you, with your excellent business sense and the pay for assisting Aunt Grace, Auntie Hen hiring out to wealthy widows as a tour guide, and me with my little jams and jellies to sell at market.'' She paused and gave Afton a sideways glance.

"Ah, but you could make a brilliant match, Binky, and then we wouldn't have to work so hard."

Afton studied Dianthe's face until she saw the twinkle of laughter in her eyes. She swung a pillow at her sister. "That's your job, Dianthe! *You* make the brilliant match, then you can take care of me in my dotage."

"I shall be delighted to do so." Her sister sighed dreamily. "There are half a dozen men I've met so far to whom I could give my heart. But where is Auntie Hen? In her last letter she promised to meet us in town and help me make a choice."

Guilt tweaked Afton and the pain crept forward. She could not give in to it yet. If Dianthe suspected the truth, she'd withdraw in mourning, and there might never be another chance to launch her in society. "She has been delayed in Greece, Dianthe. I am certain we will hear from her soon."

"Oh, I do hope so. I miss her dreadfully and I know you and she are anxious for me to make a good match. I only wish she were here to guide me."

Was a measure of desperation tainting Dianthe's enjoyment of her debut? "You know I would not have you marry for advantage alone, do you not? Swear you will not marry without affection."

"Of course not, Binky. And I do not think I will have to worry about taking care of you." Dianthe grinned. "I saw that darkly handsome Lord Glenross dancing with you, and Sir Martin Seymour seemed quite smitten."

Glenross. A queer shimmery sensation came over Afton when she recalled the way he'd looked at her. His quick flash of vulnerability when she'd teased him about his manners had touched her. She would have sworn that vulnerability went deeper than his wife's death. Ah, but she would never know. Glenross was uncomfortably intense. Challenging. *Exciting.*

She'd had enough of that. Her father had been wildly exciting, carrying his family along in the wake of his high spirits. But his irresponsibility had cost his family their fortune and their future. After her mother had died of consumption, her father had squandered what was left of their resources to bury his grief in alcohol and games of chance. Five years later he had fallen off his horse in a drunken stupor and broken his neck, leaving Afton and his sister, Henrietta, to deal with the aftermath of his excesses.

Glenross, too, made her feel as if she were falling through space, rushing toward the ground, never hitting bottom, but knowing it was coming. She was exhilarated but terrified, and she couldn't bear that feeling. After the last five years of living hand to mouth, she just wanted to feel safe, free of doubt and uncertainty. She wanted security and the assurance that her life would be calm and predictable.

Sir Martin, now, was an entirely different matter. Handsome, polite, stable, uncomplicated and very civilized. Very safe. Yes. If she had to choose a man this season, it would be Martin Seymour. Life would be simpler with someone like Seymour.

Chapter Four

Loosening the strings of her green woolen cloak, Afton took the single chair in front of Mr. Evans's desk. "Booked solid for the next few days?" She glanced at the calendar on the wall. December 15. Only sixteen more days to catch the killer.

"Yes, Miss Lovejoy. Noon through tea beginning on Monday. Only one appointment today, later this afternoon. I thought Miss Henrietta would be pleased that business is so brisk."

"Yes." Afton cleared her throat. "But could you leave her some spare time for the next few weeks? My sister has come to town and Aunt Henrietta would like to visit with her."

She wished she could tell him the truth, but the Wednesday League had agreed that the fewer people who knew the truth, the better their odds of success. If word got out that her aunt was dead, the villain would never rise to the bait.

Mr. Evans gave her a deferential nod. "I shall endeavor to direct appointments to afternoons."

Afton thought of the endless rounds of receiving and paying calls, teas, shopping and sightseeing, and relented. Someone had to keep Dianthe's spending in check. Unfortunately, Dianthe took after their father in that regard. "Perhaps a few in the evenings and a few during the day?"

"As you wish, Miss Lovejoy." The factor busied himself with copying a list of names and appointment times for her.

"And, um, she wants you to put off Glenross when he comes to reschedule."

"Was there a problem with the man?"

"Not exactly. But I—she cannot decide what he wants of her."

Mr. Evans nodded and went back to his task. As she watched him transfer the appointments to a separate sheet of paper, she was struck with an idea. "Mr. Evans? Could you…that is, my aunt noted that one of her clients left, er, dropped a possession during his last appointment, but she cannot recall who it was. It was in the last week of November or the first week of December. She has misplaced her list and asked if I could prevail upon you for a copy of her appointments during that fortnight."

Mr. Evans looked up from the paper and pursed his lips. He gave a rather pointed glance at the clock on the shelf behind him. "It will take a few moments, Miss Lovejoy."

"Thank you, sir. I will wait."

She perched on the edge of her chair, as if so temporary that Mr. Evans would not be inconvenienced beyond the moment he could produce the list. The man bent to finish his current work, then flipped the pages of Henrietta's appointment book back to the time in question and began copying the names.

Afton could not wait to tell the Wednesday League of her brilliant idea. Although Auntie Hen hadn't had an appointment the night she'd been murdered, it was possible she had seen her killer in the recent past. If Afton could give Mr. Renquist those names, he would know who to question. Who to investigate.

And, as luck would have it, she was to meet Mr. Renquist

in less than an hour at La Meilleure Robe. She could give
him a copy of the list of her aunt's appointments, and answers would not be far behind.

A few moments later, the lists tucked into her white fur
muff, she descended the single flight of stairs to the street.
A blast of cold air took her breath away as she rounded the
corner, ran squarely into a solid mass and teetered backward.

Lord Glenross steadied her with a firm hand on her elbow.
"My apologies, miss."

Afton's hood had fallen back and she noted that Glenross
was no less surprised than she. "Glenross! How...I mean,
what...oh, dear."

He glanced at the stairway. "Are you well, Miss Lovejoy?"

"Yes, thank you," she said, frozen in place.

He reached out to touch her cheek, and his finger came
away with a tear. "I have not injured you, have I?" he
asked.

"Oh, no, my lord. I just...have come from seeing my
factor and..."

"You have had bad news?"

"No. Oh, no." She gave a little laugh and shook her
head. "I was just thinking of, well, of the season, and of
how I wish I were back in Little Upton for the holiday."

"Homesick, eh?" He grinned. "One's own hearth and
home is a great comfort, is it not?"

"A great comfort," she repeated with a little shiver.

Lord Glenross lifted her hood from her shoulders and
settled it over her head again, arranging the fur-lined drape
to frame her face. His gloved hand grazed her cheek and
she caught her breath at the intimacy of the touch. He
glanced at the stairway again and she suspected he was
headed for Mr. Evans's office to make another appointment.
She did not envy the factor having to put Glenross off.

"Thank you for your assistance, my lord. I...I should be on my way now." She shivered and backed away from him, anxious to clear her head.

He took her elbow once more and led her into the busy foot traffic on Fleet Street. "Where is your escort, Miss Lovejoy? Your coach?"

"I am my aunt's employee, my lord. I have no escort, and I walked from her house."

"Mrs. Forbush allowed—"

"She tried to send me in the coach, but I told her I could use the walk to clear my head. Sometimes she tries to do too much for me, and I have to remind her that I am in her employ."

Snow mixed with rain began to fall, forming small pellets that made little clicking noises as they hit buildings, windowpanes and cobblestones. If the temperature dropped a few more degrees, there would be a heavy snowfall. The pavement had already grown slick as the sleet froze on the smooth surface. She shivered and drew her cloak a little closer.

Glenross's features softened. "I believe I passed a tearoom a few doors down. I think you need to be warmed, Miss Lovejoy. Your aunt's house is not exactly nearby." He shook his head when she opened her mouth to protest. "I will not hear any objections. If you were found frozen tomorrow, I'd never forgive myself. Come. It is nearly tea time."

Afton had no choice but to allow him to escort her the thirty yards or so to the small tearoom. A little bell above the door rang when they entered the shop, and a woman dressed in black with a white apron and dust cap came out of the back room.

"Welcome," she said, her accent suggesting a hint of cockney. She led the way to a small private booth in the back, designed to protect them from curious stares. It held a small round table and two chairs. Ladies were not served with the general population and most genteel establishments had similar arrangements to accommodate just such circumstances. "You're the first of the afternoon trade," she said, hinting that they would not be disturbed.

Afton glanced at her escort. She'd never been to tea with a man. Country living did not lend itself to such refinements, and she had not been in such a position since arriving in London. She knew she was a country bumpkin, but she took a deep breath and decided to carry it off with as much aplomb as she could manage.

The warmth of the cozy tearoom was welcoming after the cold starkness of Mr. Evans's office and the chill of the sleet. Lord Glenross lifted the cloak from her shoulders and hung it on a peg outside their booth. He held a chair for her and she sat. When she took her hand out of her fur muff, the folded sheets of paper fluttered to the floor. She had forgotten about Mr. Evans's lists in the shock of colliding with Glenross.

Glenross had closed the little curtain that would shield their privacy when he turned and noted the papers on the floor. He lifted one eyebrow in question as he bent to pick them up. "Yours?"

"Oh!" she squeaked. "My...my errand list. A-and a shopping list." She reached out to take the sheets from him. If he unfolded them, he would see the names and appointment times, and would know what she had been doing at Mr. Evans's office.

Something of her panic must have reached him because he hesitated and gave her a curious look. "Miss Lovejoy, are you certain you are quite all right?"

"Yes, of course." She extended her hand farther in wordless insistence.

He glanced at the papers as if he had forgotten them, then

looked at her and smiled. "If it is errands, I'd do you a favor to lose them."

"No! Please, my lord."

"I was teasing, Miss Lovejoy. Apparently I need more practice. I would not have suspected Mrs. Forbush is such a harsh taskmaster."

"She is not, my lord. The lists are mine. Personal." Afton hated the panic lacing her voice, but she was growing more desperate. The knowledge that he could recognize the appointment list made her dizzy with anxiety.

Slowly, almost reluctantly, Glenross offered her the papers. She claimed them and quickly pushed them back in her muff, safely out of sight. When she glanced up again, he was studying her with a puzzled frown.

"I…I had forgot what was on the lists already, and feared I would return home with errands undone," she said, compelled to offer an explanation for her behavior.

His expression grave, he nodded. "I have a theory about that."

"Yes?" she asked

"If you forget, you truly do not want to remember. And if it is truly important, you will remember."

"Yes, but I recall now that one of my errands is to buy ribbon for Dianthe's hair for the Spencers' ball tonight."

He grinned as he sat across from her. "Ah. Ribbons. Important, indeed."

The shop bell rang and the sound of another group entering the tearoom and taking seats in the main room carried to them in the back. Afton flashed Glenross a nervous smile, suddenly realizing how compromising their discovery together could be. Had she been an ordinary servant, no one would remark upon it, but since she existed on the fringe of society, her behavior should have been more circumspect. Glenross was a controversial man, and his title made him even more interesting to the ton. Ah well, too late now.

Glenross returned her nervous smile with a quirk of his own expressive mouth. She realized he was fully aware of the potential for gossip, and did not care a whit. Odd, she thought, for a man who valued his heritage and family name.

The serving girl brought a tray laden with teapot, cups, little biscuits, muffins and tea cakes, pots of jam and honey and thin cucumber sandwiches. When she'd unloaded the tray, she stepped back and asked, "Will there be anything else?"

Glenross shook his head. "No, thank you, miss. I shall ask if there is."

She bobbed a curtsy and hurried away. After an awkward pause, Afton took charge of the pot. When she had served them both to her satisfaction, she sat back and sipped from her cup. Glenross looked completely out of place with a dainty teacup in his large scarred hand and she couldn't help but laugh.

"I am sorry, my lord, but you do not look altogether comfortable. Which, of course, only indebts me further."

"How so, Miss Lovejoy?"

"That you have sacrificed your comfort for mine. I do not much fancy having to repay you by bellying up to a bar with a tankard of ale, or rum, or some such beverage."

It was his turn to laugh, a rare and unexpected sound. "I would not ask so much of you. I shall count myself well paid if you grant me another waltz."

"Then *do* count upon it, Glenross," she said, more firmly than was wise.

Conversation outside their booth stopped. His identity now known, Glenross's assignation with an unseen woman would certainly be the topic of conversation around dinner tables and dance floors. Afton gave her companion an apologetic look.

"I am sorry," she whispered. "I did not mean to call attention to you."

He did not seem perturbed in the least. "This makes an excellent argument for a less formal form of address, does it not? Please forgo my title, Miss Lovejoy. Call me Rob, or McHugh. All my friends do."

Friends! Did he really think of her as a friend? "I do not believe that would be appropriate," she murmured in a low voice, not wanting to be overheard again.

"I insist."

Afton opened her mouth and formed the "R" but could not bring herself to adopt the intimacy of the word. Indeed, the only male she'd ever called by his given name was Bennett. Why, even her mother had referred to her father as "Mr. Lovejoy."

"Come now, Miss Lovejoy. It cannot be that difficult," Lord Glenross taunted with a wicked grin.

"McHugh," she gasped at last, finding "Rob" impossible to manage. Perhaps someday, if their acquaintance lasted that long, she could try "Lord Robert."

He nodded his approval. "Good enough for now. Come, let's plump you up with cake and jam."

Using silver tongs, he placed a small slice of airy sponge cake on a plate and spooned a dollop of Devon cream and raspberry jam over the top. He placed a fork on the side of the plate and handed it to her with a flourish, as if to show her he was not lacking manners.

Catching his mood, she took a delicate bite, closed her eyes, smiled and moaned, "Mmm…heavenly," as she licked the remaining cream from her lips.

When she opened her eyes, McHugh was looking at her as if dumbstruck. He blinked, cleared his throat and finished his cup of tea in a single gulp. "Yes. Heavenly."

She took a small sip of her own tea, studying McHugh.

He seemed suddenly uncomfortable. "Are you well?" she asked.

"I have thought of something I must do, and the sooner the better."

"Oh?" Afton wondered if she had done something wrong. What could account for Glenross's sudden change of mood?

"Take your time, Miss Lovejoy. Finish your tea and I will send my coach back for you."

"But…ah, that is not necessary, my lord." She groped for words. "I prefer to walk. Really."

He opened the little curtain across the booth a crack. "It is snowing now, Miss Lovejoy. Heavily. The streets will be muddy and unpleasant." His voice was harsh, making it clear that he was forbidding her to walk.

The greatest chill was coming from Glenross, she thought. "I have several errands and will be stopping frequently."

"Where are you going?"

Afton recalled the list Mr. Evans had given her, and that she had a meeting scheduled with Mr. Renquist before her afternoon appointment as Madame Zoe. But she could not tell Glenross that. "Hatchard's, the Exeter Change and…" She halted suddenly, wondering why she felt a need to explain to Glenross. "Really, my lord, I appreciate your concern, but that's quite enough."

The glacial-moss look was back in his eyes. "As you say. I will pay the shopkeeper on the way out." He stood, keeping his hat in front of him and bowing sharply at the waist. With no more explanation than that, he turned and departed. Was this another example of the infamous Glenross unpredictability?

Breathless, Afton arrived at La Meilleure Robe at the appointed time. Mr. Renquist was waiting in one of the back fitting rooms, tapping his foot impatiently. His wife, Madame Marie, gave him a quelling glance.

"François, you are impolite. The girl is on time. Do you attempt to intimidate 'er?"

He looked suitably abashed. "My apologies, Miss Lovejoy. I have been anxious to know what you have for me. The ladies have been quiet of late and I had begun to think they had no further use for me."

She took the little list from her muff and handed it over. She had meant to recopy the names, but her encounter with McHugh had taken all her time. She had read the list, though, and would remember most of the names.

"Interesting," he murmured, scanning the lines. "It reads like a list of the ton's most influential. What is it, miss?"

Afton sighed. "Auntie Hen's appointments for the two weeks prior to her murder."

Mr. Renquist smiled up at his wife. "Marie, this one has an investigator's mind."

Madame Marie ruffled his hair affectionately. "But of course she does, *chéri*."

He grinned, obviously delighting in teasing his wife. He turned back to Afton. "I will look into this at once."

She heaved a sigh of relief. This, at least, was one thing she needn't worry about. Mr. Renquist had handled many cases for the Wednesday League and he could be trusted implicitly. "When should we meet again, sir?"

"I shall put one of my best men on this." He paused, sensing her impatience. "I will leave word through my wife when I have anything to report. Never you fear, miss. We'll find the bas…the cur who did this to Miss Henrietta."

"Thank you, sir. And thank you for installing the little bell in Auntie's flat. It gives me great comfort to know I can summon help if need be."

"No trouble at all, miss. If anything happened to you, the

ladies would skin me alive. I should set one of my men to guarding you.''

"Entirely unnecessary, Mr. Renquist," she said. The last thing she needed was to have some strange man following her or waiting outside Aunt Grace's for her to leave. How would she ever explain that to Dianthe?

"If you should change your mind, miss, just let me know. Best to be safe, eh?''

"I am always cautious, Mr. Renquist.''

He stared at her for a moment and then laughed. "That's a good one, miss. You almost had me there.''

"Oh, Madame Zoe, you *must* tell me what to do! I am so confused, and time is of the essence. I shall go mad trying to figure it out myself.'' The stunning blonde finished shuffling the tarot cards and slid the deck across the table to Afton.

Miss Barlow had been inconsiderately late. A quick glance at the clock displayed the hour. Half past six! Beneath the veils that hid her identity, Afton suppressed a twinge of anxiety. She should have sent the woman away to make another appointment. What demon had possessed her to agree to see Miss Barlow so late in the day? Afton would scarce have time to bathe before dressing for the evening out.

It wasn't that she suspected Miss Barlow of having anything to do with her aunt's death. No, it was money. Filthy lucre. Bit o' the ready. Dianthe's new gown. That's what. And Beatrice Barlow deserved her money's worth. That was only fair. "I must 'ave more information, *chérie*,'' she said in the affected French accent. "'Ow can I 'elp if I do not know the problem?''

Miss Barlow blanched at the suggestion. "I dare not breathe another word! The entire ton says you are the absolute best! Surely you can help me without knowing the particulars.''

''Hmm,'' Afton stalled deliberately. In truth, she was learning more than she cared to know about what went on behind society's closed doors. But drawing on that knowledge did her little good. She knew nothing about Miss Beatrice Barlow other than that she had made an advantageous match and would wed soon. Whatever was troubling her would have to be solved quickly.

''Very well, *chérie*. You understand that it is not for the cards to make the decision, eh? That belongs to you. The cards are only a guide, *n'est-ce pas?*''

''Yes. Yes, of course.''

Afton dealt the cards, deciding upon a horseshoe pattern, the quickest of the tarot spreads.

Miss Barlow twisted her handkerchief and chewed her full lower lip. ''Tell me everything, Madame Zoe.''

''Your first card tells past influences,'' she said. She tapped the figure of an upside-down man in a belled cap. ''You must guard against impetuosity, *chérie,* or face disaster.'' Innocuous enough, and good advice under any circumstances.

''I have not been impetuous in the least. But I must be certain, and that is why I have come to you for guidance.''

''*Oui.* I can see that this is the critical matter.'' Afton turned up the next card. ''Là! The magician! You 'ave the decision to make. You must remain clear-headed, *n'est-ce pas?*''

''Clear-headed?'' Miss Barlow appeared to be baffled.

''*Oui.* Do not 'urry to judgment. 'Ow you *Anglaise* say— 'Act in 'aste, repent at leisure'?''

''Oh, piffle! I haven't the time to mull things over, *madame.* I must decide what to do very soon.''

Another glance at the clock showed the relentless march of time. Feeling a fair amount of urgency herself, Afton turned the third card up. "The lovers! Ah, this explains everything."

"The lovers!" Miss Barlow exclaimed, leaning forward. "Oh, I knew it! Tell me more, *madame*. What do you see for us?"

"He is…'andsome. 'Is coloring is—"

"Dark! Oh, yes! The most handsome of men! You are so terribly clever, *madame*. Tell me, is it true love?"

"The card foretells love, and a choice to be made, *chérie*. Between the flesh and the spirit. Not the same things, eh?"

"No!" Miss Barlow agreed. "My flesh—my heart—tells me one thing, and my spirit and good sense tell me another."

Afton turned up another card. The moon. The card called for use of the nonrational—instinct and intuition—over rational reasoning, a poor prospect where Miss Barlow was concerned. Nevertheless, it was *her* fortune. "Use your instincts, *chérie*. Your 'eart tells you what is best."

Miss Barlow winced. "If only I could be certain."

Afton turned up the next card and was surprised at the way the cards were reinforcing one another. It was almost enough to make her believe in the tarot. Almost. "This—" she tapped the card with her finger "—is the chariot, *chérie*, and foretells travel or distance. Per'aps emotional, per'aps physical."

"Travel! Oh, yes, *madame!* I shall travel, indeed. Oh, this is what I have been searching for. Now I know what I must do," Miss Barlow resolved firmly as Afton nearly pushed her through the door of the small salon. "I shall follow my heart."

Chapter Five

Standing near the fireplace in the Spencer ballroom, Rob watched Miss Lovejoy dance a quadrille with Seymour. She was stunning in a willow-green gown trimmed at the bodice and hem with embroidered pink rosebuds. Her hair was secured at the crown with green satin ribbons and then fell in a shining, pale copper riot of curls to her nape. Had she splurged on ribbons for her own hair as well as her sister's? Money well spent, he observed.

He was still disturbed by his response to her in the tearoom. When she had savored her sponge cake with a little moan and then licked the cream from her lips, she'd been completely irresistible. He'd wondered what it would be like to have Afton moan like that for him. Rob had been seized with such a strong physical response that he'd been afraid he would fall upon her like a ravenous wolf. It would seem he was inching nearer the proverbial edge.

"Lord Glenross?"

He turned to find Mrs. Forbush at his elbow. She wore a gown of silver-gray trimmed in lavender, which displayed her sultry elegance to dazzling advantage. "How are you this evening, Mrs. Forbush?"

"Quite well, thank you. I saw you standing here and

thought to take this opportunity to invite you to attend my salon next Friday.''

An invitation to Mrs. Forbush's much-vaunted and exclusive ''Friday salon'' was an unexpected compliment, but… ''Christmas?''

''I have a number of unattached friends in London for the holiday. I thought we could make our own little family. If you'll come 'round after church, we shall have a merry celebration. Your brother is welcome, too.''

''Douglas has accepted an invitation from his fiancée's family,'' Rob said. He suspected he would find congenial company at Mrs. Forbush's gathering—a gathering of strays, orphans and wanderers. And Afton Lovejoy. ''I, however, shall be pleased to accept,'' he said, watching Miss Lovejoy curtsy to Seymour.

Mrs. Forbush followed his glance. ''I've invited Sir Martin, as well. Do you think he is interested in my niece?''

''Miss Dianthe?''

''Miss Afton,'' she said.

Rob felt a nasty flash of annoyance. ''Would his interest be reciprocated?''

Mrs. Forbush smiled. ''Afton is a paradox, Lord Glenross. She is uncommonly intelligent, and she can appear so worldly and wise, yet she is really quite innocent. At the moment, she is focused on family matters and does not realize the interest in her. I do not know if she would welcome attention from that quarter. I just pray she will not drift into the wrong relationship.''

''Wrong?'' When the implication sank in, he turned away from the dance floor to look into Mrs. Forbush's deep brown eyes. ''Do you think *Seymour* is the wrong sort? Or *me?*''

She smiled again, an enigmatic expression rife with hidden meaning. ''Oh, heavens! I would never say that Sir Martin is not the right sort. I just meant that perhaps he was…well, not the right match for Afton.''

Rob frowned. Surely Mrs. Forbush couldn't be match-making. "What—who—would be the right match?" he asked.

"Someone strong enough to protect her. Someone who has the necessary depth of character to appreciate her. Someone who has a capacity for deep and abiding love. A man of honor."

"Ah, then you cannot mean me," he muttered, startled by the slightest twinge of disappointment. After all, it wasn't as if he wanted to make a match.

Grace laughed. "Which of those things disqualifies you, Glenross?"

"All of them, I regret to say." *And if I had any intentions toward your niece, Mrs. Forbush, they would definitely not be honorable.*

"I confess I have misread you, Glenross. I thought your interest in Afton was, perhaps, more than merely superficial. So then, what *does* account for your interest in her, my lord?"

He watched Seymour lift Afton's hand to pass her beneath his arm. The willow-green fabric smoothed over her décolletage and caused the soft flesh to swell and strain against the row of rosebuds. *Oh, what honeyed heaven did those rosebuds guard?* He cleared his throat. "Can one not simply enjoy the scenery?"

"Indeed. As long as one does not mind a locked gate between himself and the scenery."

"A locked gate?"

"Shortly, by virtue of the interest she is attracting, that particular scenery will belong to someone else, and trespassers will be shot."

He studied Mrs. Forbush's bland smile. Was she issuing a warning?

"Ah well, 'tis not of a pressing nature, my lord." She waved her gray silk fan in a languorous arc. "I am certain you will have entire hours, perhaps even a day or two, to think on the matter.''

Entire hours? Was Seymour's proposal that imminent? Odd how thinking of Afton as someone else's exclusive provenance could cause Rob no little amount of irritation.

''Mmm,'' he answered in a noncommittal undertone as the dance ended and Seymour began escorting Miss Lovejoy back to her aunt. ''I am relieved I have entire hours to contemplate my future.''

Mrs. Forbush laughed, the sound warm, bubbling and entirely unconcerned, as if she already knew the outcome.

''There's the McHugh with your aunt,'' Sir Martin said, ''looking ever so fierce and forbidding.''

Afton smiled. ''Fierce and forbidding are quite ordinary for Lord Glenross,'' she observed.

''Do you suppose he is wooing her? She's quite delectable, is she not?'' He gave Afton a sideways glance, as if measuring her response to his comment.

Bemused by that notion, Afton tilted her head to one side and studied the casual posture of Glenross and her aunt. She'd have thought it congenial, but not romantical. And yes, Grace Forbush was ''delectable.'' The number of men who sent her flowers, paid calls upon her and fought over invitations to her Friday salons would attest to that. But McHugh? She couldn't picture them together—Grace with her cool elegance and McHugh with his seething, rough-edged masculinity. A poor match, that.

She repeated Sir Martin's word. ''Wooing? Do you suppose Glenross knows how to accomplish such a task?''

''May not,'' Sir Martin agreed. ''Maeve was given to him like a parcel wrapped with a bow. Their families betrothed them when they were still in the nursery. He never had to woo or win her. She was always…his.''

His. Afton sighed, wondering what it would be like to be

his. So, they had loved each other since childhood? What sort of woman had won and kept the love and devotion of a man like McHugh, even after death? A small flash of jealousy shot through her. "You knew her? Glenross's wife?"

"Aye. We grew up together, an unmanageable threesome if ever there was one. Willing partners in one debacle after another until we reached adolescence."

Afton was charmed by a sudden vision of three barefoot children roaming the Scottish countryside, causing havoc. "Indeed?"

"Aye. McHugh was our ringleader. He knew every hiding place and every forbidden door in the county, and he could pick any lock known to mankind."

Afton met McHugh's gaze across the distance. A provocative smile curved his lips and a thrill of excitement warmed her. "He was mischievous?"

"Larcenous." Sir Martin grinned.

She laughed. She had always suspected McHugh would not let mere rules stand between him and a goal.

Sir Martin slowed his pace and leaned near her ear to whisper, "So, if not your aunt, Miss Lovejoy, who do you suppose the McHugh is waiting for? Your sister?"

Afton shrugged. "I promised him another waltz earlier today. Perhaps he has come to collect."

"It would have been better if he was interested in your aunt. Since she is a widow, she is free to engage in a discreet alliance. You see, I know for a certainty that McHugh is not interested in marriage. Maeve ruined him for anyone else."

Afton was not surprised. She had suspected as much all along. "I shall warn my sister," she murmured.

"And you, Miss Lovejoy?"

"Me?"

"Did you have any hopes in that direction?"

Afton was startled by the question—both that Sir Martin had asked it, and that she had never contemplated it. Oh, she'd thought of McHugh often enough, but only to wonder what it would be like to kiss him, and if hands gentle enough to replace her hood and wipe away a tear would be likewise gentle in an embrace. She felt the heat of a blush creep into her cheeks at those possibilities.

But hope that he might make an offer for her? Absurd. Aside from the fact that he was still in love with his dead wife, he was far too…intense. There was an impalpable darkness that hovered about him, as if he knew that darkness intimately. As if he cherished it. Courted it.

"Miss Lovejoy?" Sir Martin repeated.

Afton shook her head to clear it of the troubling thoughts. "Hopes, Sir Martin? Nay. I am not that foolish."

Rob wondered what the hell Seymour had said to elicit Miss Lovejoy's delicate blush. It was all he could do to maintain his self-control as he waited for his friend to deliver her back to her aunt. Patience was not Rob's strong point. And neither, it would seem, was sharing.

He took a deep breath and relaxed his tense muscles. What had gotten into him? He had better claim the waltz she had promised this afternoon and then be on his way. Miss Lovejoy was not for him. Too sweet. Too innocent. Too damn tempting.

"Ah, Glenross." Miss Lovejoy offered her hand the moment Seymour released it. "Have you come to collect my debt?"

"What debt?" Seymour asked, his eyes narrowing.

"His lordship rescued me from the weather today." Miss Lovejoy answered for him. "We waited out a fresh snowfall at Twickford's Tearoom until duty called his lordship away. He was kind enough to order me tea and allow me time to warm up."

Rob felt slightly smug at Seymour's look of surprise. "Careful, Miss Lovejoy. Such reckless talk could ruin my reputation. You'll have people thinking I am a gentleman."

She laughed. "I shall be more circumspect in the future."

The orchestra began the first notes of the next dance. "As fate would have it, I *have* come to collect. A waltz, was it not?" Without further ado, Rob whisked his partner onto the dance floor and into his arms.

"I must admit that I am a little surprised," Miss Lovejoy began. "I feared, when you departed so abruptly this afternoon, that I had done something to incur your displeasure."

He gave her a wry smile. He could never admit that, amidst the pots of jam and sponge cake, he'd been about to bend her over the little table and take her then and there. Or how he'd fantasized about being the one to lick the cream from her lips while she moaned, "heavenly." Maeve had been right about that much at least. He *was* an animal. "To the contrary, Miss Lovejoy, I did not find you displeasing in the least. I simply had...ah, urgent business."

His downward glance snagged on the row of rosebuds at her décolletage. Thankfully, Miss Lovejoy did not notice, her attention drawn to the sidelines where a murmur was growing to a buzz. "I wonder what could be amiss," she mused.

Ethan Travis, Rob's old partner, was standing in a group of colleagues and turned to look at them. With a quick jerk of his head, he signaled them to the sidelines. Rob guided his partner off the floor.

"McHugh, did you hear? James Livingston was found murdered in a back street behind the Pultney Hotel. Is that not where you are staying?" Travis asked.

"Jamie Livingston?" Rob went still. "Shocking" news rarely affected him, but this was extraordinary. He had run into Livingston after leaving Twickford's mere hours ago. It was no secret he and Livingston had not been on good

terms since Rob had found him pulling Maeve into a night-
dark garden many years ago, but he certainly would not
have wished such a fate on the man. "Did they catch the
murderer?"

"No. He'd been dead a few hours before he was found.
The bastard took a knife to him, Rob."

A soft intake of breath demanded his attention and reminded him that Miss Lovejoy was a witness to this un-
pleasantness. He looked down at her pale complexion and
horrified expression. "Are you all right, Miss Lovejoy?"

"Yes." She nodded, her eyes wide. "Please do not worry
about *me*."

He gave her a distracted smile and turned back to Ethan.
"Are there any clues?"

"The watchman said he was clutching a button of some
kind. Had a raven on it. Jamie must have grabbed for his
attacker as he went down."

A button? A dim memory tweaked the back of Rob's
mind.

"H-how very awful for you, to lose a friend in such a
manner," Miss Lovejoy gasped.

She looked so distressed that Rob felt the need to reassure
her. Forgetting Travis in his concern, he led her toward a
vacant grouping of chairs near the punch bowl. He seated
her and quickly fetched a cup of punch laced with a touch
of brandy.

He knelt by her chair and offered the cup. "Drink this,
Miss Lovejoy. You'll be fit as a fiddle in no time."

She drank deeply and returned the cup with a sad smile.
"Thank you, Glenross. Really, I am quite all right. 'Tis just
that I lost someone dear to me in much the same manner.
It is dreadful, is it not?"

"James Livingston and I were not close, Miss Lovejoy.
Save your sympathy."

She blinked and he realized he'd been harsher than he

intended. He had a regrettable habit of speaking before considering how others would interpret his words. One of his many shortcomings. He stood again and stepped away from her.

"Oh," she murmured. "You looked so affected that I thought you…that is, well, it is a pity, nonetheless."

"It is indeed," he conceded. But not for the reason Miss Lovejoy would think. He was glad to see the color returning to her cheeks. Now he would be able to leave her and get the hell out of here. "Shall I return you to your aunt?"

"Yes, thank you. I must speak to her at once." When she looked up at him, her aqua eyes were luminous with unshed tears. "I fear I am still in your debt."

"Ah, the dance." He regarded her somberly. "I shall put it on account."

Afton waited until Glenross was out of earshot before she reported the events to her aunt and finished with her latest worry. "It never occurred to me until I heard about Mr. Livingston that Auntie Hen's killer might have happened upon her by chance. Mr. Livingston has nothing in common with Auntie Hen, and yet he was killed as randomly and in the same manner, and there was an object with a raven found at the scene. Perhaps Auntie Hen's murderer was not one of her clients, but a common burglar or thief who was surprised to find her in residence."

Grace drew her eyebrows together in a frown. "Because of the value of the raven pin and the fact that she was found in the fortune-telling salon instead of her little flat, we assumed that the murderer was one of her clients." Grace's eyes met hers. "We must not rule *anything* out, Afton, least of all this new coincidence. Still, I think it far more likely that Henrietta's killer knew her. I shall send a note to Mr. Renquist in the morning, informing him of this new development."

"But if the murder *was* random—"

"Then you are wasting your time," Grace finished for her. "He will not be back."

"And if it wasn't?" Afton shivered, somehow doubting Auntie Hen's murder was as random as Mr. Livingston's.

"Then you have barely two weeks remaining to find the villain before the Wednesday League turns this matter over to the authorities."

Rob locked his door and turned up the oil lamp on the bedside table. His bed had been readied, the fire in the grate had been banked and a foot warmer waited on the hearth for his use. The Pultney was known for its elegance, service and security, and that had seemed just what he needed after months in a hellhole. But perhaps all was not what it seemed.

He shrugged out of his jacket and tossed it over the back of the desk chair. He checked his window, three stories above the street. Locked. He'd known it would be. Just as his door had been locked. He glanced at the wardrobe in one corner, feeling his anxiety rise a notch and a fine coating of sweat dew his brow.

He poured himself a glass of brandy from the bottle on the bedside table, tossed it down in two gulps, poured another and put it on the mantel over the fireplace before crossing the room to the wardrobe. His hand shook as he reached out to turn the latch.

"Bloody hell," he snarled to himself, disgusted with his reaction to the small space. He feared what he might do if faced with that sort of confinement again.

He seized the knob, turned it quickly and opened the door wide. One after another, he examined his jackets and coats. When he came to the coat he'd worn that afternoon, he clenched his jaw. The right sleeve was torn and missing a button.

Years ago, Maeve had ordered custom buttons for his vests and jackets. The Glenross family crest included the Scottish unicorn and the Glenross raven, and Maeve had selected the raven as the emblem to be carved on buttons made of horn, bone, shell and wood.

This was not the first personal item to disappear since his return. A number of other objects, valuable and inconsequential, were missing, too. What the hell was going on?

A sharp rap on his door spun him around. "Who is it?" he called.

"Douglas! Open up, Rob."

He shoved his jacket back into the wardrobe, and when he unlocked his door, Douglas pushed his way inside. "What is it, Doogie?"

"'Tis women, Rob. Bebe is behaving deucedly odd."

"Let me get this straight." Rob exaggerated a thoughtful pose. "You want *me* to explain women?"

"Aye." His brother nodded. "You've been married, which is more than I can say for most of my friends. What accounts for the female vagueness? And why are they so variable from day to day? I vow, Monday Bebe adores me. Tuesday, I am the enemy. And Wednesday she indulges me like a three-year-old. By Friday, I am the Antichrist."

Rob cleared his throat. "Um, well, I am certain this is a very...emotional time for the young lady." In truth, he feared life with Bebe would always be filled with drama. But there was a greater question. "How much do you love her, Douglas? Enough to indulge her moods and whims?"

"Aye. She's everything to me," his brother vowed. "All I want to do is make her happy, and I fear I'm failing miserably."

Rob clapped him on the back and went to his bedside table to pour him a drink. "Here," he said, offering the glass, "you will be needing this."

"So what advice do you have for me?" Douglas persisted.

Rob raised his glass in a salute. "Buy more whiskey."

"This is normal, then? This moodiness?"

"How would I know what normal is, Doogie?"

"Aye. You and Maeve were betrothed from the cradle. She had a long time to accustom herself to the thought of marrying you." Douglas grinned. "'Tis the reason the two of you never fought. Two bodies, one mind."

Douglas was wrong. Rob and Maeve never fought because neither of them had cared enough to argue.

Chapter Six

Thursday morning found Afton brooding over her tea as she read a letter aloud to Dianthe. Outside the garden window, a cold rain replaced the earlier snow, and the whole world seemed drearier. Or was it just the news that made her feel that way?

"I am exceedingly flattered that the invitation was extended at all, seeing that our current circumstances are not as favorable as they once were." That was a colossal understatement, Afton thought as she turned the page over.

"The Sheffields are in a position to improve my standing in society and such other benefits as come with the stamp of approval from a leading family. Thus, I know you and Dianthe will understand why I feel compelled to accept Charlie's invitation."

"Well, I do *not* understand." Dianthe pouted. "Write him, Afton, and tell him the men he would meet in London, and at Aunt Grace's salons, would do him more good in society than any connections he could make in the country. Devonshire, indeed!"

Ignoring Dianthe's editorializing, Afton continued reading. "If I am to be perfectly honest, Binky, were it not as socially prominent a family as the Sheffields extending the invitation, I'd still want to accept. Christmas holiday is always more gay in the country. I miss Wiltshire diversions, and with Dianthe in London now, I do not much relish going home to an empty house, nor do I find the prospect of idling away winter days in Aunt Grace's parlor much to my taste.''

Dianthe harrumphed. "Apparently he has not heard of the popularity of Aunt Grace's Friday salon. Why, two titled members of the ton came to blows over invitations!''

Afton gave an absent nod, thinking that Bennett's decision could work to her advantage. She had been worrying how she would entertain him as well as Dianthe and still tend to her investigation. Bennett would have insisted on knowing where Auntie Hen was, and would not have quit until he had answers. He was just like their papa in that regard.

"Is that all he says?" Dianthe quizzed. "No tender of fond regards for his sisters? No promise to post us tokens of his regret? No apology to Auntie Grace?''

Afton cleared her throat and continued. "I dislike troubling you, Binky, but could you please send along ten pounds pocket money? Wouldn't want to impose upon the Sheffields for incidentals. I beg you convey my regrets to Aunt Grace and Aunt Henrietta. I shall miss catching up on Aunt Henrietta's stories of her travels abroad, but I shall send you all greetings from the countryside.''

Dianthe brightened and clapped her hands. "Oh! D'you think Auntie Hen is coming back from Greece? How lovely it would be if she could be here for the occasion.''

Afton's stomach twisted and tears prickled the backs of her eyes. Not yet. "I…I would not pin my hopes upon it, Dianthe. But perhaps we shall go a-wassailing. Or caroling.''

"I would so like Auntie Hen to meet my beaux. She is such a good judge of character that I know she could counsel me. At the very least, she could tell me who to eliminate."

"Aunt Grace is equally astute," Afton suggested. "And she has the advantage of knowing most of the men who are circling you. I wish I could be of more help."

"Yes, Aunt Grace is quite amazing, but Binky, you need your own counseling. Between Sir Martin and Lord Glenross, I cannot think which I'd choose. Sir Martin, most likely."

Despite being uneasy about her appointment with Glenross later this afternoon, Afton could not hide her astonishment. "You'd choose Sir Martin over McHugh?"

Giggling, Dianthe slapped her knees in delight. "I knew it! You prefer Glenross. Your reaction betrays you. And, in truth, I *would* choose Sir Martin. Glenross is…well, not quite civilized. He is a little too honest to fare well in society. And anyone that well-favored will always bear watching lest he stray. I vow, Binky, he is just so… overpowering. And that, I think, is what makes you his match."

Afton sat back in surprise. "*I* am overpowering?"

"No, silly. But you are the bravest woman I know, aside from Aunt Grace. I can see you as St. George to his dragon."

Brave? She almost laughed. She supposed she had been brave in the decision to ferret out Auntie Hen's murderer, but she had trembled with fear every day since. Knowing that the next person she met at the little fortune-telling salon could be the assassin had begun to wear on her nerves. And each day was one less to find the killer. Only two weeks left.

Rob McHugh took the stairs to Madame Zoe's second-floor flat two at a time. With the circumstances of Livingston's death and the possibility that someone was trying to implicate him, he was anxious to bring his grievance with the charlatan to a close. This was one little annoyance he should be able to handle without trouble.

True, he hadn't had time to gather all the facts, the names of everyone she had defrauded, all the criminally bad advice she had given, nor chronicle the harm she had done. But he had enough to make her damn uncomfortable—hopefully uncomfortable enough to quit her business and leave town. If not, he'd just have to destroy her.

As he lifted his hand to knock on the heavy door, he recalled the slender gloved hand that had dealt the tarot cards, the husky laugh when she had teased him and her naggingly familiar and subtly arousing scent. He suspected it would have been amusing to match words and wits with her. Too bad he didn't have more time to play.

Or was it? After all, the sooner he put her out of business, the sooner she would be unable to misdirect and misinform gullible innocents. He could not forget that it was her advice that had sent Maeve and Hamish to their deaths. It was not just his pleasure, it was his *duty* to prevent Madame Zoe from giving advice that could result in the deaths of yet more innocents.

He rapped three times, ready to put the little swindler in her place.

Faint floral incense coupled with seven candles infused the salon with a mystical quality, warm and somehow welcoming, Afton hoped, in the twilight of early evening. As she stood aside to let McHugh enter, she noted his quick, almost habitual assessment of the room, and wondered how he had come to that sort of behavior.

He skimmed past her, brushing against her shoulder. Was there something vaguely threatening in that action, or was it just her imagination? She closed the door and turned the lock. When she swung around, McHugh was already sitting at the table, shuffling the tarot deck.

"Bonsoir, m'sieur," she murmured.

"Good evening, *madame,"* he replied.

"You wish to get right to the point, yes?" She was disappointed. She had been looking forward to seeing him, to talking with him free of the constraints of the ton. Perhaps it was just as well. Since they shared the same circle of friends, they were likely to be running into one another over the next month or so, and she dared not risk him connecting her with Madame Zoe. Every little familiarity increased her chances of discovery. This would be the last time she would permit him an appointment.

"I do, indeed," he said. He inclined his head toward the chair opposite him. "I am ready for whatever bits of prophecy you may divine."

Afton slid into her chair. There was a difference about McHugh this evening. Something even more challenging than before. The icy green eyes were even speculative. Every instinct she had warned her to caution.

She decided on the ten-card spread, the most popular of the tarot patterns. McHugh must believe he had gotten his money's worth this time. She did not want him to have an excuse to come back again.

She turned up the first five cards and caught her breath in surprise. The queen of cups and the king of swords stared back at her. And around them, danger in the form of the devil and the moon. His last fortune was repeating itself, but with the appearance of the devil, the danger was defined—death. And the moon would indicate deception and a false friend. James Livingston?

"Again, *m'sieur,* I…I think you are in grave danger. I cannot be certain, but every indication—"

McHugh's lips curled into a sideways grin. "Ah, that's very good, *madame.* Could you be any more vague?"

Afton glanced up into the handsome face. Thank heavens for the veils that hid the heat that crept into her cheeks. *"M'sieur?"*

"Is this how you tell fortunes, *madame?* 'I think?' 'I cannot be certain?' 'Every indication?' You certainly allow yourself a wide margin. Three disclaimers in one sentence."

"M'sieur, nothing is certain. Choice always lies within us. If you could not change your future, there would be no need of fortune-tellers. No need to look ahead at all. Everything would be predestined and unchangeable. It is only in knowing what may lie ahead that one can make choices to change it."

"Interesting that you do not subscribe to destiny," he muttered, then lowered his voice in a dark challenge. "Then do you accept responsibility for the choices your patrons make based upon your fortune-telling?"

A chill ran up Afton's spine, the first uneasy stirrings of menace. He was leading her—but where? "I accept responsibility for the telling of the cards, *m'sieur,* but not for the choices others make."

"Choices made based upon your telling of the cards," he pressed.

She put the tarot deck down on the table and folded her hands in her lap. "Are you accusing me of something, *m'sieur?"* she asked.

McHugh sat back in his chair and crossed his arms over his chest. "I scarcely know where to begin."

"The beginning? Do you blame me because I could not define the danger at our last meeting?"

A muscle in his cheek jumped as his jaw tightened, and Afton realized the depth of his anger. She swallowed hard, casting about in her mind for the details of their previous meeting in the little room. "I...I warned you of danger, *m'sieur,* but I could not tell if it was *to* you or *from* you. 'Ow 'as that 'armed you?"

He sat forward and swept the tarot cards into a single pile again. "Allow me to tell *your* fortune, *madame.* I warrant I'll do as good a job as you. Better, perhaps, since I have the advantage of knowing what lies ahead for you."

Afton inclined her head at the deck of cards, knowing she had just stepped into his trap, but feeling powerless to escape it. She barely breathed. "By all means, *m'sieur.*"

McHugh made a show of shuffling. He placed the deck faceup on the table and fanned the cards across the expanse. He pulled the queen of cups out and tossed it toward her. "You, I believe?"

She nodded. *"Oui."*

"Me?" he asked, pulling the king of swords from the pile.

"Oui," she replied.

He frowned, as if trying to remember something. After a moment, he pulled the queen of wands from the deck. "The cause of my *'eartbreak,* I believe?" He mimicked her accent.

"Ça va," she said, growing colder.

He uncovered the nine of pentacles and tapped it, lifting his gaze to study her reaction behind the veils. "Danger."

She nodded.

"I see cause and effect between these cards. They are closely related, though virtual strangers," he said. "The queen of cups has accused the king of swords of being a destroyer, yet it is she who has destroyed." He slid the nine of pentacles from the deck and tossed it atop the queen of cups.

Afton remained silent. She knew he would take his time before explaining. She recognized now the smoldering anger behind the ice-cold eyes, but could not think what she might have done to cause it.

He sought another card and lifted the crowned figure of

a female holding the scales of justice. "Justice, *madame.* There has been a wrong that is about to be avenged."

No! Dear Lord, not McHugh! He cannot have been Auntie Hen's killer! But what is all his talk of vengeance and justice? And why did he connect himself with her? Afton's mind raced even as her body seemed mired in quicksand. "*M-m'sieur,* I do not comprehend."

"Aye, it took me awhile, too. But I had time to puzzle it out. A veritable wealth of time. Countless hours in a solitary box. Days on end manacled to a wall."

She swallowed hard and ignored her shaking knees to stand. "What wrong 'ave I done you?"

"You 'ave altered the course of my life." He mocked her accent again. "And not for the better."

"*Je n'ais—*"

"Enough, *madame.* All your denials ring false."

Afton's heart beat so hard it throbbed like thunder in her ears. She took several steps backward, desperate to distance herself from McHugh, who was now standing, too. "I...I—"

"You." McHugh nodded. "Aye, 'twas you."

"What? What did I do?"

"Does the name Maeve McHugh mean anything to you?"

She searched her memory, trying to make a connection. How could Afton be connected to her? The woman had been gone from England for three years, and dead for at least two, although McHugh hadn't known that until recently. But Afton had been in Wiltshire all that time.

McHugh advanced on her, his jaw clenched. He gripped her upper arms and muttered, "*Maeve,* damn it. Maeve McHugh, Lady Glenross. My wife."

His hands tightened, cutting off her circulation and making her fingers tingle. Her mind raced, frantic for a connection. Auntie Hen! *She* had been in London telling fortunes at that time. "Pray, enlighten me, *m'sieur,*" she gasped.

His voice became a low growl, as dark and dangerous as a wolf's. "You advised her to travel. You said that it was urgent and that she must escape the man she loved. He was a destroyer, you told her. Her destiny awaited, you said."

Afton tried to back away, but McHugh followed. He leaned over her, his mere size an unspoken threat. She remembered hearing that McHugh's wife and son had been aboard a ship captured by Barbary pirates several years ago, and that they had subsequently died of typhoid or dysentery. And Auntie Hen must have told her fortune—must have told her to go on that ill-fated trip.

Heavens! McHugh was bent on retribution. Did he mean to kill her? Had he thought he'd killed Auntie Hen and, surprised to hear she was still alive, come back to finish the job? Another backward step landed Afton against the wall. She glanced at the bell rope across the room.

"Well?" McHugh asked, his mouth mere inches from her ear. If he meant to intimidate her, he was succeeding. "What do you have to say for yourself?"

What could she say? "I…I do not remember 'er," she gasped.

"Good God, *madame!* Do you ruin so many lives that you cannot keep track? Maeve and Hamish are dead, and you cannot even remember their names?"

He moved ever closer and Afton felt the warmth of his body through her clothes, smelled the tangy scent of his shaving lotion, saw the agony in his eyes. What could she say? What could she do to ease his pain?

"I…am sorry. 'ad I known—"

"Precisely," he snarled. "Is that not your business? To know? And that is the crux of the matter. You are a charlatan. A conscienceless fraud who plays with the lives of others and cannot even remember the names of the people you destroy."

He released her and lifted his hand, and Afton flinched, fearing the damage he could do with a single blow. When he raked his fingers through his dark hair instead, she sighed with relief. "My lord, please let me explain—"

"No, *madame*. Let *me* explain." He turned away and went back to the table, gathering the cards into a pile again and dropping them on the smooth surface. He began turning the cards up without looking at them, slowly, methodically, his gaze never leaving her. "There is danger from the king of swords to the queen of cups. He does not like her. He thinks she is a treacherous charlatan. I see a reversal of fortunes. I see trouble ahead, *madame,* and adversity. I see someone watching, waiting for you to make your next mistake. And when you do, he will be ready. You will be exposed for the fraud you are. When the Fates are done with you, not even a madman will employ you to tell a fortune. You are on borrowed time, *madame*. And if you ever harm anyone again, you may double everything I've just told you."

He strode to the door and unlocked it. "Oh," he said without turning, "and remember to keep watch over your shoulder. Whenever you feel safe, whenever you think that I've forgotten—that's when the ax will fall."

Chapter Seven

Afton gave her report to the Wednesday League in Grace's small private parlor while they waited for the Forbush coach to be brought around for the drive to the Woodlakes' rout. She edited the account of her earlier meeting with Lord Glenross. If they knew the whole story, they might forbid her to go to Aunt Hen's salon again.

"And when I turned the cards up, they were very similar to the first time. I saw danger, deception and…and death. I have never seen a stronger caution. When I warned him, he became, well, angry, and advised me to stop telling fortunes," she finished.

Grace clasped her hands in her lap, her knuckles white against the elegant black velvet of her evening gown. "Afton, I am speechless. Did he harm you in any way?"

"Of course not," she hastened to assure her. "He is a gentleman. And I could tell this time that the danger is *to* him, not *from* him." But there was more. "Aunt Grace, how much did Auntie Hen tell you about her clients?"

"Henrietta was very closemouthed about her business, Afton. Discretion was her hallmark. She spoke in generalities, but rarely mentioned names."

"Then, you never heard her mention Maeve McHugh?"

Lady Sarah's delicate hand flew to her throat in a protective gesture. "Maeve? Good heavens! Is that why Glenross sought Madame Zoe out?"

Afton nodded. "I am not certain what Auntie Hen said, but I believe McHugh holds her responsible for the death of his wife and son."

Lady Annica's face registered anxiety. "If he holds Madame Zoe responsible, might he be the one who...that is, could Glenross be the murderer?"

"Heaven forbid," Afton scoffed. All the same, a shiver worked its way up her spine. McHugh was the closest she'd come to finding a suspect since beginning her investigation, and she was not so naive that she had missed the darkness beneath his civilized facade. In fact, she suspected that darkness ran very deep, indeed, and that the man who showed such gentleness and grace in a mere waltz, and in rescuing a virtual stranger from a sleet storm, wore a very thin mask.

"Just the same, Afton, I think you should be careful of Glenross," her aunt said.

Afton nodded, rising from her chair to peer into the hallway and make certain Dianthe had not come downstairs to join them yet. "I went by Mr. Evans's office this afternoon after telling Glenross's fortune, and left a message that he was not to make any more appointments for Lord Glenross. I suspect he will claim the dance I owe him tonight and I intend to test him and make certain he cannot identify me as Madame Zoe. If he suspects any connection between us, I shall find some way to set his mind at rest."

Charity Wardlow gathered her paisley shawl more closely around her and stood, going to the front window to check for the arrival of their coach. "If you need assistance, Afton, I stand ready to render whatever aid you need."

Grace squeezed her niece's shoulder. "I have invited Glenross to join our Christmas celebration, along with some others. I was trying my hand at matchmaking. I should have known better. I shall cancel the party, of course, begging illness.''

Afton felt a fluttering deep inside. Matchmaking? For her and Glenross? But Glenross would never seek a lasting relationship with another woman. He was still deeply in love with his dead wife—to the point of avenging her. Any woman foolish enough to love the McHugh would be certain to lose her heart.

"Please do not cancel, Aunt Grace. Dianthe is looking forward to it, and I cannot avoid him at all the parties and events before Lent. If he does not show any signs of recognition tonight, and if I do not meet with him again as Madame Zoe, I will be quite safe.''

"I think, Afton, that it would be better if you desisted in telling fortunes at all," Lady Annica advised. "We have never been entirely comfortable with this scheme, and if you can come to so much trouble over someone who is no danger to you, then I shudder to think what the real villain could do.''

Afton's resolve hardened. "The Wednesday League agreed to give me until the New Year—eleven more days— to find the murderer, and I intend to use every one of them.''

Grace threw her hands up in defeat. "Swear you will tell us if you notice any difference in his behavior toward you,'' she said.

"I swear," Afton vowed.

The crystal chandeliers, the perfectly tuned orchestra, the footmen circulating through the glittering crowd with trays of rum punch and hors d'oeuvres faded to insignificance. *It couldn't be true!*

"Are you quite certain, Lady Sarah?" Afton repeated for the third time. Her head spun and she clutched at her middle as if she'd been hit in the stomach. "Her pianoforte teacher?''

"Good heavens, Afton! It is not the sort of thing I'd likely misunderstand. Miss Barlow told the Thayer twins you advised her to run off with him, and you know that Hortense and Harriett have never been able to keep a confidence. Now the whole ton is abuzz with it," Sarah confided in an undertone.

Afton searched her memory of reading the tarot cards for Miss Barlow. "I cannot recall what I said." She glanced around the Woodlakes' ballroom, almost expecting to find Beatrice in the crush of pastel-clad women, of men in their elegant white vests beneath conservative jackets. "She would not give me the particulars of her dilemma so I told her that she must use her very best judgment and instincts, and that only she knew what was in her heart. You know— the usual sort of thing."

"Well, she took your advice seriously, my dear!" Annica whispered. "And now all hell has broken loose. Can you credit it? Bebe Barlow running off with her pianoforte instructor! And on your advice!"

"Blast! I should have known something was amiss when she became so agitated at seeing the lovers and the chariot. Now heaven only knows where she is and if she is safe and—"

"Oh, I think we can guess that," Grace said. "She is apt to be halfway to Gretna Green and a preacher. And I'll wager she is safe in all regards but her virtue! Still, there is another who might blame you, Afton."

"Who?"

Lady Sarah raised her fan to cover her mouth to shield her words from strangers. "Robert McHugh, Lord Glenross. I believe you know the name."

"Lord Glenross." Afton spoke it slowly, dread building in her heart. Wasn't she already in enough trouble? "But why should he care what Miss Barlow does?"

"Because he is devoted to his brother," Sarah said.

Afton frowned. "I do not understand."

"His brother, Douglas McHugh, was Bebe's betrothed," Sarah informed her. "They were to be married in January."

"A McHugh was affianced to *Bebe?* Fickle, flighty Bebe?"

"Odd, is it not?" Grace agreed. "Yet more proof that love is blind."

"And yet another crime to my name," Afton murmured, looking at Sarah questioningly. "Even so, how can he hurt me?"

"He does not tolerate insults to his family. The Scots' honor, you know. Aside from that, there is the matter of Maeve. And he believes Zoe is a fraud. He hates frauds. In fact, tolerance is not a virtue I would associate with Rob McHugh."

Afton felt slightly nauseated. Now she knew why he had behaved so strangely in the fortune-telling salon. But why hadn't he come after her before? Then it occurred to her that he had—that very day! "I...I suppose he is very angry?"

"That is an understatement," Sarah said. "I have never seen him so...so furious. And so, I gather, are her father and Douglas McHugh. But this is different." Sarah glanced away and refused to meet her gaze. "Having lost his wife and heir, Rob McHugh has little left of his former life but his fortune and his pride. He has declared that he will not marry again, thus Douglas's children would be his heirs. That is very important to him, and your advice to Bebe has barred that door and made the McHughs look foolish. He will not forgive it."

Lord! They were right; she should cease telling fortunes at once! But she really had no choice. Only eleven more days, and she needed every one! Surely the culprit would come forward by then. She would avoid Glenross in the meanwhile.

"The McHughs are relentless," Annica agreed. "I'm of a mind to think *they* are the real reason Bebe ran off with Mr. Dante Palucci."

"I do not understand. Why would Miss Barlow flee? What did she have to fear?"

Grace gave an odd little smile. "I do not know Douglas, but I do know Robert. I admit, Afton, Glenross has the form of a Greek god and the features of an angel, but he has a darkness to him. He is too hard, too single-minded. He can be charming, but that is merely surface."

Sarah nodded in agreement. "I do not think he has a frivolous fiber in him. I cannot see him reciting poetry or composing pretty speeches for his lady love. But Douglas is different. He is more vulnerable. And he will produce the Glenross heir. *That* is the reason Glenross will come after you, Afton."

She stiffened her spine and lifted her chin. Business. Heirs. Marriage always came down to that for men. "Well then, I cannot feel badly if Bebe has found something better."

"Better? Dante Palucci? He is an Italian wastrel! A fortune hunter. Oh, the McHughs will go after her and bring her back, but Bebe is thoroughly ruined."

Afton cast about for a way to salvage the situation. "Might it be possible for Douglas to wed her anyway?"

"Never," Grace said. She arranged the drape of her jet-black gown in preparation for rejoining the party. "Aside from the question of Bebe's infidelity, Glenross really is not the forgiving sort. A man in his elevated position must have a care to the mother of his heir. She must be a woman who will not subject the McHugh name and title to scandal and ridicule. And he himself must be vindicated, else his public credibility will suffer. A man like McHugh sets great store on reputation and credibility."

Afton's stomach clenched again as she thought of the

lives she had altered with her innocuous advice. "I will find a way to make this come a-right."

"A-right? Are you mad? Can you un-ruin Bebe? Or resurrect Maeve and Hamish? There's nothing you can do, Afton. And, despite what you are feeling, it is not your fault. McHugh and Mr. Barlow must share the blame. When a woman is betrothed for convenience, she is apt to do something desperate."

"Convenience? But you said Douglas was fond of Bebe."

"He is. 'Tis her father's convenience I mean. But really, Afton, the best thing—the *only* thing—for you to do is quit. Retire at once and disappear quietly."

Afton frowned, thinking of her family—winsome Dianthe with high hopes of making an advantageous match, and ambitious Bennett, determined to rebuild the family fortune and care for his sisters. Was there anything she would not do for them? Any risk she would not take?

No, if she was in for a pence, she was in for a pound. "I cannot quit," she said with desperate finality. "There is too much at stake."

The orchestra struck up a reel and Grace tugged her hand. "Come, then. We shall find Dianthe and pay our respects to our host. Enjoy yourself tonight, Afton. It may be your last party before Glenross calls Madame Zoe to public account."

It was impossible for Rob to ignore the titters and whispers behind fans and the suddenly hushed voices that followed in his wake as he crossed the ballroom toward his target. The news of Bebe's defection was now public knowledge. He could cheerfully strangle the silly little chit for her shortsightedness. She did not have to ruin herself to escape marriage to Douglas. A simple "I've changed my mind" would have done the trick. A bitter blow to Douglas, perhaps, but it would have left his brother's pride intact.

Now Bebe's father and Douglas were off in hot pursuit of the eloping couple. Rob prayed they would find them ere they stood before a smithy in Gretna Green. And that Douglas did not kill the Italian on the spot. Rob's brotherly pride was pricked by Bebe's defection and he would deal with that, but less forgivable was the insult to the McHugh name and Glenross title. Common little Bebe could have been mother to an earl, and she had thrown it all away for an anonymous Italian music teacher.

Rob needed to enlist Mrs. Forbush's help again. If he could convince her to assist him in salvaging what was left of Bebe's reputation, it would have been worth running the gauntlet of pitying glances. But that was only part of it. He needed to salvage what was left of the McHugh reputation, as well. He'd be damned if he'd let society pity them. He could better stomach their scorn. He could hear the gossip now. *First the McHugh lets his wife and son be killed, then his younger brother is made a cuckold before his wedding! Are the McHughs so inept that they cannot keep a woman?*

A woman... And that brought him full circle to Miss Lovejoy. He wanted to see her again. He needed to know which camp she would join—the rumor mongers or the pitying sympathizers. It would be interesting to see how the ton would line up, but there had been something in Miss Lovejoy's quiet, strong bearing that made him believe *she* would make her own decisions. He could not say why, but her opinion mattered to him.

His trepidation grew when he noted that Miss Lovejoy was, indeed, with Mrs. Forbush. They were accepting wineglasses from the tray of a liveried footman. Rob was close enough to know, even before she turned, that she was stunning. The mass of coppery-blond curls arranged at her crown exposed the graceful arch of her neck and slender

line of her back. But when she actually faced him, she took
his breath away. Her lilac gown was trimmed in pristine
white lace, a perfect frame for her beauty. He took her politely offered hand to find it soft but not yielding. She met
his gaze without flinching. There was no hint of pity or even
titillated curiosity about her. To the contrary, there was
something faintly challenging in her study. When she curt-
sied, she did not drop her gaze as was customary, but held
his in open study. Her voice, when she said his name, was
soft and husky, and the sound of it brought his blood up.

"Lord Glenross," she acknowledged.

The stirring in his loins gave him a moment of discomfort. Unable to resist the urge to test her, he lifted the delicate hand and grazed the soft flesh with his lips. He felt,
rather than heard, her intake of breath.

"Miss Lovejoy," he replied.

Mrs. Forbush cleared her throat, pulling him back from
the brink of yet another scandal. He released Miss Lovejoy's
hand and turned to her, bowing at the waist.

"Mrs. Forbush. I hoped I might find you here tonight."

"Did you?" she asked, a note of mild surprise in her
voice.

"Once again, I require your assistance." He would find
some way to repay her. He did not like being in anyone's
debt.

"How, Lord Glenross?"

"You, ah, may have heard the recent rumors regarding
my brother?"

"I have heard whispers," Mrs. Forbush admitted.

"Yes? Well, I would like to change the tone of those
rumors. Considerable damage could be done if the current
story is allowed to run unchecked."

"I see," Mrs. Forbush said. "But why have you come
to me?"

"Your consequence in society, Mrs. Forbush. 'Tis well

known you are a woman of integrity. No one would doubt your veracity.''

Mrs. Forbush looked uncomfortable at his praise and he began to wonder if she would help him. ''There is no reason they should, my lord. But how can that be of help to you?''

''I would like you to correct the current rumor to one less damaging. You may, of course, quote me as the source.''

''Correct? In what way?''

Rob shot a quick glance at Miss Lovejoy. He had never before found himself in the position of trying to manage society's impressions, and he loathed the necessity now. ''I would like you to let it be known that Miss Barlow and my brother had come to an amicable parting of ways prior to her, ah…''

''Ill-advised elopement?'' Mrs. Forbush finished for him.

''Well, yes.''

''Hmm. I can see how this would mitigate the damage to Miss Barlow's reputation, but how will it help your brother?''

''He will not seem like a fool. And perhaps my brother *is* at fault,'' he hedged.

Mrs. Forbush gave him a stern look. ''If you want my help, you will have to tell me the truth, Glenross.''

She was too perceptive by half. ''Very well. There is someone at fault here, Mrs. Forbush, but it is not my brother, and it is not Miss Barlow.''

''Your brother is quite the gentleman to shoulder any part of the blame. Does he realize that Miss Barlow's reputation will not escape blemish altogether? When all is said and done, Mr. Palucci is scarcely a suitable match, is he?''

''I have thought of that, Mrs. Forbush, but I am flummoxed. There is nothing I can do about Miss Barlow's choice.''

She smiled at him. ''My last question, Glenross. Why have you involved yourself in Miss Barlow's bad judgment?

Your brother has been betrayed, after all and, should I do as you ask, speculation will have it that *Miss Barlow* was on the rebound from a cruel jilt. Your brother's reputation will suffer and he will be hard-pressed to redeem himself.''

''If we do nothing, Miss Barlow will face consequences more dire than she could have envisioned due to someone else's machinations. Douglas is better equipped to weather this particular storm, and at least he will be spared the humiliation of having been publicly jilted.''

Grace sighed. ''I have no objection to helping you salvage Miss Barlow's reputation, but how shall I reconcile that with the unjust damage to your brother's?''

''By knowing that it was his wish, as well as mine.''

Mrs. Forbush expelled a deeper sigh. ''Very well, Glenross. You may consider it done.''

He nodded, relieved to leave it in her capable hands. He bowed to the ladies, on the verge of excusing himself when Mrs. Forbush stopped him with an astute question.

''So, Glenross, if neither your brother nor Miss Barlow are responsible for this debacle, who is?''

''That damn meddling Madame Zoe,'' he growled. ''She actually advised Miss Barlow to 'follow her heart'! Run off with the foreigner! Whatever happened to duty and obligation? And what, in God's name, does the French crone have against the McHughs?''

''I…I am sure I don't know.'' Her voice was so meek he could scarcely hear her.

He frowned, recalling his second order of business. ''How can I find Madame Zoe? Do you know where she lives? I would prefer not to lurk outside her salon until she turns up.''

He intended to stalk her! Afton grew light-headed and her wineglass slipped from her hand to stain her lilac gown. Grace offered her handkerchief. ''Afton dear, perhaps you should go to Lady Woodlake's retiring room? Shall I take you there?''

Lord Glenross glanced down at her hem. '''Tis barely visible, Miss Lovejoy. No one will notice.''

"She should not have come tonight," Grace interjected. "I think she is coming down with something. She has been a little unsteady."

Glenross tilted his head to one side. "Is that so, Miss Lovejoy?"

Afton cleared her throat. For better or worse, she had to know if McHugh suspected she might be Zoe. "I am better, Aunt Grace. Thank you for your concern, but Glenross is right. The stain is insignificant."

"Are you up to dancing, Miss Lovejoy? I hear a waltz."

She met her aunt's gaze and forced a casual smile. She was about to risk the entire future of her family on a single dance. '''If it were done when 'tis done…'''

'''Then 'twere well it were done quickly','' Grace answered with an unhappy look.

As Glenross led Afton onto the dance floor, he leaned toward her and spoke in a tone of confidentiality, a wicked smile on his face. "Am I something to be done with quickly, Miss Lovejoy? And here I was thinking women considered slowness a great virtue in men."

Afton was uncertain what he meant, but suspected it was something risqué. "I referred to the dance, my lord. And my own misgivings about dancing. As your feet will attest, I am a novice. Indeed, I would be pleased to give you twice the time you request of me, since you have been my most patient partner. It was not I who ran off Saturday night."

"Extraordinary circumstances, I assure you. I was rude, and I have no excuse."

"But you do. It is not often that someone you have known since childhood is murdered."

Another guest opened the French doors to the terrace, and

a cool breeze made the candles in the chandelier flicker as the air around them freshened, clearing away the mingled scents of foods, flowers and exerted dancers. Chill bumps rose on Afton's arms and she tilted her head back and laughed with exhilaration.

McHugh breathed deeply, as if to cleanse his lungs of a poison. A curious look passed over his face and he leaned closer as he led her into a turn. His breath was warm on her neck as he leaned closer still. "Now that I can sort out the smells in this closed-in room, Miss Lovejoy, I must compliment you on your perfume."

"Thank you, my lord," she said, feeling the heat rise in her cheeks.

"Does it have a name?"

"Vent de Lis." She smiled, thinking McHugh did not seem like the sort of man who would remark upon a woman's perfume.

"Ah. I knew I caught the scent of lilies," he murmured in a husky voice. "I find I am more attuned to scent recently. When one is denied movement and light, one's other senses become heightened. I learned to appreciate all manner of things I never used to notice at all."

Did he refer to his captivity in Algiers? She looked down at the hand that held hers, wondering how he had come by the livid scars on them, but afraid to ask. She could only imagine what sort of horrors he must have endured in that foreign prison. She had overheard Auberville, Travis and Lord Barrington whispering about torture, deprivation and isolation. Surely such things would not leave a man unaffected.

"May I ask where you get it?"

She blinked, trying to recall the thread of their exchange. *"Vent de Lis?* Monsieur Le Blanc's Perfumery, my lord."

"In Oxford Street?"

"You know it?"

"I have seen his sign. I shall go tomorrow."

"Are you looking for a gift, McHugh?"

"You might say that."

She realized it would have to be a gift for a female, and was annoyed by a little flash of jealousy until she recognized the absurdity of it. Had McHugh been looking for a love token, a poor relation like Afton Lovejoy of Little Upton would never have been a recipient. And had she been looking for a suitor, she would have avoided Robert McHugh like the Black Plague. He was none of the things she needed in a husband—manageable, predictable, gentle, civilized. Oh, but it was thrilling to tease him when he had no idea how he'd been tricked.

She shrugged and gave him a saucy smile. "If I can be of assistance, my lord, you need only ask."

His lips twitched. "I shall remember the offer, Miss Lovejoy, and may prevail upon you again in the future. The very *near* future."

The candlelight flickered again and dimmed. How extraordinary that the glass globes protecting the flames seemed to offer no protection from that errant wind. A soft murmur rippled through the crowd and the orchestra faltered. Glenross, however, did not falter for a second. He waltzed her toward the sidelines with an amused look on his face.

"Do you suppose anyone will think to close the doors, Miss Lovejoy?"

"Too simple a solution, Lord Glenross." She laughed, tilting her head back to look into his eyes. A thrill sliced though her and she caught her breath.

The look on Glenross's face sobered and grew intense. He came to a sudden stop beside one set of closed French doors and released her hand long enough to open them wide and then innocently rejoin the dance, skirting the outer edge of the dance floor.

"What are we doing?" she asked, caught up in his little prank.

"Tempting fate," he said in a husky drawl.

Almost immediately another blast of cold wind billowed the curtains and sent dead leaves skittering along the marble floor among the dancers. Glenross halted in a dim corner away from the fireplace just as the candles guttered and died. Afton could only distinguish his outline as voices raised in laughter and shouted directions filled the room. The orchestra, deprived of their music, waned in a discordant clash.

"And fate has taken the challenge," he whispered. His head lowered and his breath was warm against her cheek.

Fate? Her mind whirled. She knew what was coming, and knew she should prevent it at all costs. Instead, she tilted her head back farther and parted her lips just the tiniest little bit. "Who am I to deny fate?" she asked.

"Who, indeed?"

Masked in darkness, his lips brushed hers, tentative at first, then firmer, more certain. His arms tightened and drew her up against the solid wall of his chest, her breasts aching for that contact, her thighs against his thighs, her belly against his. Something stirred in her center, turning her liquid in his embrace.

She was startled by the invasion of his tongue, at first probing, then coaxing, insisting, but she was even more startled by her own response. When she thought he would consume her, she gave him access—sustenance to his hunger, abandoning herself to the moment.

One heated hand against the small of her back held her fast, and the one that had cupped her head traveled across her shoulder and beneath her arm toward her bodice. Panic licked at the edge of reason. Though unseen, they were in public! He meant to...to—

He groaned. "The candles! Where are the damn candles?'' he whispered. "If someone does not light them soon, I shall lay you on this floor, and nothing would stop me then.''

Oh, Lord! If he did, could she stop him? Would she? His fingers brushed across her breasts and her knees went weak from shock and a sweet yearning. She sagged against him and heard his curse, muffled against her throat.

A dim glow grew brighter and the room began to come into focus again as servants brought new candles to relight the lamps and chandeliers. Glenross stepped back while supporting Afton with one arm until she steadied. Laughter and banter swirled around them, but none of it made sense. As the musicians attempted to find the place they had left off, Glenross looked down at her with sharp, glittering eyes.

"Have you been warned about me, Miss Lovejoy?"

She nodded, incapable of subterfuge in the face of that extraordinary kiss.

"I am everything my detractors say, and more. If you have a care for your future, you will stay as far away from me as you can.'' His voice was a harsh whisper as he added, "And do not count on me—*never* count on me—to rescue you from yourself. I would despoil you in an instant.''

Afton's heart twisted when she recognized his words as the absolute truth. And given that he would treat Afton Lovejoy, who had never caused him a moment of concern, with such disregard, what might he do to Madame Zoe? Thank God he did not suspect her.

Chapter Eight

"A list?" Monsieur Le Blanc repeated. "You want a list of women 'oo purchase *Vent de Lis?*"

Rob jingled the coins in his pocket to make a point. "That is precisely what I want," he confirmed.

The wraith-thin man wrung his hands and frowned. "But I do not keep lists of such things, *m'sieur. Vent de Lis* is not one of my more popular perfumes. The scent is too light and delicate for most of my clients."

Damn! Now what? He couldn't even describe Madame Zoe other than to say she wasn't old *or* French. "If you do not know who, then how many?"

The man gave a typically French shrug. "Per'aps seven, per'aps ten? They are not my usual clients."

Rob tried a different tack. "What sort of woman buys that scent?"

"Hmm." Monsieur Le Blanc frowned and glanced at the ceiling as if consulting some astral chart. "Discriminating? Subtle? Uncomplicated? It is not my most expensive scent, but neither my least expensive. Gentility, per'aps, if not nobility."

Rob nodded, thinking of Miss Lovejoy. That description fit her perfectly. But not Madame Zoe. *She* was a diametric opposite to Le Blanc's description, being indiscriminate, cunning, deceptive, elusive and secretive. Yet she wore the same scent.

"Do you have any delivery records?" he asked.

"*Mais non.*"

"Surely you must recall a name or two?" Rob withdrew his hand from his pocket and laid a crown on the counter.

"Hmm." The man tapped the coin with one fingertip and slid it toward himself. "There is a woman of depth and many layers. She comes 'ere with 'er aunt. Miss Lovejoy, I think."

Rob nodded. "She sent me here, Monsieur Le Blanc."

"Ah, you know 'er."

"Yes. But it is not her I seek."

"*Très bien,*" Le Blanc said. "I shall make the list of those 'oo purchase *Vent de Lis* as they occur to me."

"Thank you, Monsieur Le Blanc. I will pay you handsomely upon delivery." Rob turned toward the door, anxious to get out of the impossibly small shop. The walls were beginning to pulsate around him.

The merchant beamed as he began walking Rob to the door. "You know, I 'ave considered addressing Miss Lovejoy myself."

That piece of news stopped Rob. He studied the man with new interest. Though he was no judge of what women found attractive, he knew he wouldn't find Le Blanc attractive if he were a woman. And Miss Lovejoy was far above the touch of an obsequious immigrant shopkeeper. Still…

"I 'ave the weakness for *cheveux rouges,*" Le Blanc confided.

Oddly annoyed, Rob nodded. But he wanted to encourage the man to keep talking. He might remember other names.

"Miss Lovejoy 'ides many secrets. Each time I meet 'er, she reveals a little more. I am fascinated, I confess, by 'er contradictions."

"Contradictions? How so?"

"'Ave you ever 'ad a *prostituée,* my lord, and found she is a beauty when she is cleaned up? 'Ave you ever removed a woman's rough wool gown to find a silk chemise beneath? Surprising. Erotic, eh? Miss Lovejoy is like that."

Unaware of how close he was to a broken nose, Le Blanc continued. "'Er appearance suggests fire and passion, but 'er manner is cool and aloof. Beneath the surface, what will you find? Fire or ice? 'Oo knows? But there will be silk, I think. Much silk."

Silk. A vignette of Afton Lovejoy tilting her mouth up to Rob while he brushed his hand over the exquisite softness of her breasts flashed through his mind. Then, illogically, he wondered if Madame Zoe wore silk beneath the dark widow's weeds and veils.

Bloody hell! It was worse than he'd thought! He was teetering on a sharp edge again. His treatment of Miss Lovejoy the night before was evidence of that. The only decent thing he'd done was to warn her away from him because, God knows, *he* did not have the will to stay away. Her sweetness, her humor, her quiet strength and her commitment to her family all combined to make her incredibly irresistible.

His conscience, or what was left of it, had been pricking him all day. Perhaps Travis and Seymour were right—he should make use of a Covent Garden abbess to dull the edge before he did some irreversible damage.

"*Oui.* When next Miss Lovejoy comes with 'er *tante,* I will ask permission to call upon 'er. I am certain she will welcome my interest."

"You do that," Rob said. *Damn French,* he thought.

Afton dropped the veils over her face, opened the door and stood aside for Lady Enright to glide into the room on a lavender-scented cloud for her weekly visit. Eloise Enright was a well respected member of the haute ton, known for her wit and charm, and had been Aunt Henrietta's favorite client. "Madame Zoe. So good to see you again. I confess I nearly canceled twice today. Still, I felt it was important to come." The woman unpinned her hat and tossed it on the table, then began peeling away her white kid gloves.

Afton was grateful she hadn't canceled. At the moment "Madame Zoe" was buried in cancellations. She had become anathema to the ton once the news of Bebe's elopement came out. It seemed no one wanted to employ a fortune-teller who gave such ghastly advice, and the bill for Dianthe's new gowns would be arriving any day.

According to the notes in her aunt's most recent journal and her own observation, Lady Enright often simply wanted to talk, to air her problems and perhaps solicit a second opinion. Afton suspected the process allowed her to sort through her thoughts and put them in order in an atmosphere of confidentiality. "My pleasure, *chérie,*" she said in her husky French accent. "Shall we use the tarot—"

"Ah, yes—the trappings." Lady Enright waved impatiently. "Use the crystal orb, *madame.* I have no patience for shuffling and dealing today."

This was as close to acknowledging that fortune-telling was a pretense that Lady Enright had come since Afton had taken over for her aunt. Suspecting something unusual was afoot, she took the small crystal orb from the cupboard, removed the black velvet covering, and placed the object on a little stand in the middle of the table. "Will you 'ave tea, m'lady?" she asked.

"Not today, *madame.* If you have a glass of sherry, I'd be very grateful."

"But of course," she murmured. Whatever was bothering Lady Enright must be quite out of the ordinary. Afton went to her meager cupboard, poured a rich sherry into a crystal goblet and placed it on the table in front of her patron. When she was settled in the chair opposite her, she instructed, "Make your wish, *chérie.*"

"Wish? To be frank, I do not know what I should wish for. Tell me what you see if, indeed, you see anything."

Afton pretended to gaze into the ball. If she watched it steadily for a few moments without blinking, she could often conjure clouds and some vague impressions of forms and movement in the depths, a trick of the eyes due to the hypnotic effect. When that happened, she allowed her mind to put words to the impressions. "I see a man…" She waited for the inevitable response.

"Of course you do, dear." Lady Enright sighed. "Is there not always a man, if not two?"

This was not like her client at all. Whatever was bothering her was sufficiently important that she was hesitant to discuss it. Keeping her eyes on the orb, Afton agreed, "Always, *chérie.* Great beauty can be a curse, *n'est-ce pas?*"

"*Oui,*" Lady Enright responded with a sigh.

No help there. Afton frowned as something dark swirled in the depths of the crystal orb. "There appears to be troubling times ahead."

A humorless laugh met this pronouncement, so unlike Lady Enright that Afton blinked and lost the vision. "You are troubled *now, chérie?*"

"Troubled…" Lady Enright said the word as if she were trying it on for size. "Yes. 'Troubled' would be a fair assessment."

"And it concerns a man," Afton said. The fog in the crystal was back and the dark figure split. "Two men," she corrected. Then one figure split again. "La! Three men?"

"Three? I can think of only two. Fie! Just what I need at the moment—another man to muddy things up."

Afton's head began to ache and she felt a numbing cold all the way to the bone. "M'lady, there are many forces at work in your life. Some you know, some you do not. There is a threat, and the possibility of danger. You must be very careful in your decisions. And...and in your actions.''

"Danger, yes. And betrayal." Lady Enright pressed her fingertips to her temples and winced. "That is the very crux of the matter, dear Zoe. So many decisions looming, and no way to know the right one."

She sighed and sipped her sherry before continuing. "You see, I have come here today because of you—because of the friendship we have forged over the past years. I shall not pretend I have not heard the gossip, and that you are out of favor with the ton. Such silly people, really. They toss this way and that with every little change in the wind."

Afton sat back in her chair. She had not expected Lady Enright to broach the subject. And there was still another problem. "What I saw in the crystal 'ad nothing to do with me, Lady Enright," she said, certain there was some sort of menace to her patron.

"Zoe, I do not care about the pretense. I do not care that you are a fraud. Your common sense and discretion are all I have ever expected of you. You have given me an avenue to air my most private problems, and have always tendered excellent advice. But others care. Most notably—"

"Miss Barlow's father and 'er betrothed," Afton finished. She nodded through her veils. "Were there a way to change things...to call back my words...I would do so in an instant. I 'ave never intended any 'arm. While I sought to reassure Miss Barlow that all would be well in 'er upcoming marriage, she was interpreting my words in quite another way. I 'ad no inkling, no warning, that she 'ad fixed 'er affections on another and would elope."

"Oh, that." Lady Enright waved one gloved hand in a dismissive gesture. "I never cared much for Bebe. She is a silly girl with little but a pretty face to recommend her. Not at all suitable for Douglas McHugh. No, 'tis not the broken betrothal I mind, but the foolish way another woman entirely chose to interpret your words, and the resulting danger it has brought to you."

Afton licked her lips, gone suddenly dry with anxiety. "Danger?"

"Yes, and my very presence here has brought me conflict, dear Zoe. You see, Lord Robert McHugh means to hang you out to dry. He is bringing all his resources to bear on this problem. Because of him, you are in grave danger. You stand to lose your reputation. Worse, you stand to lose your livelihood."

Lord, was she about to lose the only client she had left? "What other woman, Lady Enright? And 'ow has my blunder caused you conflict?"

"McHugh never fails, you see. He is single-minded and quite without conscience when pursuing a goal. 'McHugh the Destroyer,' Maeve used to call him. Your only hope is to leave town and not return for several years."

Years? Afton could not even contemplate such a thing. In years Dianthe would be past her prime for making a match. In years, Bennett would have been sent down from Eton for lack of tuition, and his future would be dim indeed. Most important, in years Auntie Hen's killer and any clue to finding him would have long vanished. No. Afton could not afford to take Lady Enright's advice.

"I would not advise you to leave if I thought there were any other way to avert this disaster," the woman continued when she remained silent. "You have been a good friend to me, and I will miss you dreadfully. But go you must."

Afton sighed. "'Ow has this caused you conflict, Lady Enright?"

"You may as well call me Eloise, my dear. Might as well be done with the pretense. I know you are not French. I suspect you are well educated and not foreign to society. No!" she exclaimed as Afton lifted her hand to protest. "I do not want to know who you are! You see, that is where the conflict comes. If I know, McHugh will have it out of me. I've never been able to resist him when he is on one of his crusades. And he has enlisted me, along with several other society matrons, to flush you out of hiding.''

''You know him well?'' Afton asked, dropping her fake accent.

''As well as anyone knows him, and better than most.''

Afton's heart began a downward spiral. Was McHugh one of Lady Enright's discreet paramours? And why did that thought disturb her more than that he was bent on her destruction?

''I am a close friend of his family,'' Lady Enright announced with a mixture of pride and regret. ''His mother was my dearest friend before she died giving birth to Douglas. And I sponsored his wife, Maeve, when she came to London.''

Afton shook her head, astonished at the odd twists and turns of fate. How had she missed the Enright-McHugh connection? If only she had taken the time to go through her aunt's older journals! Perhaps she ought to have gone out in society more. But it was too late for that now. She pulled off her dark gloves and massaged her temples through her veil. ''I see. Then the other woman of whom you spoke would be Lady Maeve McHugh?''

''Yes, my dear. Robert is furious with me for recommending you to Maeve. He holds me partially responsible for what happened to her and Hamish. He believes they are dead because of my interference. And your fortune-telling, *madame*.''

Afton nodded. McHugh had said as much the last time he had visited her salon. Tears stung the backs of her eyes. How could she ever undo such a tragedy? How could she ever make things right again? Telling McHugh that it was her aunt who had told Maeve's fortune would not make the man relent. *She* was responsible for Bebe's fortune.

"If I am ever to redeem myself in his eyes," Lady Enright continued as she stood and retrieved her hat and gloves, "I shall have to stay far away from you. I cannot come here again, but neither will I help him destroy you."

"You are very kind," Afton replied mechanically, analyzing her chances of preventing him from finding out if he was so bloody single-minded.

From his position in the opposite box, Rob watched as the plump soprano hit an extended high C and Miss Lovejoy pressed her fingertips to her temples. The opera had just begun, and if she was already wincing, she'd never survive the entire thing. In fact, unless he missed his guess, she'd never make it to the intermission.

On cue, she leaned toward her aunt and whispered something behind her fan. Mrs. Forbush frowned with concern and began to stand. Miss Lovejoy shook her head and held her down with a hand on her shoulder. A short discussion ensued, ending with Miss Lovejoy sweeping her green velvet cloak from the back of her chair and exiting the box. The attention of the other occupants of the box—Martin Seymour, Dianthe Lovejoy, Lord Ronald Barrington and two or three other nameless swains dancing attendance on Dianthe—remained riveted on the stage.

If Rob hurried, he could intercept her at the entrance to the theater. Without apologies to his own companions, he slipped through the curtain to the mezzanine.

He found her standing on the front stairs, hugging herself against the cold. He touched her shoulder and she whirled on him, her aqua eyes wide and sparkling with unshed tears.

"Miss Lovejoy," he said as he cupped her elbow beneath the green velvet, "are you ill?"

"No," she gulped. "You…you just startled me."

She was lying. Those luminous tears had not been caused

by surprise. "I saw you leaving and thought you might need a ride home," he offered cautiously.

"I am not going home," she said as she wiped at her eyes with one gloved hand. "I hoped a short walk in the cold air would clear my fuzzy head. I promised to be back by intermission."

He smiled. So he was supposed to ignore those tears? He could grant her that much now, but he would eventually know what had upset her. "A fuzzy head, eh? The opera has a similar effect on me. Allow me to escort you on a short stroll, Miss Lovejoy. 'Tis still early enough to avoid scandal."

"Said the hound to the fox." She returned his smile. "Was it not just last night that you warned me not to trust you? And that you would despoil me in an instant?"

"Hmm. Did I say that? How uncharacteristically sporting of me. But, in fact, Miss Lovejoy, I rarely ravish young ladies on dance floors. It is considered bad form in our circle."

He was surprised when she chuckled. "I can see how such a thing might curb future invitations."

Damn! He'd followed her to apologize for his behavior in the Woodlakes' ballroom last night, but once again he'd let that rough edge take control. He'd have to do something about that. "So," he asked, "since huntsmen release the fox before they release hounds, shall I give you a head start?"

"Will I need it, my lord?"

"I shall try to behave myself, but the choice is yours. Risk, madam, or safety? You cannot have both." He offered his arm with a small bow and was just a little surprised when she took it. "So you are the adventurous sort, eh, Miss Lovejoy? Not afraid of a risk?"

She gave a choked little laugh and replied, "More adventurous than you could possibly know, my lord."

"I had thought we were past the formalities. I'd rather you called me Rob, but I'll settle for McHugh."

"McHugh." She nodded, as if remembering their agreement.

He gauged that they would have time for a stroll to Seven Dials and back before intermission, so he led the way toward the square at a leisurely pace.

They had walked in silence for a few moments when she said, "You are doing your level best to distance me, McHugh. You never miss an opportunity to warn me against you, or to attempt to shock me with some reference to your past."

"I do?" he asked, but he knew he had.

"Why is that?" She tilted those startling eyes up to him, then veiled them again by dropping her impossibly long lashes.

"Why?" he repeated, a little bemused. He could hear Maeve's voice in his ear. *Tell her, McHugh the Destroyer. Warn her before…* "I suppose it is because I have ulterior motives and, should I act on them, I would not want you to say you were not warned."

"Ulterior, McHugh? In what way? Do you mean me harm?"

Her voice held a note of uncertainty that somehow accused and put him on the defensive. "Good God, Miss Lovejoy, you cannot be that naive."

"There are many ways to present a danger. Prithee, McHugh, in what way are you a danger to me?"

"I'm trying to act a gentleman—not an easy task for me—"

"There! You've done it again. Am I now supposed to go running for safety?"

He laughed. "Would you prefer not to be warned?"

"I have been sufficiently warned, McHugh. By you, my

aunt and half of society. And still I would prefer to make
my own judgment. Tell me what your ulterior motives are.''

"Another of those kisses we shared in the Woodlakes'
ballroom. Quite extraordinary.'' And much more than that,
he thought. Next time, he would not stop at a kiss.

She blushed and her hand on his arm trembled, but she
did not respond. He did not speak again until they turned
up Mercer Street and saw the lights of Seven Dials ahead.
Guessing at the reason for her earlier tears, he asked, ''Are
you still missing home, Miss Lovejoy?''

She sighed. "I long for the simplicity, but I think those
days are gone forever.''

It struck him that Miss Lovejoy and he were facing the
same prospects, but with different expectations. ''Is there
nothing waiting for you in Wiltshire?''

"Nothing but memories, I fear,'' she murmured. "Dianthe will marry and remove to her husband's lands. My
brother, Bennett, will finish at Eton and come home to run
his estate or, if we can find the resources, will go to Oxford
or Cambridge. And I...well, once I have kept my promise
to my father, I will stay with Aunt Grace as long as she will
have me.''

"Have you no hopes for your own future? Not to put too
fine a point upon it, Miss Lovejoy, but are you so ambitious
for your siblings that you do not see opportunity passing
you by?'' he asked. It had not occurred to him that Miss
Lovejoy might not desire what he had thought every woman
desired—a husband, children, her own home.

Her lashes dropped demurely and her lips curled up in an
introspective smile as color suffused her cheeks. "I have
noted a few opportunities, McHugh. It remains to be seen
whether I shall take them.''

Martin Seymour, he thought. Miss Lovejoy and Seymour?
The phrase "pearls before swine'' came to mind. Something

would have to be done about that. He was still pondering that problem when Miss Lovejoy changed the subject.

She clasped her gloved hands together and blew into them. "Brr," she said with a small shiver. "I left my muff at the theater."

A vendor wheeling a cart with a steaming brazier of hot coals pushed by them on his way to the square. "Chestnuts! Hot roasted chestnuts!"

Rob cupped her hands, small and delicate, in his and lifted them to his lips. When he blew into her palms his breath rose in a vapor. She looked up and he recognized his own uncertainty in her eyes. Neither of them, then, knew what his intentions were. One thing was certain. He was perilously close to kissing her again.

Knowing he would not be able to resist her a second longer, he turned to the chestnut vendor and called him back. He exchanged a coin for a paper cone filled with the roasted delicacies and offered it to her.

"Thank you," she murmured, holding the warm chestnuts between her hands.

He turned and started back to the theater. He did not have to look to know Miss Lovejoy was beside him. "Would you like a little nibble, McHugh?" she asked.

Damnation! Why did she ask questions like that? He cleared his throat and took a chestnut, relieved to find that the skin had been split and the nut slipped out easily. He heard the rustle of paper and suspected Miss Lovejoy had done the same.

"Has your brother sent news of Miss Barlow yet?" she asked conversationally.

"I expect her father and my brother back tomorrow or the day after. I hope they will have Miss Beatrice in tow or, at the very least, have news of her."

"I pray so." Afton expelled a soft sigh. "The whole event is so unfortunate."

"Criminal," he corrected. "'Tis criminal."

"Surely not. Why, Miss Barlow is of an age of consent."

"Indeed she is, and she *consented* to marry my brother, Miss Lovejoy. She is in breach of that contract."

"Would you hold her to it?"

Would he? Likely the woman had gone too far to turn back now. Likely his brother would never be able to trust her fidelity again. Likely Douglas would not want society regarding him as a cuckold and so desperate for Beatrice, so lacking in pride, that he would take her on any terms— even unwillingly and as another man's leavings.

Maeve's face flashed through his mind. Maeve, who'd confessed that she'd been forced into marriage to him. "No," Rob admitted at last. "*I* would not hold her to it, but I cannot speak for Douglas. Aside from that, every instinct I have demands retribution for this insult."

"Insult, McHugh, or a prick to your family pride?"

"Are you calling my motives into question, Miss Lovejoy?" he asked, hoping the tone of his voice would be sufficient to warn her away from the topic.

"Yes, I am," she admitted.

Taken aback, he stopped and turned to face her. "Be that as it may, I shall have my 'pound of flesh.'"

Though her expression was solemn, there was an odd glint in her eyes. "You are an unforgiving man, McHugh."

"Do you think I take this situation too seriously?"

She hesitated. "Possibly."

No one except Travis had ever called him to account for his behavior before. "Impertinent chit." He hid his grin.

"Perhaps I have nothing to lose, McHugh."

He leaned closer to her face, his mouth mere inches from hers. "More than you realize, Miss Lovejoy," he said, leaving little doubt as to his meaning.

"Do not presume to know my circumstances, McHugh."

Was that a challenge? How interesting.

What the hell was wrong with him? He'd followed Miss Lovejoy out of the theater to apologize to her for the kiss they'd shared. He sure as hell hadn't meant for it to happen again. And it looked as if he wasn't going to succeed in either intention. His skin hummed in anticipation of feeling her against him.

Afton Lovejoy had the potential to make him forget himself, to make him believe that he was capable of something good again. But that was madness. She might be the only woman he'd met who'd been undaunted by his reputation, but she was also an intelligent, principled, responsible woman who'd sacrificed her own future for that of her family. A woman who would want nothing to do with him if she knew the depths to which he had sunk.

"McHugh? Lord Glenross? Are you well?"

The voice—soft, musical, genuinely concerned—stopped him. He took her arm and spun her around to face him. Startled, she dropped the paper cone and chestnuts rattled on the ground, bouncing and rolling around them. He leaned in, thinking he would steal that kiss now.

He brushed his lips against hers tentatively, hoping to keep his hunger in check even as he could feel it surging upward, demanding to be satisfied.

She gave a throaty moan as she tilted her head back farther to accommodate his kiss. The sight of her heavy-lidded gaze nearly pushed him over the brink. Had she been reclining when she'd looked at him so, she'd be impaled on his shaft by now. Instead, he gave an answering growl and tightened his arms around her as he claimed those offered lips with a ferocity that startled them both.

A party of drunken revelers rounded the corner on Long Acre, exchanging good-natured shouts and buffoonery. They staggered past them, making ribald remarks and inviting them to join their group. Rob refused with a wave of his hand.

He stepped back from Afton, his jaw tight. "What will you do when no one is near to rescue you from me, I wonder?"

She gave a short, humorless laugh. "Yes. I wonder, too."

He hesitated when he realized that little admission could be construed as an invitation. He gave her a sideways glance as they started walking again. "I like your honesty. I value it. I have not had much of it from the fairer sex."

She gazed up at him, a stricken look in her eyes. "Please, McHugh. I...I am not what—"

"Be glad of your principles, Miss Lovejoy. If you were not so honorable, I'd find little reason to behave myself."

She shivered again and gathered her cloak closer before heaving a deep sigh. He'd give half his fortune to know what she was thinking.

Chapter Nine

Afton hung back near the heavy velvet draperies of the Grants' music room. Her attention was riveted on the quartet playing on the little dais Mrs. Grant had specially constructed for the occasion. Diffused light washed the room with an ethereal quality and softened the outline of the seated guests in front of her. Standing apart from the tableau, Afton felt oddly alienated and vulnerable.

Her hand fluttered up to her coiffure, where she'd attached the onyx raven stickpin to her yellow hair ribbon, wearing it like a challenge. *Come and get me,* it cried. Would anyone take the bait?

She was desperate. Her time was running out, only ten days remaining before the end of the year, and she'd made no progress in finding Auntie Hen's killer.

The air stirred beside her and a soft voice whispered in her ear. "Do you not like the music, Miss Lovejoy?"

Drats! Just Sir Martin. "It is divine," she whispered back.

"Then you should sit and enjoy it with the others," he said.

She turned to face him and smiled. "I think Mrs. Grant invited more guests than she could accommodate, Sir Martin. I gave my chair to Mrs. Eliot the elder."

"Your kindness is a part of your charm, Miss Lovejoy. I believe there is still a chair next to mine," he offered.

She muffled a little laugh. "That is very kind of you. But I think that would shock my aunt."

"I see. You'd rather hide back here? As if you are afraid someone might notice you?"

I am, she thought, resisting the impulse to touch the raven pin again. She gave what she hoped would be an elegant shrug. "I am more concerned that people should notice Dianthe. I would like to see her satisfactorily situated."

"Shh!"

Afton winced in response to the rebuke from the back row of guests. "Sorry," she whispered.

Sir Martin lifted her hand and tugged her toward the corridor. "I would like to speak to you, Miss Lovejoy. Shall we have a cup of punch?"

A protest was on the tip of her tongue when she realized Sir Martin had more on his mind than a cup of punch. They had been speaking of Dianthe. Perhaps he wanted to discuss her sister. Her hopes soared. Oh, if she could just secure Dianthe's future, half her problems would be over!

They found their way to a large reception room where buffet tables laden with punch bowls, tea- and coffeepots, tea cakes and biscuits, fruit and cheeses had been readied for the reception at the conclusion of the musicale. A few discreet servants stood ready to serve, hands clasped behind them in silent expectation.

Sir Martin waved one footman back as he helped himself to the punch. He offered the first cup to Afton and then took one for himself. With a small nod, he indicated a conversational grouping of chairs in one corner. As she followed his direction, she noted that his expression had changed.

"Is something amiss, Sir Martin?" she asked as she sat in a straight-backed chair.

"No. I was bemused. The little ornament you have on

your hair ribbon gave me a moment's pause. I know I've seen something like it before, but I've forgotten where. Doesn't look like a woman's geegaw.''

Afton's heart raced and she fought to maintain her calm. ''The blackbird? It was my aunt's.''

He looked surprised and a little wary. ''Mrs. Forbush's?''

''No,'' Afton admitted. ''My father's sister.''

He leaned closer to study the pin. ''I'd say it was a raven, Miss Lovejoy. Raven. Hmm.''

''Yes?'' she said encouragingly.

''I recollect…ah, never mind.''

He knew something! She blinked ingenuously. ''Does someone you know have one similar?''

''I wouldn't think there are many like it,'' he murmured, a frown creasing his forehead.

''If you know where I could get another, I would be most grateful. Dianthe has always admired it, and I would like to give her one of her own.''

''If I recall it, I shall be happy to let you know.''

She could not risk forcing the issue. She had more to lose than gain if Sir Martin started asking her questions about her aunt or where she had acquired the pin. Afton sipped her punch. ''What did you wish to discuss, Sir Martin?''

''Discuss?'' he asked, as if he'd forgotten why he'd led her from the music room. He glanced at the raven pin again. ''Ah, yes. I was thinking of Rob McHugh. I know he followed you from the theater last night. I think he may be, ah, misleading you.''

''Misleading?'' she repeated, thinking of that extraordinary kiss outside the building. She'd wanted it to go on forever.

''Yes, Miss Lovejoy. I am sorry to be the one to tell you, but nothing can come of his interest.''

''I am aware of that,'' she said, trying to keep her embarrassment under control. She did not need Sir Martin's reminder that she was not a suitable match for McHugh. Nor that his heart still belonged to his deceased wife.

"You are? But that is excellent. I feared you had fallen under his influence. He has always had that effect on women. But, of course, *now* things are different."

Her insides twisted when she thought of McHugh as a womanizer. Odd that she hadn't seen evidence of that at the events they'd attended. Still, a man as good-looking as McHugh could likely have his pick of women. "Really, Sir Martin, I do not think—"

"It's the blasted Moors, you see." Sir Martin gave her a sideways glance.

"This is really none of my...what have the Moors got to do with McHugh's intentions?"

"Well, nothing to do with his intentions, precisely. More a matter of the execution, if you catch my drift."

Her curiosity aroused now, Afton leaned forward. "No, Sir Martin, I do not 'catch your drift.' What execution?"

"Children, of course. That and, er, marital...obligations. 'Tis why Douglas must now provide the Glenross heir. There will not be another from Robbie."

"Heavens." She breathed deeply as she sat back. "I knew he loved Lady Maeve deeply and was mourning her loss, but I never suspected he had lost his *desire* to...to..." She could feel the burning of a deep blush spreading upward from her throat. But why had he kissed her so ardently? What had been the point?

"Gads! The desire is still there. And so, to some degree, is the equipment. But the *ability* is gone! He cannot get a babe on any woman, Miss Lovejoy. He hasn't got it in him. The damn Moors, you see." Sir Martin stopped in his discourse to look over his shoulder, then leaned forward and lowered his voice. "They did things to him when he was their prisoner. Torture. The worst that can be done to a man. If, in fact, you can still call McHugh a man in the truest sense.''

Afton went cold all over. She knew the blush of a few moments ago had drained and a lump formed in her throat as the horror of Sir Martin's words sank into her dazed mind. She could not even imagine what the poor man must have endured. It was no small wonder then that he was so...so oddly at variance—one moment kissing her as if his life depended upon it, and the next warning her to stay away, to not trust him or depend upon him. Oh, it all made perfect sense now. Tears welled in her eyes.

''There! I've upset you,'' Sir Martin growled. ''I knew you had hopes—''

''I am not upset for myself, Sir Martin, but for Lord Glenross. How awful for him to suffer such a fate. How devastating. Has he not lost enough in his family? I feel so guilty for some of the unkind things I have been thinking. I shall have to be more kind, more forgiving, for his occasional lapses in good manners.''

Sir Martin shot her a look of consternation. ''I warned you of this so that you could avoid him, Miss Lovejoy. His, ah, inabilities have given him a rough edge. He could, um, snap, and I would hate to see you hurt in any way.''

''Thank you for your concern, Sir Martin, but what, really, can he do? Surely you do not think he would strike me?''

''One cannot be too sure. McHugh has always been a ruthless man, but now he is an angry man, as well. Being confined to a small box for days on end is bound to have some sort of effect on a fellow. He might be...well, unhinged.''

Unhinged? Lord! Perhaps she had not known McHugh at all. Afton placed her punch cup on the side table next to her chair and clasped her hands together to keep them from trembling. She could have wept for all that had been lost in that Moorish prison.

Douglas McHugh burst into Rob's hotel room, his hands clenched into fists. "She's just gone, I tell you! The little chit and her Italian paramour have disappeared off the face of the earth," he ranted.

"Calm yourself, Doogie," Rob cautioned, holding the door and glancing down the corridor to see if they'd been overheard. The last thing he wanted was for his brother to wake the neighboring guests with this conversation.

"I hoped I would return home to find my fiancée, abashed and repentant, in her room, begging forgiveness for her idiocy. Tell me she's come back, Rob. Tell me this was all just a grotesque joke." Douglas ran his fingers through his thick dark hair and fell into the club chair by the fire.

Rob glanced into the hallway again to see if Mr. Barlow had returned with Douglas. When he found no sign of the man, he closed the door, went to the small side table, poured a stiff brandy and took it to Douglas. He tightened the belt of his dressing robe and glanced at the mantel clock. Half past two in the morning. Evidently his brother had come directly to the Pultney when he'd failed to find Bebe at home.

Rob sighed. "Wish I could tell you she was jesting, Doogie, but I haven't heard a word from her."

"Christ! What was she thinking?" He shook his head. "This whole affair is humiliating for all of us. You are a saint, Robbie! You've been better to me than I deserve. To honor Bebe with your consent, and then for her to treat it with so little regard is more than an embarrassment, it's a goddamn *crime!* And then to have you attempt to save her reputation is more than she deserves. How could she do that to us? She ought to be pilloried!"

That was going a little too far, Rob thought, and spoke volumes about the nature of Douglas's devotion to his ladylove. Perhaps all love was like that—fleeting and wholly dependent upon the other person's behavior. Since he'd never been in love, he wouldn't know. "Calm yourself, Doogie. I will survive the insult, but will you? The match was obviously not a…a grand passion—at least on Bebe's part. And where is Mr. Barlow? Did you leave him in Scotland?"

Douglas snorted. "Once we found they'd arrived in Gretna before us and that the deed was done, I headed back. Barlow is trying to trace them, though what good that will do now is beyond me. He said he intended to bring them back and force them to face society as if there were no shame in what they'd done."

Rob suppressed a sharp stab of fear. Pray God that Douglas did not kill the pianoforte teacher on the spot the first time he saw him. Rob could not imagine compounding this debacle with a murder trial. Just one more tragedy to lay at Madame Zoe's door.

"Tell me what you've learned, Rob. What are people saying?"

The last thing he wanted to do was add fuel to Douglas's public humiliation, but it was late. He'd lost at faro and had too much to drink. And he'd spent the whole evening regretting not going to Mrs. Grant's musicale, where he could have tortured himself with the sight of Afton Lovejoy.

Regardless, this conversation was bound to be painful, so he poured a glass of brandy for himself. "The gossip mill has begun to grind. I enlisted Grace Forbush and Eloise Enright to plead Beatrice's case."

"Has her name been removed from any guest lists?"

He shrugged. "Too soon to tell. But I believe Douglas and Rob McHugh may have been."

"Damn it, Rob! Say you didn't take the blame."

He could only nod. Douglas would learn the truth by tea time tomorrow, regardless. "Shared it. That's only fair."

"How the hell is that fair?" his brother roared, his face suffusing with volcanic color.

"Because your proposal was a complete surprise to Bebe. It's not as if you had been courting for a season or two. Like as not, she couldn't think how to say no. Her recent actions show clearly enough that fondness was not her motive in accepting."

"Just as it was not your motive in giving permission. I was the one that swore ours was a destined love. Motives are of little consequence," Douglas pronounced with youthful sangfroid. "You were in want of an heir. I was in want of a wife. Beatrice was in want of a husband. Seemed like a logical bargain to me." He tossed his brandy down his throat as if it was water. "Now I suppose I am persona non grata in society."

"Do not be absurd." Rob took a healthy swallow from his own glass. "The only persona non grata is Madame Zoe. And I intend to inform her of it very soon."

"Have you found the crone?" Douglas asked with surprise.

"She is avoiding me," he admitted. He took the chair facing his brother. "I gather she has instructed her factor to refuse me an appointment. In spite of that, I will eventually catch up to her."

"Ah. At least you are not alone in this endeavor, what with Mrs. Forbush and Lady Enright lending their influence," Douglas muttered, his gaze fastened on his empty glass.

Rob smiled, thinking of his other ally—Miss Lovejoy. He had to agree with the French perfumer. There *had* to be hidden depths beneath that innocent exterior. His body stirred with the memory of how he'd been momentarily drunk from the heady intoxication of her lips. Had they been private—

"Rob?" Douglas interrupted his thoughts. "What are you thinking?"

He gave himself a mental shake. "Just that Madame Zoe is not the only one I shall investigate."

Chapter Ten

Afton rounded the corner and headed toward Madame Marie's dress shop, her head down as she remembered the few names of her aunt's last appointments. Some she had heard before, some were strangers and a few were actual acquaintances. What surprised her was how many were men, and that James Livingston had been one of them. He had consulted her aunt and within weeks both were dead. Yet another coincidence?

She glanced up as she reached for the doorknob to La Meilleure Robe and caught a glimpse of a furtive movement across the street in the late afternoon shadows. A chill went through her and she stepped over the threshold and closed the door behind her.

The chime of the little bell above the door had not faded when Madame Marie hurried from a back room to greet her. "Ah, Miss Afton! You come for Miss Dianthe's new gown, yes? I will 'ave it ready within the hour."

Another gown? Afton bit back her dismay. She would have to have a word with Dianthe. One more gown and Afton would be trapped into telling fortunes beyond finding Auntie Hen's killer. She forced an unconcerned smile and shook her head. "I have an appointment upstairs, *madame*."

''Ah.'' The woman nodded. She held open the door to a private fitting room and waited for Afton to enter. ''Go on up, *chérie*. I will leave the gown on the little table so you will 'ave it on your way out. Oh, and my 'usband wishes to meet with you tomorrow to discuss your little list, yes? 'Ere at two o'clock?''

Afton nodded, intrigued by the prospect that Mr. Renquist had news about the names on the list. She slid a wall panel back to reveal the hidden staircase. ''Thank you, Marie,'' she said before sliding the panel closed behind her.

Once upstairs, she lit a candle and the fire that had been prepared on the hearth, then retreated to the small dressing room to don her disguise. Her mind was still engaged with deciphering the only connections between her aunt and James Livingston—each other. And a raven.

She went to the mirror over the mantel and checked her appearance. She studied her reflection, trying to determine if any part of her was visible, or if there was something wrong with the disguise. No, everything was in place.

Shaking off her brooding, she readied the room for her client—tarot cards, crystal orb and tea leaves. She placed a kettle on the hearth to heat and went to the single window overlooking the street to close the heavy velvet curtain.

Something out of place stopped her with her hand on the drape. There, on the street below, stood Lord Glenross. His stillness was absolute, and she would not have seen him from the street level. But from her vantage above, the outline of his form stopped her. The set of the wide shoulders, the tensile readiness of his muscles, the stillness that was anything but still, betrayed his identity. But for that, he could have been any man waiting for someone's arrival.

Madame Zoe's arrival.

Very slowly, his hand came up to his mouth and the end of a cheroot glowed in the winter dusk. His head dipped in a nod to acknowledge her. He knew she was there! Her hand fluttered to her veil, reassuring herself that she would not be recognized as Afton. Before she could think, she stepped back and pressed herself against the wall, as if that would somehow save her.

He was stalking her! He had *wanted* her to know he was outside, waiting to waylay her as she departed, or to follow her home. His posture promised that he would wait as long as necessary. Thank heavens she would be exiting Madame Marie's shop instead of the public stairway to the narrow street door. Even so…would he think it too odd for coincidence that she would be in the building at the same time as Madame Zoe?

She inched back to the side of the window and risked the slightest peek. Glenross had stopped her client, Mrs. Murray, with a hand on her arm, and was speaking with her. She listened for a moment, recoiled and turned back the way she had come.

Blast! He was sending away the few clients Afton still had. He glanced up at the window and tipped his hat. The bounder was challenging her! Did he expect her to come out and take him to task for his interference? She would never give him the satisfaction. Actually, she didn't dare.

Glenross settled into the shadows again, clearly prepared to wait for her to come out, as he knew she must, sooner or later. But he was wrong. Madame Zoe would never leave this little flat. Afton Lovejoy would leave La Meilleure Robe.

She pulled the heavy drapery over the window with an angry snap. Hurrying to the curtained-off dressing room, she began changing her clothes again. Determined to leave nothing out of place, she took the time to fold and put her disguise away in the small clothespress.

Before she left, she blew out the candles, banked the fire and checked the bolt on the door. Satisfied that nothing was out of place, she went through the closet door and descended the steps to Madame Marie's back dressing room.

True to her word, the dressmaker had left a box tied with string on a fitting stool. Afton smiled, glad that she would have something to carry away. If Glenross should notice her leaving, she would have a perfect excuse for her presence at the shop.

She stepped onto the street and pulled the hood of her cloak up to cover her hair. A moment more and she would make a clean escape, with Glenross none the wiser. She tucked the dress box under one arm while she pulled on her gloves. She had taken no more than three steps when she felt a hand on her shoulder.

"Miss Lovejoy? Ah, I thought that was you."

The sound of his voice raised goose bumps on her arms. "Glenross?" She affected surprise as she turned to face him. "What a surprise to find you here."

"We seem to cross paths fairly often, Miss Lovejoy."

She tried to detect any note of sarcasm in his comment, but it seemed innocent enough. "One might begin to wonder if you are following me, my lord."

He grinned. "Might one?"

She nodded and shifted the box to her other arm.

"Allow me, Miss Lovejoy." He reached for it. "Once again I find you without a carriage. You must allow me to give you a ride home this time. 'Tis almost dark. Winter solstice, you know."

She glanced around in surprise. She'd been so consumed with her deception that she hadn't even noticed that darkness had come on suddenly. "I…I would not want to take you away from your errand, my lord."

"It will wait."

Yes, she suspected it would. He could wait all night for Madame Zoe to come out and nothing would come of it. "The—the alterations must have taken longer than I thought. Dianthe and Aunt Grace will be expecting me,'' she admitted.

"Another good argument for accepting my offer,'' he said with a slight bow.

She smiled. "Is that McHugh the Ruthless speaking, or Glenross the Gentleman?''

"'Tis Rob the Selfish,'' he quipped. "Did you ever think I might welcome the opportunity to have you alone in a coach?''

The memory of Sir Martin's revelation rose to her mind. The tragedy was staggering when she saw before her the evidence of the man he could have—*should* have—been. She fought her pity and relinquished her package to him with a nod of consent. After all, there was nothing to fear. The little deception seemed important to him, and she would not deprive him of that. "You must not tease me so, McHugh, or I might fear for my virtue if I were to accept your offer.''

"If you do not fear for your virtue, then I will have to try harder,'' he said.

She laughed, more comfortable with his lie than she would have been had it been the truth. Pride was not an insignificant thing, and a man like McHugh had nothing if not his pride.

He led her around the corner to a waiting hired coach. Such a vehicle did not come cheap, and she was scandalized by the cost he had incurred to stand watch for Madame Zoe. She counted that as a measure of his determination.

He opened the door and handed her up, calling directions to the driver. His hand, cupping her elbow, was so strong yet so gentle that she smiled. How like the man himself. In appearance and manner, he was brusque and powerful, but at heart, so peculiarly vulnerable. She wondered if he even realized it. Or was she woefully wrong?

The coach rocked as McHugh stepped up to sit opposite

her and place the box on the seat beside him. He took the lap robe from his seat and leaned forward to place it over her knees.

"One could wish for snow," he said.

Afton detected an edge of self-consciousness in his words. What had changed to give her the advantage? "Yes, in the country it is often warmer when it snows. This is my first winter in the city, though. I hope I will find things much the same."

"You will, Miss Lovejoy. 'Tis still England, after all."

"Yes." She waited for him to speak again, feeling awkward with the silence. After a scant moment, she felt a need to fill it. "Before Papa...fell on hard times, and when Bennett was still a baby, Father took us all to Spain one winter. I still recall how desperately I did not want to go, and how homesick I was for wassail, plum pudding and caroling." She closed her eyes at the memory. "But I can still feel the warmth of the sun on my bare arms and the sand between my toes as Dianthe and I waded in the Mediterranean and hoarded pretty pink shells. Those were blissfully indolent days, and they are good memories now. I would not trade them at any price."

He cleared his throat as she opened her eyes again. Leaning forward, he rested his forearms on his knees. "I envy you, Miss Lovejoy. I would pay any price for the peace of pleasant memories."

There was no doubt in her mind that he was referring to his wife and son. What could she say? How could she ease his pain? "Please, McHugh, give yourself a little time. Eventually..."

"Eventually I will heal?" he scoffed. He leaned back and crossed his arms over his chest. "I will heal, Miss Lovejoy, the moment the instigator of this travesty pays. I will find her, and when I do, I will unmask her in front of all of society so that everyone will know her for the charlatan she is.''

Afton nodded even as her stomach clenched. She seized on the first thing that came to her mind as a change of subject. "How…how is your brother, my lord?"

"Douglas is well. He returned from Scotland last night."

"Oh," she squeaked, feeling more and more trapped. "Was he…"

"Successful?" McHugh seemed adept at finishing her sentences. "Yes and no. Miss Barlow—now Mrs. Palucci—did not return with him. In fact, Mr. Barlow is in pursuit of the newlyweds at the moment. Douglas is attempting to salvage the remnants of his pride."

"Oh…"

"I say, Miss Lovejoy, do you have any personal knowledge of Madame Zoe?"

Her heartbeat sped. "Um, who—that is, why would you think—I mean…"

"Why ask you?" he interjected. "Because you and your aunt Grace seem to know damn near everything that goes on in the ton."

"Oh. Well, I know the woman is a fortune-teller. And that some of the most influential people in London frequent her salon."

"Have you ever consulted her, Miss Lovejoy?"

She felt a hot blush creep up her cheeks. "I…yes. She told my fortune once a long time ago."

"Was it good? Did her fortune come true?"

"I cannot recall exactly what she said." But she did recall that distant rainy summer day quite clearly. "We…I thought it was a parlor game. Not to be taken seriously. It amazes me that anyone does."

"Levelheaded of you." He smiled, leaning close enough to cause her to grow slightly dizzy. "Just one of the many things I find admirable about you."

She swallowed hard, uncertain how to reply to such a blatant compliment. "Really, Lord Glenross, I think—"

"Don't think, Afton," he whispered, leaning closer still.

Afton? Oh, how sweet the sound of her name from those lips. When his mouth took hers, it was unlike any of his other kisses. No challenge here, no ferocity. This was soft, cherishing, with the promise of sweetness to come. This was a kiss that revealed his vulnerability. Knowing what she knew, what Sir Martin had warned her of, how could she allow McHugh to delude himself? Her heart was breaking with the unutterable pain of his loss. Of *her* loss.

The coach rolled to a stop as their lips parted and, embarrassed by the slow tears filling her eyes, she placed her palm against his chest to hold him at bay. "Please, McHugh. Do not do this to yourself. You know nothing can come of it."

He reeled back as if she had delivered a slap. "Nothing, eh? Very well, Miss Lovejoy. Never say I am a beggar."

He threw the coach door open and stepped down to give her a hand. When her feet were solidly planted on the street outside Grace's house, he got back in and departed without another word.

Lady Annica, Charity and Lady Sarah met Afton and Grace at La Meilleure Robe at two o'clock the following afternoon. Madame Marie's buxom assistant led them to the back fitting room, where Mr. Renquist was waiting. A row of chairs circled a tea table holding a steaming pot and a platter of little sandwiches. Madame Marie knew how to keep her favorite clients comfortable.

"Mr. Renquist, do you have something to report?" Grace asked when they were all seated.

Lady Sarah arranged the drape of her gown. "I do hope so. There are only eight days remaining before we must notify the authorities of Henrietta's death, so time is of the essence,'' she said.

Renquist regarded them all somberly. ''My *lack* of progress is daunting. I had hoped to be further ahead by now. Instead I have precious little. The most common thread connecting these names is a high death rate and the fact that they traveled in the same circles.''

''Anything else?'' Charity asked. ''Any little tidbit?''

Mr. Renquist squirmed uneasily. ''They must have had acquaintances in common. Perhaps they shopped at the same places, or employed the same person, or frequented the same establishments. I have not had time to make those connections. But they have to be there. I know it in my bones.''

''And Auntie Hen is the link between them?'' Afton asked.

''I cannot say if she was the link, or if she was linked to someone else who is the common thread, Miss Lovejoy. There have been other deaths in London. All with the same hallmarks.''

''What deaths?'' Afton asked. ''What hallmarks?''

''The authorities have been keeping it secret. They are afraid there will be panic if it comes out. There has been a rash of murders in the upper classes. Someone is bludgeoning and stabbing victims, as if one method is not enough—''

Afton gasped. ''Like Auntie Hen.''

''Yes, Miss Afton. And there's another thing. I believe you said that you found a raven stickpin near your aunt?''

She nodded.

''All the victims have been found with some object representing a raven.''

The raven again. Mr. Livingston had been found with a raven button. Afton frowned, trying to remember what Sir Martin had said. That he had seen carved ravens before? She must find some way to pique his memory.

"All the victims, you say?" Lady Annica asked. "How many might that be, Mr. Renquist?"

"Seven."

Seven? Good heavens! Afton glanced around the circle to see the other ladies' eyes widening. This was worse than they had thought. "When did the killings start, Mr. Renquist? Seven victims since when?"

"The first of December," he admitted.

"Then Auntie Hen was one of the first?"

"Yes, Miss Lovejoy."

Lady Sarah leaned forward and asked, "If you cannot find an association between the victims other than the manner of their deaths, could it be a madman on the loose?"

"Undoubtedly it is a madman, Lady Sarah. There does seem to be a pattern, but I cannot quite make it out yet. The deeper I look, the more I will know. I hope to have more for you by next week. In the meantime, I thought it best to warn you."

"Warn?" Grace asked. "What an odd word. Whatever do you mean?"

"The victims cross boundaries of wealth and gender, but they have all been members of polite society. I must conclude that no one in your circle is safe. And you, dear ladies, are in the gravest danger, because you are on the murderer's trail."

Afton fought to clear the lump in her throat. Had she drawn the entire Wednesday League into danger?

Chapter Eleven

Lord Millerton was noted for his exclusive little dinner parties. To be invited to a Christmas Eve supper was a stamp of approval within the ton, and Afton had been pleased when the Lovejoys had been included in Grace's invitation. Now Dianthe would be seen as even more desirable.

After dinner, when the men had rejoined the women after their secret male rituals in the library, Afton scanned the gathering, picking out various young men who had shown interest in Dianthe. Here a baron and an earl, there a wealthy shipper and a banker's scion. Her sister's prospects were good indeed.

As for Afton's prospects, here was Sir Martin and there was…no. Lord Glenross was not a prospect. She suspected she could have loved him anyway, devoid of the physical aspects of the married state, but she knew a man of his mettle could never settle for half a marriage. Nor would he marry a pale copy of his beloved first wife. And Afton would never be content to live in Lady Maeve's shadow.

Glenross's intense eyes met hers across the room and a thrill went through her. He gave her a polite nod—cordial, no more—but his gaze was so piercing she felt as if she had been undressed. Her hand came up to check the row of tiny glass buttons running from her décolletage to the hem of her overdress. His last words to her echoed in her mind, as they often had since he'd spoken them. *Never say I am a beggar.* No, she would never say that. She was the beggar.

They hadn't been seated near one another at dinner, Glenross's position being above the salt, while she and Dianthe were far down the table. But Afton had caught him looking in her direction three or four times, while she had watched him every opportunity she had. The woman to his left, Lady Enright, and Glenross bowed their heads together to share a few whispered words. She was pleased for Lady Enright that they were mending their rift.

"A penny for your thoughts, Miss Lovejoy," a voice whispered in her ear.

A guilty heat burned her cheeks. "Too high a price, Sir Martin," she answered. At that moment, McHugh turned toward her and a flash of annoyance crossed his face. Perversely, Afton returned her attention to Sir Martin and beamed her brightest smile. "But I would be delighted to bore you to stupefaction with them, if you wish."

"You could never bore me, Miss Lovejoy. Put me to the test," he invited, gallant to a fault.

She took his arm and allowed him to lead her toward the large front parlor, where guests were gathering for a game of charades. She hoped McHugh noted her preoccupation with his friend. She did not want him to think she was pining away for want of him.

She gave Sir Martin a sideways glance, measuring his sincerity. "Stop me when you've heard enough, my lord. I was thinking that we might be receiving an offer for Dianthe soon. I then tallied the interest in her, trying to determine who will offer, and which offer I should consider most seriously. Upon deciding that, I pondered if Dianthe has a preference, and if we would agree, or if I am in for a struggle. I then considered the most advantageous time of year for the wedding, and wondered if I might be able to put an anxious swain off until autumn, which would be most convenient for me to put a wedding together in Little Upton.''

''Ah.'' Sir Martin nodded sagely. ''Weighty matters, indeed. Always fascinating to have a look inside a woman's mind. But you must not worry overmuch. If Miss Dianthe has not formed an attachment by Lent, she will just have to stay on in London until after Easter. The spring season is best for husband hunting.''

Afton laughed at his helpful advice. ''How would you know that, Sir Martin?''

''I have extrapolated that information by the embarrassing number of invitations I receive at that time of year. Indeed, I have been 'hunted' in spring more than any other season, I am bound to say. You have not forgot that I am considered highly eligible, have you?''

She grinned at so blatant a ploy. ''Certainly not.''

''Excellent! Then perhaps you will consent to be my partner for charades?''

She glanced to the side and found McHugh escorting a pretty brunette toward the parlor. ''Not if you wish to win, sir.''

''Hmm. I shall have to think on that.'' His forehead creased in a thoughtful pretense. ''No. I believe I would rather lose with you by my side than win alone.''

''Very well, Sir Martin, you have been forewarned.''

''Forewarned? Ah, yes.'' He hesitated as if debating the wisdom of continuing. ''I have been meaning to tell you, Miss Lovejoy, that I recalled who had a pin exactly like yours. 'Twas McHugh.''

Not McHugh. The raven pin could not belong to him. She turned to see the man in question being assigned partnership with Hortense and Harriett Thayer for the game of charades. She held her voice steady. ''How interesting. I would like to compare the two. When did you last see him wear it, Sir Martin?''

"Don't know, Miss Lovejoy. Had to have been last winter before he went to Algiers, eh? Don't think I've seen it since he returned."

He'd returned about the time of Auntie Hen's death. About the time the murders began. "How did you remember such a thing from so long ago, Sir Martin?"

"I should have recalled it at once. After all, the raven is the McHugh's emblem. You will find it on the family crest, on McHugh's buttons and everywhere there is room for them."

A sharp pain pierced Afton's temple and she closed her eyes to visualize the carved head of his walking stick. Yes. Ravens. Why had it not registered in her brain before now? How had she missed something so obvious? She recalled his agitation when Lord Ethan Travis had brought the news that Mr. Livingston had been found dead clutching a raven button. Dear Lord. If the murderer was McHugh, she needed to know at once.

Sir Martin caught her arm as she stumbled. "My dear, are you ill?"

"Sudden headache," she murmured. "Something I ate did not agree, I think. Please, continue without me."

"Won't hear of it, Miss Lovejoy. Allow me to escort you back to your aunt."

Afton nodded absently, planning her next move—to liberate McHugh's key from his cloak in Millerton's anteroom. Grace would excuse her and even give her use of the coach. After all, Lord Barrington would stand ready to rescue her at a moment's notice. But who would rescue Afton if her suspicions were true?

Afton pulled her hood forward to shadow her face and alighted from the coach at the Pultney Hotel's side door.

She crept up the rear stairs, pausing intermittently to glance over her shoulder. If anyone recognized her—alone and sneaking up to a man's room—she would be beyond redemption. Thanking the Fates for the dim light in the hotel corridor, she prayed she would not encounter anyone at midnight. The tired and elderly would have retired long ago, and the young and adventurous would still be abroad for many hours.

She pulled the pilfered key from the little pocket inside her muff. Before she could think better of it, she inserted the key in the lock, turned it and edged through the door, breathless with excitement and fear. She secured the lock behind her, scarcely believing that she had just illicitly entered a man's rooms. McHugh might still be at the party, but she could not be sure for how long. She had to work quickly.

A glance around in the soft firelight betrayed nothing unusual. The room was extraordinarily tidy, even sparse, until she recalled that he had just returned from eight months abroad. Under the circumstances, he would not have many possessions. That should make her search all the easier.

Her attention snagged on the bed, a wide expanse boasting a tall canopy hung with heavy midnight velvet draperies. One could sleep all day with those draperies drawn. Her heartbeat raced when she thought of lying abed with McHugh. The sudden sound of laughter and the shattering of a bottle in the corridor made her jump.

Filled with new urgency, she shook herself and recalled herself to duty. She dropped her muff on the tall highboy dresser and slid the top drawer open. It was narrow and contained collars, a few cravats, gloves, handkerchiefs and a few other male accessories. McHugh was not an extravagant man.

She could feel herself blush when she opened the second drawer and found men's underclothes. Heavens! She took a deep breath and searched quickly through the personal items, her fingertips tingling when they came in contact with the fine linen. Nothing.

She wondered at her quickened breathing and stared at the remaining drawers in dread. If such simple items could stir her senses, what might the rest of McHugh's possessions do to her? Deciding a change might be in order, she went to his closet, intending to return to the highboy once she had regained her composure.

She opened the door and stared at the few items within. Two heavy woolen coats, a soft, dark blue velvet robe, the simple elegant vests and jackets that defined his style, and, on a shelf above them, three fashionable tall hats. On the floor in a gleaming military row stood several pairs of shoes and boots. Nothing there, either.

Just as she moved to close the closet door, she caught sight of a small wooden box on the shelf beside the hats. With scarcely a moment's hesitation, she lifted it down and removed the carved lid. Ah, his cuff links, pins, studs, a watch chain and fob, a set of small angled instruments and a ring. Flushed with guilt for her violation of his privacy, she nonetheless inspected and inventoried the pieces. Their value was obvious from the excellent quality and workmanship. She lifted the heavy gold-and-onyx ring from the box to examine it more closely.

It appeared to be old—a seal with the pattern in recess. The intricacies of the design carved into the onyx would only be evident when pressed into wax, but Afton was certain she could make out the form of a bird with its wings spread for flight. A raven? Her heart skipped a beat. She dropped the ring into the box, replaced the lid and pushed it back on the shelf in one fluid movement.

Perhaps more important than what she'd found was what she hadn't found—his raven pin. Was it missing because he had dropped it in Auntie Hen's salon? Suddenly urgent to leave, Afton stepped back to close the door, and landed against a solid wall of bone and muscle.

Light-headed with shock and fear, her knees buckled. A strong arm caught her around the waist and spun her about. The McHugh!

"Looking for something, Miss Lovejoy?" he asked in a sardonic tone.

"I…you."

"Me? In the closet?" Rob glanced over her shoulder to look into the darkened nook and consider this thought. She was lying, of course, but what other motive could she have? Why else would a woman like Afton Lovejoy come to a man's rooms? Could she have been drawn there by the desire he knew they both felt? A doubtful warmth crept into his chest.

She gave him a timid, tentative smile, looking charmingly disconcerted. Deliciously vulnerable. Freshly innocent. By the pink stain on her cheeks, he guessed she had read his thoughts. But she wasn't dashing for the door. No, Afton Lovejoy held her ground. He admired her valor.

Why, when he tried to behave himself, did God only send him more temptation? Lust literally pounded in his blood, pulsed through his veins. Could it be that little Miss Lovejoy did not want to be safe? That she was not as innocent as she appeared? That she had come to be seduced, regretting her rejection of the night before?

He tested the waters. "The only charm a closet would hold for me, Afton, is if you were in it with me."

"Oh." The word came out as a squeak and she looked down at her hem as she cleared her throat. "I…I do not know what possessed me to think I could invade your privacy in this manner, Lord Glenross. I—"

"The less formal I become, the more formal you become.

Is that your counterpoint to the liberties I have taken, Afton?''

"I…this is just so…so unusual for me, my lord. It isn't as if I am often in a man's rooms. I have behaved completely out of character, and—"

His voice was low and raspy. "Completely? Are you certain?''

She looked up and met his gaze, her eyes wide. One trembling hand reached out and touched his sleeve. So many emotions passed over her face that he was easily convinced of her confusion and embarrassment. Could Afton Lovejoy really want him? Did she feel even half the measure of desire he felt? A fourth of the wonder at the miracle of emotions running so deep? God! He hadn't felt anything so profound and true since…ever. Desire, yes. Lust, need and hunger, yes. But a passion so intense it beggared expression? Never.

He lowered his lips to within inches of hers. "Are you certain?'' he asked again.

"F-fairly certain. I have never done this before. I shouldn't have come.''

"No. You shouldn't. But you are here now, and there's nothing for it but to pay the consequences.''

"What consequences?''

He dropped his mouth the remaining inch to meet hers. This time, tutored by his previous kisses, she parted her lips very slightly. Timid as it was, the action was as bold as a woman of Afton's upbringing would dare. But before this night was over, he would see that she would dare more. Much more.

His answer to her invitation was hungry—half moan, half growl—as he swept her up and carried her toward his bed. He cradled her against him with one arm and worked at the fasteners of her cloak and hood with the other. They fell away as he placed her on the bed and stood back to discard his own coat.

He could not take his eyes off her. She was glorious. Her eyes sparkled with unknown emotions. Excitement? Fear? Or, if it please the gods, desire? Her ivory skin was luminescent in the candlelight, and her face was framed by wisps and curling tendrils of coppery silk. She was the most beautiful thing he'd ever seen as her lower lip trembled, curving a timid smile.

That a woman of Afton Lovejoy's warmth and integrity could want him woke an unexpected and fragile hope he had thought dead. Forgotten passions surged upward, burning and branding his heart with wonder and gratitude. Perhaps he wasn't the animal Maeve had accused him of being. Perhaps there *was* something within him worth loving. Perhaps he did have more to offer than an unholy pride, a title and a fortune. Perhaps, oh glorious notion, he could reach with Afton the destination he had sought his whole life.

Afton's senses reeled in a dizzying spin as she watched McHugh unbutton his shirt. Now she could think of nothing rational as she took note of the light matting of hair that spread across his pectoral muscles and dipped in a downward line to disappear into the waistband of his trousers.

Her gaze snagged on a fading scar at the base of his throat that stretched the width of his neck. Then she saw the crosswise scars on his chest, still livid against the paleness of his flesh. The scar tissue was thick and reddened, as if it had been damaged again and again. As if his torturer had enjoyed his job and had been good at it…. She'd seen Rob's other scars, the ones on his hands and arms, and knew what they meant. Resistance. Defiance in the face of death. What horrors he must have endured, what sheer strength and determination he must have possessed to survive. She shivered, a sudden cold invading her soul for what he had suffered.

McHugh must have read her expression because he pulled his shirt together in a self-conscious gesture. "Afton, dinna ask about my scars, if you regard me at all. I could not bear your pity."

She fought the tears threatening to well in her eyes. That he could bear the pain and the scars, but not her pity, told her much about the man he was. "I hold you in the highest regard, McHugh," she confessed in a soft breath.

Leaving his shirt open, he leaned over her, one knee on the bed beside her. His large, rough hand traced the line of her jaw to her throat, and his attention focused on that spot. "I can see your pulse, Afton. 'Tis as rapid as a sparrow's. Are ye frightened?"

Frightened? She knew she should be. But all she could think of was how his brogue became more pronounced as he let his guard down and lay beside her, pressing her against him, flattening her breasts to the hard wall of his chest. Of the seductive way some part of him pushed into the V of her legs, causing her to shiver with bittersweet yearning. And, oh Lord, of the way his tongue slid past her lips and claimed her with an intimacy so strong, so complete, that she heard herself urging for more with little moaning sounds, encouraged to meet his tongue, taste him, take him into her in a way that was entirely foreign to her.

"Are ye?" he insisted.

"Frightened? No," she whispered against his ear when he gave her the chance. She found the boldness to touch that magnificent chest. "I know you will not hurt me."

"*Thank God,*" he murmured in a voice so faint she thought he had not meant her to hear.

He began undoing the row of glass buttons to reveal the nearly transparent chemise beneath her dress. Reticence made her squirm when he lifted himself to one side in order to examine the prize he had uncovered. His breathing deepened and he applied his mouth to the swells above the edge of her chemise. She closed her eyes, both to shield her modesty and to better experience the sensations he evoked. Warmth washed over her, languorous and lazy, rendering her incapable of protest.

Impatient or careless, McHugh tore the fragile cloth of her camisole when he moved down to expose what lay beneath the fabric. Then he froze. "I'm sorry, lass," he mumbled against her flesh.

She choked back a small laugh. "My mistake entirely," she whispered. "I had no idea how to dress for seduction."

Muscles in his back that had stiffened a moment before relaxed. "Ask next time. I'll gladly give ye advice."

Afton seized the moment to satisfy her own curiosity. She pushed his shirt out of the way and traced his scars with her fingers. They were valiant, smooth and strong, like the man himself. She bent to press her lips to the one at his throat, then left a trail of little kisses along the thickened scar tissue of his chest. She heard him gasp before he twined his fingers through her hair and cupped the back of her head, holding her to him like a lifeline. That gasp resonated in her heart and she knew she had given him some sort of gift. But she would not stop there.

By the time she was finished tracing his scars with little kisses, McHugh had abandoned his reticence and returned to his earlier quest. Her chemise tore further, but she scarcely had time to register that fact before his mouth fastened over one aching nipple. Her breasts tingled and firmed into tight buds in response to his attentions. She arched to him, wanting deeper contact, needing more of the exquisite feelings. When she made involuntary mewling sounds, he relinquished her breast and moved up to her mouth again, murmuring nonsensical soothing words—Gaelic poetry, by the sound of the rhyme, and she loved that he would recite it to her. Later, when he was done with her, she would ask him what he'd said.

He reached down and slid his hand beneath the hem of her underskirt, sweeping it upward until he could slip one knee between her thighs and move over the top of her.

Shock ripped through her, but she was so deeply aroused that she could not frame a protest when his hand inched farther up her thigh. In a tangle of gown and bedding, McHugh drew her knee up to ride his hip, then traced the curve of her bottom to find the now-exposed center of her passion. At his first searching touch, she obeyed her instinct to raise her knee farther.

"Aye," he whispered. "Yes…that's th' way of it, lass. Gi' y'self over to it. T' me."

That affirmation gave Afton confidence and she pushed his shirt off his shoulders to bare his upper body, heavily muscled and perfectly formed. She could feel the coiled, hard strength beneath his skin and scars, and marveled at the intensity of his attentions coupled with his deliberate tenderness.

Then his hand unerringly found the root of her yearning, and reason departed. She could only think of the wildfire running through her veins, consuming her. Rationale, logic, sanity—all disappeared in the flames of McHugh's passion. She wanted to wrap her legs around him, trap him there forever.

He stroked downward, parting the fleshy petals shielding her passage. One finger found and forced a shallow entry, and it was her turn to gasp. She twisted beneath his touch, trying to get closer, to deepen the contact, dimly aware of McHugh's murmured approval. She knew instinctively that there would be bliss at the end of this questing, but she needed more…ever more. And more.

McHugh deepened his stroke, drawing her closer to the edge of sanity, while raining kisses downward. "I want t' taste ye, lass. I want t' memorize ye with all my senses. D'ye trust me?''

She arched her back, trying to mold herself to him. "With my very life," she moaned, breathless from the excitement coursing through her.

Afton felt a deep shudder go through him. A moment before, he had been fire and ferocity, and now he was ice and stillness. He lifted himself away from her and rose, cursing darkly under his breath.

He stood stock-still, tightly controlled, his face in shadow. A long moment passed and she wondered what had changed in that space of seconds. When he did speak, it was not what she expected.

His voice was hoarse and raspy in the clipped English tones, as if he were forcing the words against his will. "Repair yourself and go, Afton. Quickly, ere I change my mind.''

"Why—"

"Too easy, Afton. Are you not sensible to what is happening here? You'd trust me with your life, you said. This would change your life forever. I cannot do it to you. I'll not be responsible for that. I've warned you before." He went to a side table, seized a carafe and poured a deep amber liquid into a glass. Lifting it with a shaking hand, he tossed the contents down in a single gulp.

Confused, her breathing still out of control, every nerve thrumming, Afton sat up and gathered the front of her gown together. She pushed the torn edges of her camisole into the dress as she refastened the buttons. What had she done? Or was the fault McHugh's?

Her body pulsed with unquenched passion. She still burned for his touch between her legs, and through the frustration she realized what had gone wrong. McHugh *would* not, because he *could* not. How had she forgotten that? How had he?

She stood on legs still wobbly and weak, straightening her skirts. Tears rolled down her cheeks as she swept her cloak up from the floor. She had left her muff on the high-boy dresser—too close to McHugh. She would have to leave it. She was halfway through the door when his voice gave her pause.

"I'd take ye home," he said from far across the room, the rough Scottish brogue back. "But I'd likely change m' mind in the coach and have y' heels over y' head then and there. You're safer alone than w' me, Afton Lovejoy."

Keeping her back to him, she pulled her hood over her head and closed the door. She had not made it to the rear stairs before she heard a loud explicit curse followed by the shattering of glass and the crash of furniture.

Chapter Twelve

Rob frowned when the wheels of their coach slipped on the icy cobbles as they rounded a corner. Across from him, his brother gripped the hand strap to prevent a sidelong tumble to the opposite door.

"Fortunate the streets are nearly empty," Douglas observed.

Rob looked out the window without answering. Christmas. It was supposed to be a day of rejoicing, but he hadn't wanted to go out at all today. He'd rather have stayed alone in his room getting quietly, morosely drunk. Or better yet, finding some fresh-faced prostitute to take the edge off his irritation. That was the only way he knew to forget the tantalizing lure of what could never be.

He'd been better off in the Dey's dungeon. Then he'd only been haunted by his own guilt at what his indifference had cost, and by his fury at the forces that had directed Maeve down that path. McHugh the Destroyer—aye, that was him, and that was bad enough. Now he was haunted by the knowledge of what could never be, and the pain of knowing he could never love Afton without destroying her, too. He'd tasted her passion, lost himself in her guileless responses, daring to believe, for just a moment, that he could make love to her without loving her. He hadn't known it was already too late.

"With my very life," she'd said, responding to his plea for trust. That had stopped him. Maeve had put herself in his hands and had forfeited her life. He couldn't—wouldn't—do that to Afton. Nor could he risk alienating her with his excessive passions and sensual needs. Or risk having her turn away from him in disappointment and revulsion. Or watch her love turn to loathing. That would be more than he could stomach. Ah, for the dulling, numbing nectar of forgetfulness!

He shifted his weight on the leather squabs to ease the hard aching in his groin. The edge he'd balanced on for months had just narrowed to a thread.

Well, he could never go back and unmake that mistake. Never unlove her. Never unsmell the lily scent of her hair, untaste the sweetness of her lips, untouch the slick heat of her sex…

And now he found himself speeding toward a destination where he knew she would be. She would not be pleased to see him. She would expect him to have the decency to send his regrets and not stand in her parlor as a reminder of her lapse in judgment. But no, he was completely shameless. Even if it were not for Douglas, he doubted he'd have the strength to stay away from Afton's siren call. He'd never be able to make it right again, or undo the damage, but he'd have to find a way to make amends. The sooner the better. Tonight.

"You're in a surly mood, Rob," Douglas observed, interrupting his thoughts. "D'ye think you can leave it behind for the party?"

"I'd not have inflicted my mood on anyone today had you not insisted we attend Mrs. Forbush's gathering," he lied.

"I didn't fancy moping about my rooms," Douglas admitted. "Besides, it was your invitation. You are my entrée. You had to come."

"And why, Doogie, did *you* have to come?"

Douglas gave the crooked smile that made the ladies swoon. "She's the fairest in the land, Rob. Her eyes shame a summer sky. Her hair is threaded with liquid gold. When she laughs, the angels sing."

"When we call her, we call her…*what,* Doogie?"

"Dianthe Lovejoy. Even her name is pure poetry."

Rob closed his eyes and muttered a prayer for forbearance. Was he doomed to having a Lovejoy everywhere? There was no use reminding Douglas that he'd said almost the same words about Bebe Barlow barely two weeks past. His brother would only swear this was different—this was real. Well, why not? Wasn't that always the way with Douglas? Quicksilver emotions, quick to fall in love and quick to heal.

"Don't go rolling your eyes at me, Robbie McHugh. We lesser mortals make mistakes. Only godlike creatures such as yourself are blessed with restraint and eternal love."

"Eternal love? Is that what you think Maeve and I had?" he asked. "You think I am *mourning* her? That no others can compare to her?"

"Is that not the way of it?"

No, not mourning. The word *acquit* came to Rob's mind. Was he trying to acquit himself of her death, or find a reason, other than her disgust and fear of him, for her to abandon her home and position? But that was between himself and Maeve. "Have it your way, Doogie."

His brother looked as if he would question him, but the coach drew up in front of the Forbush mansion. It was time for Rob to reckon with his sins.

Afton knew she'd go mad if she dwelled on the events in McHugh's room. She had been keyed up and on edge since her return home last night, a sense of heightened anticipation keeping her on the edge of an imaginary precipice, unable to think of anything but what McHugh had done to her. And of her shockingly wanton response. Who was she? *What* was she? She scarcely knew herself since McHugh had come to town.

She took a deep breath, smoothed the lilac-sprigged ivory satin of her gown and tightened the lilac ribbon that fastened her hair on top of her head. It was time to join the party. Sir Martin was wending his way through the guests toward her, and she intended to flirt shamelessly. Anything to forget McHugh and put last night behind her. But Afton hadn't been able to help herself. A depth of emotion she hadn't known she possessed had overwhelmed her, and she hadn't been able to get enough of him.

Heat swept up from her toes to her face at the thought of McHugh's kisses, his touch, and her breasts tingled with the memory of the intimacy of his mouth against her flesh. She had to stop and steady herself. Lord! How could she have allowed him to believe she had come to be seduced? But was that not better than the truth—that she had come to expose him as a murderer?

Alas, the truth was also that, no matter how it had started, they had both wanted it. She'd been ready to throw caution, her reputation, Dianthe's future and the family name to the wind—all to find what lay at the end of that questing. Well, she hadn't found out, and she still felt as if she might jump out of her skin at the tiniest provocation.

From the confident smile on Sir Martin's face as he came forward, he must have thought her blush was for him. "About time, Miss Lovejoy! The party hasn't truly started for want of you." He offered his arm and a cup of hot mulled wine redolent with cloves and cinnamon.

She accepted his arm and the cup. She hadn't eaten yet today, and the wine hit the bottom of her stomach and spread a warm sensation through her. The party truly was underway.

Dianthe rounded the corner from the parlor and stopped, smiling at her. "There you are, Binky. I have been looking all over for you. You've missed the games, but we are going wassailing after supper. Say you'll come."

Perhaps the cold air would douse the heat in her limbs. She nodded. The ringing of the doorbell brought her around with a feeling of expectancy. She had hoped she was safe, but only one guest had yet to arrive. It had to be McHugh. She looked around for Mr. Dewberry, Grace's butler, but he was occupied in overseeing the buffet. Grace was in the parlor, urging the guests toward the dining room.

Afton went forward reluctantly and opened the door. "My lord," she said with due deference and a formal curtsy.

He stepped into the foyer, stomping snow from his boots, followed by a younger man with the darkly handsome McHugh looks. Rob studied her, and she knew that had they been alone, he would have made some reference to the night before. An apology? A taunt?

"The McHughs!" Sir Martin said in greeting. "By George, now we shall have a full chorus for wassailing!"

"Af—Miss Lovejoy. Have you met my brother, Douglas?"

Ah. So this was the youth whose life Madame Zoe had ruined. He looked so open and vulnerable that Afton's heart twisted. "Pleased to meet you, Mr. McHugh," she managed to reply. She turned for help. "Have you met my sister, Dianthe? And...and Sir Martin."

Seymour laughed, stepping forward to ruffle Douglas's hair. "Met? I changed the lad's nappies."

Douglas grinned and swatted at Sir Martin's hand. "You never! I had a nurse for that."

"Aye. Well, I remember you in nappies," he insisted. He took Afton's arm and turned her toward the parlor, leaving the others to trail behind. "You're just in time for supper," he told the late arrivals.

"Smells wonderful," Douglas declared. "You cannot imagine how dreary it is to eat hotel food day after day."

"Oh." Dianthe fluttered her eyelashes. "You poor things. You must come more often."

Afton felt a deep groan building in her center and hoped she had not uttered it aloud. She would have to have a word with her sister.

The McHughs excused themselves to offer their regards to Grace, who was circulating among the guests. She moved with such elegance and poise that she did not give the impression of being a harried hostess. Lord Ronald Barrington acted as her host, offering the male guests the refinements of brandy and quiet conversation centered on business and politics after dining.

Two agonizing hours later, the buffet was cleared in favor of fruits and desserts. The snowfall had increased and there was muttering that the weather was too foul for wassailing. Instead a cry went up for more games.

In the parlor, Afton waved a cup of tea away in favor of more mulled wine, feeling more and more unsettled with every passing minute. She could detect the weight of McHugh's long glances, and feared he would give her away.

She tensed when he came to stand beside her, lowering his voice to be discreet. "Miss Lovejoy, I owe you an apology. I should not have taken such liberties last night."

"No, you shouldn't," she snapped, and then felt churlish with the knowledge that no one had dragged her to his room. She'd gone uninvited. Late at night. Alone.

"And you should not have come to my room."

She studied the toes of her ivory slippers. "Yes. That was a mistake."

"Shall we agree to forget the whole incident?"

Forget? How could she ever forget the unendurable inti-

macy of his mouth? How could she disregard his sure and
steady touch, the strength of his embrace and the masterful
stroke of his hand? "What incident?" she retorted, the wine
making her contrary.

McHugh's laugh was cut short when Grace clapped her
hands to claim the attention of her guests, and announced a
game of hide-and-seek.

"Choose your partners," she said. "Quickly now. The
count has begun."

Sir Martin took a few steps toward Afton, but Grace intercepted him with a quick request to partner a dowager
whose family had gone to the Continent for the holidays.
He shrugged and gave in with good humor.

Having seen the byplay between them, McHugh com-
mented, "So. You and Martin, eh?"

On the verge of denying it, Afton stopped herself. It
would be best if McHugh believed her attentions and affections were otherwise engaged. She offered her own shrug.

"Well, fate has paired you with me." He seized her hand
and pulled her out of the parlor into the long hallway. "You
have the advantage, Miss Lovejoy, since you know every
nook and cranny. Where is the closest hiding place?"

They were passing a storage closet hidden beneath the
main staircase, and Afton gave the paneling a little push.
The spring latch released and the door popped open. Before
she could think better of it, she stepped inside and drew
McHugh after her. "Hurry! The count is almost done." He
resisted, but she tugged harder.

She pulled the door closed by the little strip of leather
fixed to the edge. A narrow band of light rimmed the door,
affording just enough illumination for her to make out
McHugh's form facing her. The warm wine and the odd
yearning that had not eased since last night made her bold,
and she pulled him to her by his cravat and fitted her mouth
to his.

He resisted for only a second. Before she could regret her impulse, his arm tightened around her and his tongue slipped past her lips, eliciting a soft moan. The darkness heightened her senses, making her more aware of the size of his hands as they splayed out on her back, of the masculine smell of his cologne and the steady thump of his heartbeat in the stillness.

He had ducked to clear the doorway of the closet, and now he straightened, knocking his head against the ceiling and nearly tripping over a trunk pushed into a corner.

"Bloody hell!" His soft curse sounded slightly panicked.

"Shh," she whispered. "They'll hear you."

"What is this place?"

"Aunt Grace's storage closet. Trunks and old hat boxes. That sort of thing."

"How...how do I get out?"

"There's a strap halfway down. Push to trip the spring, then pull the door open by the strap. Are you giving up?"

"Giving...up?"

What was wrong with him? "Yes. Quitting the game?"

He stiffened as footsteps passed outside the closet door, then he stepped closer, almost toppling her. He pulled her against him with a breathless thud. "I—no."

"Then be quiet."

She could feel his muscles twitching beneath the smooth fabric of his jacket. "*Keep* me quiet, Afton," he challenged, almost desperately. Without waiting for a reply, he bent his head and kissed her again.

She pushed against his chest, whispering angrily, "You cad! How can you make free with me after last night?"

"Aye, I'm a cad. And a beast, and a rutting bull. Ye're not the first to tell me so. But I thought ye *were* free, lass," he muttered against her throat. "Then what's the price?"

"More than you have, McHugh. More than any man has. Now release me!"

"No, Afton. I'll not let ye go. Ye'd best hold on tight."

"Are you mad?" she asked in outrage.

"Mad? Aye. I canna stomach the dark, the confinement. But you, now—*you* make it tolerable."

Sir Martin's words echoed in her brain. *Being confined to a small box for days on end is bound to have some sort of effect on a fellow. He might be…well, unhinged.* Somehow, the physical scars she had seen last night were less upsetting than this betrayal of dread and horror.

But she did not fear him. She was only afraid he would seduce her here, in the closet, with Aunt Grace's party in full progress outside. *Lord! If this was unhinged…*

"McHugh," she murmured against his lips. "We cannot—"

"Aye. We can." His kisses trailed from the corner of her mouth to the hollow of her throat, and she nearly swooned. "We should," he said, his voice a deep vibration in her chest. "It's our obligation." His heated breath left her flesh scorched in its path.

She was past dissembling. Some primal part of her wanted to find, at last, the end of what he'd started last night. "Do it then," she invited.

He made a rumbling sound deep in his throat as he bent to the task, sweeping the ivory silk up her legs. His hand sought that softness at her center and she went limp in his arms, clinging to his shoulders so she wouldn't collapse in a boneless puddle.

He moved her, adjusting her position to fit her against him. A firm pressure pushed against her core and she knew she was close—so close—to that elusive destination. Close enough to want to scream. The darkness of the closet made his touch all the more intimate, and she was damp and ready for whatever came next, and fearful it would never come. "Hurry," she urged.

The spring clicked and the closet door popped open, admitting a band of light. Afton gasped, knowing what she and McHugh must look like. McHugh spun toward the light and glared at Sir Martin.

Disbelief followed by hurt and embarrassment registered on the man's face before he said, "Nothing in here, Lady Norcroft," and shut the door again.

Now accustomed to the dim light, Afton glanced into McHugh's eyes. The world receded and she felt herself floating among the stars, moons and suns of a vast universe. Then his eyes grew dark and intense, and she recoiled from the bottomless depths of the glacial green, falling back to earth with the harshness of a physical blow. Shaken, she pushed him away.

A commotion from the vicinity of the front door gave her the diversion she needed to regain her composure. "We…we should—"

He nodded. "You or me?"

"You," she said. "I shall need a moment."

He nodded again, looking truly frantic to escape the tiny room. He opened the door quietly and slipped out, leaving Afton to compose herself and put her gown to rights. That was the easy part. The more difficult task was wondering how she could explain her behavior to Sir Martin.

As she slipped into the corridor, she heard excited laughter and questions from the foyer. She found half the guests gathered around a beaming man with sandy hair, an angular face and hard jaw.

"But what does that all mean, Mr. Barlow?" Grace asked.

"That Bebe is safe and sound," he proclaimed. "Her mother and I are overjoyed! To find that Mr. Palucci is, in fact, Comte Dante Palucci, is the very best possible news. The man is no fortune hunter at all, but a romantic Italian looking for 'true love.' The fool could have found himself shot had I caught them before Bebe broke the news."

The ladies sighed and even Dianthe looked dreamy-eyed. The gentlemen exchanged suspicious glances and cast sideways looks at the McHughs.

"I came here straightaway to set Glenross's mind at ease," the man continued.

"Oh! This is too marvelous, Mr. Barlow," Lady Norcroft declared. "Why, this means that dear Bebe is not ruined at all. She has managed the coup of the season!"

"Precisely," he confirmed. "And everyone thought she was a silly chit."

Afton's head spun and she heard snippets of conversation around her pronouncing the whole affair wildly romantic, a true love story and an excellent argument for following one's heart.

"Why, Madame Zoe is an absolute genius!" Lady Norcroft continued. "She knew all would come a-right. Did she not tell Bebe as much?"

"Heavens! I had forgot about that," another guest said. "I must make an appointment with her at once."

"Yes," another affirmed, "and quickly, before this news gets out and one cannot secure an appointment for months!"

A murmur of agreement went up and Afton felt the walls begin to close in on her. She met Grace's gaze across the foyer and was surprised to see something akin to panic in the usually unreadable face. The older woman shook her head quickly, as if warning Afton not to speak. Her gaze snapped toward the McHughs, and Afton followed her lead.

Douglas seemed unaffected, his attention riveted on Dianthe, who was gazing at him with a sweetly sympathetic smile. Rob looked thunderous, but tightly contained. Afton knew he would focus that fury on the hapless Madame Zoe. *On her!* He spun on his heel and headed for the door.

Afton lifted her hand to her throat. She could almost feel his fingers closing around it.

* * *

McHugh took the steps in the main lobby of his hotel two at a time. Fury roiled in his gut as he contemplated plans for revenge against the infamous French fraud. The fortune-teller would not get away with this latest debacle. Through some twist of fate, Beatrice's fortune had come true, and now the swindler would benefit—but only for as long as it took him to catch up to her.

Uneasiness raised the hair on the back of his neck when he reached his room. He pushed his door open and glanced around before entering. Nothing was out of place, but the single strand of hair he'd placed in the gap between the door and the jamb was gone. Someone had entered his room in his absence. He lit the oil lamp by his bed and threw his coat over a chair.

He had selected the Pultney Hotel because of its reputation as a quiet, secure and well-run establishment, and he'd questioned the management and staff of the hotel after Douglas had charmed his way in. Rob had been assured that such an occurrence was strictly against policy and would never happen again. Nevertheless, they said, they could not guarantee a professional cracksman wouldn't succeed in entering.

Rob opened the closet door. His few belongings were in place. He took the small wooden box down from the shelf and lifted the lid. His lock picks were missing, and two more of his raven shirt studs. He knelt to inspect his seaman's chest. That, too, had been rifled. His midshipman's dagger was gone. This was not good.

If he were a betting man, he'd give odds his missing items would show up very soon. At murder scenes. If any more of his enemies were murdered, he was sure to be arrested.

Enemies? He wondered if he should warn Madame Zoe. Or let her stew in her own juices.

Chapter Thirteen

Afton rubbed her temple, still feeling the effects of last night's mulled wine as she read the letter delivered this morning by way of her factor. "...have, no doubt, heard the news about Miss Barlow by now. I must see you at once. It is urgent, and I am certain I needn't tell you why. I shall be at your salon this evening at half past six. L.E.E."

"Lady Eloise Enright?" Grace asked. "This will have to do with Rob McHugh, will it not?"

Afton nodded. "Yes. She told me she would not come again, so this must be to warn me about him. She needn't have bothered. I could see last night when he left so abruptly that he was enraged with the knowledge that this would enhance Madame Zoe's reputation and business, and that he had fixed the blame for this latest development at her door."

"What are you going to do, Afton?"

"I shall meet Lady Enright tonight, then close up the salon."

"Can you do that?"

She nodded and winced. "I shall send a note to Mr. Evans and instruct him to cancel my appointments and refuse to make more until further notice. He can say I have returned to the Continent, or that I am overbooked. I do not care.

But we shall have to find another way to track down Auntie Hen's killer. Perhaps we should work more closely with Mr. Renquist.''

Grace let out a long sigh. ''Thank heavens. I was afraid I would have to insist you quit. What with only six days remaining, I was afraid you would refuse. I am glad that you see the sense in ending the charade as Madame Zoe.''

''The charade, Aunt Grace. I value my neck. But I will not give up the investigation.''

''McHugh would not—''

''Things are worse now. I have never seen him as angry as he was last night.''

''Avoid him, Afton. I see it in your face. You are on the verge of loving him, are you not?''

On the verge? It was already too late. In fact, it had been too late from that moment in the Woodlakes' ballroom when he had opened the French doors to blow out the candles, just to steal a kiss from her.

''If…if I were, Aunt Grace, I would soon come to my senses. And it would not matter if I were. He is devoted to his wife's memory. And his…his injuries in Algiers left him…ah, unable to be a husband.''

Grace's dark eyes widened. ''What?''

Afton could feel heat rush to her cheeks. How could she explain to her aunt that she would know such a thing? ''Sir Martin thought I might have developed a tendresse for McHugh, and he felt obligated to warn me that McHugh could not—''

Grace's face dissolved in laughter. She covered her mouth and laughed until tears came. Dabbing delicately at her eyes with a lace handkerchief, she finally managed to say, ''Oh, Afton. That is priceless. I have heard many stories of underhanded courting tricks, but this tops them all. I must congratulate Sir Martin on his ingenuity.''

Afton gasped. ''You think it is untrue?''

"Society thinks I am party to privileged information, but I am simply a keen observer. My dear, I must confess that I am quite appreciative of the male form. I have observed that certain postures, actions and, ah, appearances betray what a man is thinking almost as certainly as words. Let me just say that Rob McHugh is very attracted to you, and that he is generously equipped to do something about it.''

"Are you certain? I mean, I know that he was the victim of rather vicious torture. If, in the course of it, or as a part of it, he had been emasculated, or damaged in some way…''

Composed now, Grace sat back in her chair. "I am as certain as I could be without testing the matter for myself. Still, if you think there is truth to what Sir Martin told you, perhaps there could be another problem with McHugh. But not, I think, with his, ah, ability. My observations would contradict that.''

Still doubtful, Afton thought back to their times together. There had been moments when she had entirely forgotten about his limitations, had even suspected… But then why had he always backed away? Always behaved as if he were tormented when he could have had her for the taking?

Much to Afton's dismay, as she prepared for her meeting with Lady Enright, Dianthe came to her room to announce that Sir Martin Seymour was in the back parlor, requesting an interview. Afton wished there were some way to put him off, but she had known from the moment he opened the door under the stairs that this conversation would come. She needed to know what he intended to do with that knowledge.

She smoothed her hair, pinched color into her cheeks and hurried downstairs to the small parlor. Sir Martin was standing at the window overlooking the back gardens, seen now through a fringe of icicles hanging from the eaves. Afton closed the parlor door behind her, hoping Grace and Dianthe would honor that subtle request for privacy, and he turned at the sound. Preparing herself for an awkward interview, she sat in a side chair and folded her hands in her lap.

"Sir Martin?" she breathed in a soft voice. She could not meet his gaze for shame. She still could not understand what had possessed her to conduct herself in such a manner. In a closet. With a party in progress. And she certainly couldn't lay the blame at McHugh's door. She'd been somewhat more than a willing accomplice. She'd been the instigator of that particular episode. Mortification filled her at the thought.

Sir Martin cleared his throat and took the chair opposite hers. "Miss Lovejoy…Afton, I know you must realize how, ah, fond of you I have grown over the past months. I—"

She could not let him go on. It was bound to be painful for them both. "Sir Martin, I am very much afraid you—"

"One question, please," he interrupted.

Afton nodded, but she still couldn't look up from her folded hands. Answering a question seemed the least she could do. And a question was bound to be less humiliating than a denunciation.

"It is McHugh. From what I saw, it would appear he had taken advantage of your innocence. If your honor should need defending…"

That brought Afton's gaze up immediately. Sir Martin's face was hard, as if he had been reluctant to say those words. Did he mean to fix the blame for her behavior on McHugh?

"It would not be the first time he has imposed himself on an unwilling woman. Please try to understand, I do not blame you in the least. What I must ask you, however, is somewhat indelicate, so I pray you will bear with me."

Speechless anyway, she nodded.

"How far…that is, he did not manage to…"

Afton's cheeks burned and she fought for control over her surging anger and indignation. "Lord Robert McHugh did not ruin me in that closet, Sir Martin,'' she told him truthfully, ''and this is the first I've heard that he is a despoiler of women.''

''But you—''

''I cannot say what incited my behavior last night, but whatever it was, McHugh forced nothing on me. Perhaps it was the wine. Perhaps the season. Whatever it was, I accept the full responsibility for my behavior.''

''Too much mulled wine—''

''I could easily have sent him away,'' she insisted.

''Nevertheless,'' he sighed, ''I also accept a measure of the responsibility for not speaking sooner. I thought there would be time. I had no idea McHugh had set his sights on you.''

Set his sights? Heavens! McHugh had warned her away at every opportunity. He had made it glaringly clear that there would be no future with him.

''I have come today hoping it is not too late to correct my error.'' Sir Martin glided effortlessly off his chair into a kneeling position before her. He took her knotted hands in his and gazed up into her eyes with something more closely resembling cunning than affection. She longed to pull away and break the contact he seemed intent on forcing.

''As I have grown to know you, Miss Lovejoy, my admiration and affection for you have also grown. You have become so much a part of my heart that I cannot imagine my life without you. Please say you will be my wife.''

Afton was astounded. Whatever she had expected when Sir Martin requested this interview, it was not a proposal. She was about to deny him outright, but then felt churlish and ungrateful for his higher emotions. He had been willing to forgive her indiscretion with McHugh. He had proposed marriage despite that indiscretion. He had been willing to defend her honor. He had declared his love and admiration, *all of which she had encouraged*…until she'd met Rob McHugh.

"I…I am honored by your proposal, Sir Martin," she stammered. "However, I fear you could never fully trust me—and rightly so. If I accept your proposal now, I would be unworthy, and I cannot come to you being inferior to all you deserve."

"I have thought of that, Miss Lovejoy, but nothing will do but that I must have you."

Time. She needed a little time. At least the six remaining days the Wednesday League had promised. She could not even think of other matters until then. But how to divert Sir Martin?

She still believed he was good husband material, so perhaps she could transfer his attentions to Dianthe. First, she would have to shift her sister's affections away from Douglas McHugh, who was too fickle to make a good husband. If not, through inattention, she could wean Sir Martin away from his affection for her over the next several months. By spring he would be ready to fix his attentions elsewhere. Yes, that was the solution. Delay until Sir Martin's ardor cooled.

"I need time, Sir Martin, to sort out my thoughts and feelings. I cannot be hasty when we are speaking of our entire futures."

The hope that filled his eyes shamed her. "I shall wait as long as it takes you to make that decision, Miss Lovejoy, and I shall pray it is in my favor."

Although only six o'clock, it was fully dark by the time Grace's coach dropped Afton at La Meilleure Robe. Marie was just locking up when she arrived. "Shall I stay, *chérie*, or 'ave François come until you are finished?"

The Renquists lived in the first-floor flat adjacent to the shop. They would hear the emergency bell, so there was no reason for Mr. Renquist to sit in the fitting room beneath the salon. "No need for concern, *madame*. I have only one appointment, with a long valued client, and shall be leaving shortly after. I will be closing the salon until further notice. I am afraid it has become too dangerous to continue."

"Dangerous, *chérie?*"

"Oh, do not be alarmed. Please tell Mr. Renquist that the ladies will be contacting him tomorrow for a meeting to discuss our plans to proceed."

"*Oui.* Oh, I meant to tell you, *chérie*. There was a Lord Glenross 'ere the other day. 'E was asking questions about you."

"Me?" Afton gasped. "What did you tell him?"

"Not you, *chérie*. Madame Zoe. I told 'im that I pay little attention to my neighbors, and that you are very quiet and cause no trouble."

"Thank you, Marie." She breathed a little easier.

"That one." The dressmaker smiled with worldly wisdom. "'E is much man, eh? If not for François…"

Much man, perhaps, but one bent on her destruction. Now he was questioning Madame Marie. How long would it be before he discovered the truth?

"Take care, eh?"

"*Oui,*" Afton responded, already on her way to the hidden closet that led to her salon.

Once she had a lantern lit and the fire crackling on the hearth, she hurriedly donned her disguise. Though Lady Enright knew she was not what she seemed, Afton still felt the ruse necessary to maintain anonymity. She was bound to be introduced to her one day, and did not fancy an awkward recognition.

The little mantel clock chimed the half hour and Afton glanced out the window. No carriage in the street below, and no sign of anyone with Lady Enright's prominence. She frowned. The woman was always on time. Still, the weather might have delayed her.

Deciding not to waste the time merely waiting, Afton lifted her veil back, put a kettle on the hearth to warm and went to the alcove that held the cot and small bureau. She opened a small portmanteau stowed beneath the cot and began to fold the contents of the drawer and pack them away. She intended to leave no trace of Henrietta or Madame Zoe when she locked the door tonight.

As she lifted a small stack of hankies from a drawer, a whiff of Henrietta's lilac *eau de toilette* swept her back to her childhood—memories of sitting in a soft lap, nestled against a fichu of linen bearing that scent. A rush of emotion too long suppressed caught Afton by surprise. Tears flooded her eyes and a sob burst from the depths of her soul. She sank to her knees and gave herself over to the grief, truly feeling it for the first time. She leaned her forehead against the edge of the cot and cried until she could cry no more, finally slowing to an occasional shuddering hiccup.

She was so absorbed by her grief that she was not aware she was no longer alone until hands closed around her throat and a voice rasped, "One mistake too many, Zoe."

Afton clawed at the hands, but her attacker wore thick leather gloves. The fingers tightened, crushing her windpipe. She twisted and flailed, trying to break the assailant's grip, but it was ungiving.

She had not unlocked the door, but had undone the bolt in preparation for Lady Enright's arrival. Had he picked the lock? Was that how he had he gotten in? She opened her mouth to scream but could make no sound.

"You could have had it all," the rasping voice taunted.

She made one final effort to reach the bell rope, knowing her life was at stake, yet fearing the bell would not be heard as far as the Renquists' flat, despite her assurances to Madame Marie. But it was her last, her *only,* chance. Desperation lent her unnatural strength and she managed to dislodge the man's fingers. She lunged for the rope, coughing and gulping for air.

Before she could reach it he tackled her, bringing her down with bruising force, rolling sideways, his arms around her knees. The weight of their bodies falling sounded unnaturally loud in the silent room and rattled the teacups on the wooden table. A chair toppled as her attacker's leg slipped outward.

Afton rolled over to face the man who meant to kill her, but her veil fell back over her face. She tried to free her arms and legs from the tangle of cloth to clear her vision.

"What the hell?" a muffled voice snarled from the direction of the doorway. Had Mr. Renquist been alerted by the noise and come to investigate?

She felt her legs released suddenly and then heard the sounds of a violent scuffle, the table overturning and glass breaking. She pushed herself into a sitting position. Then there were running footsteps and a clatter in the stairwell. She sat up and took a moment to catch her breath. Mr. Renquist. He had come to her rescue. Oh, bless him!

One set of footsteps returned from the hallway and came toward her. "Are you injured, *madame?*"

That voice… Lord! The McHugh. Could her luck be worse? She shook her head, still trying to clear her vision through the veils. *"Oui,"* she croaked, her throat raw.

He cupped her elbows and helped her to her feet, then left her leaning against the wall as he went back to lock and bolt the door. "I don't think the son of a…blackguard will come back, but if he does, let's not make it easy for him, eh?"

"No," she gasped. Where had he come from? What was he doing here? Had he been watching since leaving Aunt Grace's last night?

"Damn!" he swore, combing his fingers through his hair. "I'd have gone after him but I was afraid you…"

"Would escape?" she finished for him.

"Needed help." He advanced on her, reaching out to take her arm. "Here. Let me see."

She spun away and moved toward the fireplace. Her skin was humming again, with no more than the brush of his hand and the timbre of his voice to start it. Oh, what was wrong with her? Seeking refuge in anger, she asked, "Why would you care what becomes of me, *m'sieur?* You 'ave declared on our last meeting that you wish to destroy me, no?"

"Yes," he admitted. "And I still do. But I would prefer to do it myself."

She took another step backward. "Now is your chance. We are 'ere, alone. The door is locked and no one will 'ear. Do it then."

He frowned. "Do not tempt me, *madame.* It would not take so very much. A little squeeze on your windpipe. A little twist of your neck. Or perhaps—" he bent and drew a wicked looking dirk from his boot "—the slightest pressure against your throat."

She knew she should be terrified, but the attack had pushed her past reason. "*Oui.* And why, *m'sieur?* I am sorry for your loss, but your wife made the choice, no? And she took your son with 'er. That is 'er shame, not yours, and certainly not mine."

"No, *madame,* 'tis yours. And I hold you responsible for my brother's fiancée's defection, as well."

"Oh, *le pauvre bébé.* 'E did not get what 'e did not want. *Quel dommage!*" She ridiculed the concept, given what she'd observed of Douglas's infatuation with Dianthe.

"*Quel dommage?* What a pity? Are you mad to mock me so?" He took a few steps closer, his size and presence menacing.

One last step backward brought Afton's spine against the wall. No more retreat. There was nothing left but to stand her ground. "So. *Madame* is to blame because she said some words that Lady McHugh took wrong. Not for the first time, *m'sieur,* and certainly not the last. Where was *'er* responsibility in all this, eh? 'Ow is she not accountable for 'er decisions, and yet I am?"

He matched her retreat with his advance, step-by-step, until he was close enough for her to see the rise and fall of his breathing. Slowly, inexorably, he reached out and fingered the fine silk of her veil.

"Do not do this, *m'sieur.*" She hadn't the physical strength to stop him, and had too much pride to fight a losing battle. She was no match for his determination.

He lifted the fabric slowly, prolonging the moment when she would be fully exposed—his moment of victory. "I have been waiting for this, *madame.* Once I see your face, I will know you anywhere. You will never escape me, never be free of me."

She closed her eyes as he lifted the veil, not wanting to see his anger.

It could not be! Not Afton. Please God, not Afton.

But it was. That flawless face framed by shining copper hair, those brilliant eyes now shrouded by dusky lids edged in feathery black lashes, was bared to him, and the vision cut like a knife through his heart.

The how of it, the why and what of it, became jumbled in his head, demanding answers or explanations, but he could not frame the questions. He could only think of one thing: Afton. Sweet, straightforward, honest Afton was Madame Zoe. The woman he was destined to love was the woman he had sworn to destroy.

Those impossibly long lashes fluttered and opened to reveal eyes dilated with fear. Her lower lip trembled as if she wanted to speak, but he could detect no other trace of emotion. It would seem he did not know her at all.

"Explain yourself," he said in a voice that was harsh to his own ears. He dropped his hands to his sides, fighting the impulse to shake her until her teeth rattled.

"I—I…" She blinked and swallowed. "What do you want me to say, Lord Glenross?"

"The truth," he prompted. "And call me McHugh. God knows you've earned that right in the last few days."

"I…I don't know what—"

"Do not lie, Miss Lovejoy. I still have the taste of you on my tongue. Your scent still fills my nostrils. My hands remember the feel and weight of your—"

Pink flooded her cheeks. "Yes, then. *C'est vrai.* I *am* Madame Zoe."

Bloody goddamned hell! Then everything else was a lie! Everything! He couldn't trust a single word she'd said, a single emotion she'd revealed in his arms. He couldn't trust that she hadn't been horrified by his scars and willing to love him anyway. He couldn't believe that she hadn't seen something vile and repulsive when he'd let his passion show. Aye, the night in his room, she'd come to search it, not to be with him. She was a consummate actress in her roles of Madame Zoe and would-be lover to Lord Glenross. The sting of her betrayal was all the worse for her counterfeit affection.

The cold shock was wearing off and fury was building in its place. He turned away from her and fisted his hands at his sides. "Good God, madam! I can scarcely credit your duplicity. All this time you've been playing a double game! Playing me for a fool."

"That was never my intention," she exclaimed. "But you deceived me, too. You said you wanted to know the future, and all along you only wanted to entrap me. You have been trying to destroy me, McHugh, without a care as to what will happen to Dianthe and Bennett.''

He couldn't believe she would try to turn this debacle on him. "I had no idea Dianthe and Bennett had any connection to Madame Zoe,'' he snarled, "though it would have made little difference to me if I had. Then any means, fair or foul, were justified in your mind?''

"Means? What means? I did nothing but keep my identity secret. What harm have I done you?''

"My wife and son, madam, are dead because of you. My brother is bereft because of you.''

"Your brother has cast his attention elsewhere already, McHugh,'' she reminded him.

"To another damn Lovejoy!''

"He could do worse. Beatrice Barlow would have bored him within months. Dianthe, I'd wager, would have kept him interested at least a year. But a man of Douglas's ilk hasn't a constant bone in his body.''

"That is not the point!'' Rob roared.

"What *is?*''

"You are a charlatan. You dupe the ton, then dance with them at soirees and the like. You perpetuate the myth that you are omniscient, and give advice as if you were an oracle. You lead poor, pathetic, vulnerable people to bad decisions, and then trade on it and collect money. You encourage people to place their trust and faith in you, Miss Lovejoy, and betray that trust. Who the hell do you think you are to play God?''

Afton dropped her gaze and shook out the coils of her hair to remove the pins that had held the veil in place. They scattered across the floor, freeing long strands of copper that glowed like banked embers in the firelight.

A watchman's bell rang in the street and the guard called that all was well. Somewhere in the distance a church bell rang seven times, and she glanced up again to see huge, heavy flakes falling as thick as eiderdown outside the window. Coaches would stop service and horses would be stabled soon.

She sighed. She supposed she could inform McHugh that she hadn't told Maeve's fortune, but what good would that do? She was guilty on all other counts, including the telling of Bebe's. Yes, who the hell *was* she to play God?

She hesitated a moment too long in her reply and McHugh stepped closer again. The scent of his shaving lotion made her head swim and melted her inside. Her heart thumped against her rib cage and she couldn't catch her breath. "I am no one, McHugh," she whispered.

"Then why?"

"To eat."

"Balderdash!" he replied, obviously struggling to keep his anger in check. "Mrs. Forbush would never have let you starve. She is quite fond of you."

"She offered. I refused."

"Pride has a price, Afton."

"And you are here to collect? What do you mean to do, McHugh?"

His voice when he answered was a low angry purr, working its way under her skin, setting it to humming and tingling again as it had since the night in his hotel room. "What could you possibly have to interest me, Afton?"

Her gaze snapped up to meet his icy eyes. There had been a challenge in his voice, and an insult. He could never love her, and that ripped at her insides. On the verge of crying and screaming with frustration, she realized that she loved him, needed him as he could never need her.

Even worse, she could not rid herself of the memory of the sensations he had evoked in his hotel room and again in the closet at her aunt's house. Afton kept returning there in her thoughts, wanting more, *needing* more, and knowing she could never submit to such intimacies again if they did not come from him.

She lifted her chin in defiance, daring him to carry out his threat, both dreading and needing the answer to her question. *What did he mean to do?*

He closed the remaining distance between them and pulled her roughly against him. "Damn it! You know what I want, Afton. You've always known, and you've used it against me."

She sighed. "How could I when I wanted it, too?"

"You're a bloody deceitful liar. I cannot trust anything you say."

He had backed her against the wall and she had to lift her arm up and push against his chest to look into his eyes. The pain and betrayal she saw there made her gasp. Darkness ran deep in his soul, and she doubted she could ever reach him. But she couldn't think about that when he was standing so close and looking so wounded.

"You can trust this," she murmured, coming up on her tiptoes and lifting her lips to his.

He met her challenge with intensity. His mouth closed over hers, demanding that it open, finding and entering in a ritual marking of his territory. His kiss was angry and fierce, and Afton met it with her own frustration, slipping her arms around him and pulling him closer when he would have drawn away.

His muscles tightened and he lifted her so that her face was level with his. "Don't do this, Afton," he growled.

"I cannot stop." The naked truth of her answer astonished her as much as it did McHugh.

His eyes darkened further and he leaned into her, pinning her against the wall. His hand slid down her back and cupped her buttocks. In a very few motions his other hand dragged her skirts up and bunched them around her waist, drawing her knees up to wrap around his waist. Once that was accomplished, he moved his hand back to the vulnerable heat at her center.

She exhaled with an involuntary cry of encouragement when his fingers found her passage. She tightened her legs around him and made mewling sounds each time he invaded and withdrew again. Her breathing quickened until she was panting, unable to catch her breath for the tumultuous sensations washing over her. She did not know where this would lead but she was willing to follow wherever it took her.

McHugh's voice rasped against her ear in short breathless gasps. "My God…you are…so hot and ready…you melt on my hands."

"Ready," she repeated, grasping that word as her means of finding the end of this unrelenting need. "What is next, McHugh? Show me what's next."

"Y've gone too far t' stop me this time."

"Then dinna stop," she whispered in his own brogue.

His answer was a deep groan, as if he were giving up his last hold on control. His hand left her long enough to fumble with his own clothing, and then something hard and thick took the place of his fingers. He rocked against her, slowly letting her slide downward.

She drew her breath in a gulp as that other object pushed and probed her vulnerable core. Aunt Grace's words came back to her: *Rob McHugh is…generously equipped to do something about it.* Aunt Grace was right.

Afton had been prepared, ready for days, and after a few tentative probes, he slid inside her with one sure stroke. She cried out in surprise at the sharp pain that shot through her, but McHugh's voice would not let her dwell on the meaning of that.

"Hold tight, Afton. Wrap y'self around me. Le' me bear yer weight."

He withdrew slowly, causing her to shudder, and when

he rocked upward again, he filled her with an exquisite thickness that sent chill bumps up her spine. Oh, yes! This was what she needed—this melding of flesh and heat.

Then his stroke quickened, leaving her to ride the crest of his passion, on the verge—ever on the edge—of knowing the reason for all these overwhelming emotions. She was speeding to an unknown destination and desperate to arrive.

McHugh's breathing became shallow and quick, keeping pace with his penetrations. "Little Miss Lovejoy…my lying little…fortune-teller," he murmured. "Ye feel like a velvet fist around me. Hot, tight, greedy. But can ye take all o' me?"

"Aye," she vowed with an uncertain laugh.

He covered her mouth with his as he drove deeper, impaling her to his hilt and swallowing her surprised squeal. She threw her head back and squeezed her eyes shut to keep from crying out. The pain dulled to an ache, then rapidly built to need again as his rhythm drew out desire. A deep shudder went through him and he stilled, the tension leaving his muscles.

Afton's own breathing slowed, her breasts aching, her skin humming. She still felt vaguely unsatisfied. The quick and violent nature of the coupling had left her trembling and weak, but she was not repulsed. Not remorseful. She knew full well what she'd done, and she'd do it again. She was still yearning, her body questing for something more—there had to be more.

Slowly, he withdrew from her, his arms tightening to support her weight as he stepped back from the wall. He carried her to the little cot in the alcove and laid her carefully upon it, smoothing her skirts down over her legs. He adjusted his own clothing and sat on the cot beside her.

"Now that we've got that out of the way, Miss Lovejoy, shall we get down to business?"

Chapter Fourteen

"B-business?" she repeated.

McHugh gazed down at her, his face unreadable. "What we just did, Afton, does not change anything. Don't mistake me—I took great satisfaction from it, and given a chance, I'd do it again in a second. A lovelier piece of arse I've never had, and the fact that you are Madame Zoe just sweetens the pot. There's something poetic in it, wouldn't you agree?"

Tears filled her eyes and she turned away, blinking them back frantically. He mustn't see how deeply he'd hurt her. She couldn't bear to look that big a fool. Everything had just changed for her, and it meant nothing to him. He'd warned her not to trust him, but she'd listened to her heart—her blind, foolish heart. Well, it wouldn't happen again. Never again.

"Yes," she mumbled. "Poetic."

"So, what shall we do with you, little Miss Lovejoy? It was always my intention to expose you for the charlatan you are. But now that I know your identity, I cannot do that without damaging other people. People who don't deserve the disgrace you'd bring to bear. Mrs. Forbush has never had a breath of scandal attached to her name. Your sister, though innocent, would share your dishonor. She *is* innocent, is she not?''

A cold shock went through Afton. Dear Lord! He would not turn this on Dianthe, would he? "Yes," she squeaked. "She knows nothing of this. She thinks I have been clever with our little stash of money. Do not tell her, McHugh. Please do not tell her."

He narrowed his eyes suspiciously. "And your brother? Well, he might never recover from the public humiliation. His future was made from swindling the ton of their hard-earned money. What would they make of that at Eton, I wonder?''

"McHugh—"

"How have you sunk so low? Why do you do it, Miss Lovejoy? The truth, damn it."

"M-my father was not a wise investor, especially after Mama died. Then, when Papa... We were very frugal, but the inheritance was eaten by death taxes and expenses within two years. 'Twas then that Auntie Hen came to town and began telling fortunes. She and I fabricated a tale that she had hired out to wealthy widows as a traveling companion and tour guide. Thus Dianthe and Bennett did not ask to visit her, and we were able to keep the scandalous details of our finances secret.

"I stayed in Little Upton with them, selling what produce we could grow, and bartering for goods and services. Dianthe made jams and jellies to sell at market. Bennett carved and painted signs before we saved enough to send him to Eton. That paid our expenses in Little Upton, but it did not pay Bennett's tuition or for Dianthe's season. Grace offered to help but we refused. She is not actually our aunt, only our mother's cousin. But when she offered to hire me as her companion, it came as a godsend. I arrived in London and—"

"And turned to fleecing the ton," he finished for her. "A

good plan, Afton, until I came along. Now what am I to do? How shall I acquire my 'pound of flesh'?''

Her heart sank. ''I am certain you must have something in mind.''

''Why, yes, I do.'' He smiled.

''What is it you want from me, my lord?''

He laughed. Actually laughed. ''Damn near everything. But let's start with your promise to cease fortune-telling immediately.''

Fortune-telling! She had forgotten her appointment with Lady Enright. She looked toward the mantel clock. Half past seven! She sat up so quickly that her head spun. ''I have an appointment,'' she wheezed. ''Lady Enright. She was supposed to be here an hour ago. She should be here any moment!''

McHugh stood up and turned his back to her. ''She won't be coming, Afton. She's dead.''

Dead? No. Certainly not. She'd just seen Lady Enright at Millerton's Christmas Eve dinner party. She'd been well and happy. ''When…how did she die?''

''She was murdered. Barely two hours ago.''

Afton grew light-headed. She covered her mouth, holding back a horrified cry. She watched the rigid line of McHugh's back, heard the wooden tone of his voice, and she knew he was not as unaffected as he wanted her to believe.

''You must be mistaken. We have an appointment. She is never late.''

He turned back to her. ''I am not mistaken, Miss Lovejoy. She'd been strangled and stabbed.''

Afton's hand trembled and a chill came over her entire body. Like Auntie Hen! Nearly like her! What had the killer meant?

Afton did not realize that the trembling had filled her entire body until McHugh gripped her shoulders to steady her.

"What does this have to do with you?" he demanded.

Dear Lord! What would McHugh do to her if he knew her connection to the deaths? He would use that against her, too! Then the less he knew, the better. "Nothing," she swore.

He released her so abruptly that she fell back against the pillow. "Do you lie when the truth is easier? Well, let me tell you what I think."

He started pacing in front of the cot, lifting his hand to smooth his hair back. For the first time, Afton noted a splatter of blood on his coat sleeve. Lady Enright's blood?

"I think there is a connection. I followed a trail of footsteps in the snow from Eloise's home in this direction. By the time I lost the footsteps in a mix of others, I realized I was close to this address. I decided to see if the infamous Madame Zoe had something to do with this, and I came here straightaway. You'd have been the second victim tonight, Afton, if I hadn't arrived when I did."

She tried to swallow, but her throat had constricted in fear. Should she tell him about Auntie Hen? Or that there were more victims than he had counted?

"So the question is, what have you done to get yourself murdered?" he asked.

Afton's azure eyes took on a hunted look. She glanced toward the door as if expecting to see Eloise walk through it, then back at him with the dullness of resignation. Had things been different, he might have comforted her. He might have gathered her close to his heart and murmured soothing endearments. But things were not different. Things, in fact, were about as bad as they could get.

His stomach turned at the thought. Losing a dear friend like Eloise had been bad enough, but if he had lost Afton... Ah, but he *had* lost Afton. He'd seen to that rather thoroughly. He'd lived up to Maeve's expectations, despoiling

Afton with barely a by-your-leave, even deliberately deny-ing her climax as a prelude to his vengeance. *McHugh the Destroyer*. But how the bloody hell was he supposed to have resisted her? He'd been raw and ready when she had smiled and teased, and made him believe for a fraction of a second that there might be something inside him worth loving. And she would pay for that as much as anything else.

The "edge" that Ethan Travis and Martin Seymour were always talking about hadn't eased at all for indulging it. In fact, it had grown sharper for honing it on Afton's unprac-ticed wantonness. If he made love to her day and night for a thousand years, would he have his fill of her? Doubtful. But he'd never find out, because what they'd just done would never happen again. She wouldn't want it, and he wouldn't be able to stop with that. Even now his desire for the deceitful little chit was rising again, threatening to de-stroy his plans. But he wouldn't let it. He'd lived for retri-bution too long to give up now.

He had her right where he'd always wanted her—wanted Madame Zoe, rather—under his thumb and entirely depend-ent upon his whim. Aside from Maeve, he owed her for all he had endured in that Algerian prison. All those long days and nights manacled and locked in the Dey's sweat box, he'd been planning this moment, fantasizing how sweet his revenge would be. How Zoe would pay for every second he'd spent in confinement, every lash of the whip, every day Hamish and Maeve had lost. Rob's goal had always been to destroy her income, force her to cease telling fortunes, and perhaps require her to leave England and return to France. Ah, but now things were different.

Afton was intimately connected to people he cared about. Grace and Lady Sarah Travis would have his heart for sup-per if they thought he had done anything to harm her. Doug-las would be furious if he caused distress to the newest object of his affection. And there was no way around it—Dianthe would suffer if Afton was exposed.

Rob stopped pacing and looked back at her, to see her brows were furrowed in an attempt to frame an answer to his question. Perhaps she needed a little help. ''If you cannot decide what you have done to get yourself murdered, Afton, perhaps you can decipher which one of the many with motives might have attempted it.'' A little flame flickered behind the brilliant eyes. He was pleased to see that she still had fight in her. He did not want this to be too easy.

''I do not know, m'lord. The veil had fallen over my face and became tangled on a button. I suppose it could have been anyone who knew I'd be here tonight. For all I could see, it could have been *you.*''

''Were it me, we would not be having this conversation, Miss Lovejoy. Were it me, you'd be halfway to hell by now.''

She gave him a calculated smile at the hollowness of his threat. ''There are moments, McHugh, when I *do* think it was you. After all, how convenient for you to arrive just in time to frighten my attacker away. How propitious to find me alone and vulnerable to your...revenge.''

The chit! He laughed and shook his head. ''No, Miss Lovejoy. That wasn't revenge. That was just a prelude. Revenge is going to be much more interesting.''

She did not look intimidated. ''Do your worst. It cannot be as bad as what I've imagined. Even so, you are the only one I know who might wish me harm, and I am not entirely convinced it was not you.''

''Believe me, we shall have to look elsewhere. I have every reason to think your attacker is Eloise's murderer.''

''Aside from jumbled footsteps in the snow, why?''

He hesitated for a moment, then reached into his jacket pocket and removed another of the raven buttons. He held it out for her to see. ''This was beside her body.''

Afton's eyes grew round and her hand went up to her throat. "A...a raven? What significance does that have, McHugh?"

"It is mine. Someone is trying to lead the authorities to me. Someone wants me to hang."

"Then what have *you* done to get yourself murdered?" she challenged.

He gave her another unrepentant smile. "Half of London might want me dead for all I know. But no one has made an attempt on *my* life."

Afton swung her feet off the cot and made a shaky attempt to stand. He reached out to steady her but she shrank away from his hand and sat again. That simple reaction told him more than mere words what her state of mind was. After a moment, she stood and went to turn the little table and two chairs upright. When she sank to her knees on the floor he hurried to her side.

"What—"

"If you are being set up to take the blame for these murders, McHugh, and I was to be one of them, there should be some trace of the villain's attempt, should there not?"

He admired her logic. He joined her on hands and knees and began searching the perimeter of the round braided rug.

She gave an exclamation and crawled toward a corner next to the cupboard. Sitting back on her haunches, she held up a small round object. "Like this?"

His stomach lurched at the sight of another of his raven buttons in Afton's hand. Then it was true. Someone *had* meant to murder her and frame him for the crime. He did not know which fact enraged him more. "Like that," he admitted in a tight voice.

She muttered something incomprehensible and stood and went to a little box sitting on the bureau in the private section of the room. She stared at the box and then at him.

Finally she opened it and took something out. She brought it to him and uncurled her hand.

He looked down and frowned. "How did you get this?"

"Is it yours, then?" she asked.

He nodded. "I haven't seen it since…since I left London for Algiers."

Tears shimmered in her eyes and her shoulders sagged. "Dear heavens," she whispered, "I've been chasing a shadow."

"Where did you get this, Miss Lovejoy?"

"I…" She glanced up at him again. "I found it."

"Where?" he demanded. "Tell me where."

Reluctantly, she pointed to a spot beneath the table.

"Did one of your clients drop it?"

"Yes. I suppose they did."

"Who? Who was it?" He watched the confusion play across her features.

"I wish I knew, McHugh."

He believed her. "What do you mean by 'chasing a shadow'?"

"I have been trying to find the owner of that pin."

"How was that chasing a shadow?"

"Because you were here all along. Under my nose." She backed away from him, looking wary and uncertain. Her guilty glance said she knew more than she was saying.

"You'd better tell me everything, Miss Lovejoy. Otherwise I have no reason to keep *your* secret."

She rubbed her temples as if she had a raging headache. He could see her waging an internal battle before she finally sighed deeply and surrendered. "Whoever dropped that pin killed my aunt Henrietta."

Little surprised him these days, but he hadn't expected that. "When?"

"Barely three weeks ago." She met his gaze and issued

the next words like an accusation. "About the same time you arrived back in England."

He grinned. He had to admit the circumstances looked bad for him. The timing rather stretched credibility. "So you think I murdered your aunt Henrietta by mistake and then came back for you?"

She frowned. "You've said you want to destroy me, McHugh. Is that not the ultimate destruction? Has your raven emblem not been found both times?"

She had a good case. And damned if he had an alibi for the time of Livingston's murder, and Eloise's. "As I've said, Afton, if I wanted you dead, you'd be dead."

"Perhaps," she allowed.

"But what is the connection? Henrietta, Eloise, you—is it the flat? Or did someone kill your aunt thinking it was you?"

"Or the other way around, m'lord. Someone may have tried to kill me thinking I was my aunt. That *was* my ploy to flush the killer out." She took a deep breath and squared her shoulders. "But either way, the result is the same. I am determined to find Auntie Hen's killer."

He gave her a grim smile. "I intend to find Eloise's killer and whoever is trying to get me hanged. It appears as if it may be the same man."

"Yes. It would appear so," Afton agreed. She reached out to steady herself on one of the chairs. He felt a twinge of guilt when he remembered that she had been through quite an ordeal tonight—first an attack on her life, and then his attack on her virtue.

"So," he said, softening his voice, "at last we have something in common."

"My lord?"

"An enemy."

She sat, looking dazed.

"Until I deal with this new development, I will not have

time to finish with you, so you have got a reprieve. Meantime, you will cease telling fortunes and coming here. Do you understand?''

"I do not think *you* understand, McHugh," she said as she wiped her reddened eyes on her sleeve. "I have been engaged in looking for my aunt's killer. I am not going to stop just because you have gotten in the way. I think now that my fortune-telling is the key to that information."

The shimmer in her eyes unmanned him. He slammed his hand flat on the table's surface and shouted, "Damn it, Miss Lovejoy, have you learned nothing tonight?"

"Yes, McHugh. I've learned you do not lie, because I should have let you walk away the first time you warned me against you. I've learned that I am close to finding the murderer, or he would not have risked an attack on me tonight. I've learned that I am the only one I can rely upon. So stay out of my way."

What had gone wrong? That tactic had always worked before, making seasoned soldiers and longshoremen quail. Rob had thought she was weak and defeated. He had thought she had been subdued. Evidently she'd just been gathering her resources.

"Have you forgotten who holds the future of your family in his hands?" he asked.

"No. Have you forgotten who knows the connection between you and a number of unsolved murders?"

"It's too dangerous for you. You could have been killed."

"So could you."

"A compromise, then?" he offered. "You can gather information, and I shall follow it up."

Her lips twitched. "Shall we share information, McHugh?"

She had him. "As long as you do not take chances."

* * *

Afton entered the morning room and found the ladies of the Wednesday League gathered around the breakfast table. But this was Sunday. Before church. Had they somehow gotten wind of what had happened last night?

Aunt Grace stood and came to take her hand. "Afton! I was going to send someone to wake you. We have just heard horrid news."

"News?" Afton repeated. She felt slow and sluggish, having arrived home last night escorted by Rob McHugh, who now seemed determined to oversee her activities. She'd heated water for a warm bath to soak her bruises and aches from the near fatal attack. By the time she'd bathed and fallen into bed, she'd slept like the dead. She simply couldn't register what news she should know about.

"Of Eloise Enright's death," Grace said. "No one knew she'd been ill. But you had an appointment with her last night, did you not?"

"Yes, but she did not come," Afton admitted. "And she hadn't been ill. She was murdered in the same manner as Auntie Hen and the others Mr. Renquist told us about."

Lady Annica stood and came to Afton's side to lay a comforting hand on her shoulder. "I am sorry to hear it, Afton. I realize how difficult this must be for you. Would it distress you too much to tell us what you know?"

She shook her head. "I'm afraid I do not know much more than I've told you. I must assume that, since the investigators are saying it was illness or an accident, they have decided to keep the actual cause secret to prevent panic."

"Well, I'm feeling a bit panicky just the same," Charity Wardlow declared. "If it could happen to Henrietta and Lady Eloise, it could happen to anyone. You might be next."

If the killer had had his way, it *would* have been Afton. She couldn't tell the ladies that, of course, or they would fly into a frenzy of outrage and protectiveness. No, if she was to make any progress in her investigation in the handful of days left to her, she would have to keep everything that had happened to her last night a secret.

"Dare I ask how you learned the truth, Afton?" Grace asked.

"The usual sources," she hedged, knowing they would think she referred to Mr. Renquist. Not a lie, but not the entire truth. "I also learned that there was a raven button found at the scene."

"Another raven," Lady Sarah mused. "We *must* discover the significance of that if we are to find the murderer."

Grace studied Afton's face. "If Lady Eloise did not come, dear, what kept you out so late?"

Afton went to the sideboard to pour herself a cup of strong coffee and help herself from the chafing dishes. She spoke over her shoulder, glad of the chance to hide her emotions. "I was cleaning the flat, searching through Auntie Hen's belongings for any clues I might have overlooked. I brought some of her things home. I have decided to leave as few personal items there as possible in the event a thief breaks in or the killer comes back to search for the raven pin when I am gone."

"Good strategy." Lady Annica nodded.

"I thought you said you were going to quit, Afton." Grace sipped delicately at her teacup and studied her niece with a critical eye.

She blushed, praying her aunt was not as astute as she appeared. She braced herself and explained as best she could. "It occurred to me that I am in a position to gather useful information as Madame Zoe. And it isn't as if I shall be going there often. Only occasionally. For a few carefully selected clients."

"Hmm," Grace mused. "Well, so long as you work closely with Mr. Renquist, I suppose it will be safe enough. Glenross is your chief problem."

No, Afton thought, *the killer poses the greatest threat.* McHugh already knew the worst, and somehow she had survived with no more than her wounded pride and a ruptured maidenhead. Oh, but the feel of his hand, his skillful caress, his instinctive knowledge of her needs—how would she survive that?

"Rob McHugh would not hurt her, Grace," Lady Sarah said. She smoothed the fabric of her gown over her slightly rounding stomach. "He saved my life once, and I cannot believe that, angry or not, he would harm a woman."

"Yes, I wouldn't worry about Glenross, Aunt Grace. I...I will manage him," Afton lied.

On his fourth cup of strong coffee, McHugh gestured to a chair in the small study of his club on St. James Street. "Good of you to meet me on a Sunday, Dawson," he said. "What have you got for me?"

"You are not going to like it, Lord Glenross." The small, wiry man sighed as he sat and took a sheaf of papers from his jacket pocket.

"I'm not paying you to make me happy, Dawson. I'm paying you for information."

"I've got that, right enough." He unfolded the papers and began sorting through them. "More to come, certainly, but this is a start. I am curious, Lord Glenross, why a man of your, er, talents should hire an investigator. Like carrying coals to Newcastle, it is."

"My attentions have been recently diverted to other areas." Such as surviving the attempts to frame him for murder. Rob sat back and waited for the man to arrange himself.

"Yes, well. Which information do you want first? The men or the woman?"

"The men," he said, deciding to save the best for last.

Dawson rearranged the papers. "Nothing remarkable, sir. To all appearances, the first man seemed perfectly normal.

But then he caught on that he was being followed and gave us the slip a time or two. The blighter's clever, I'll give him that."

"Yes, but did you find anything to implicate him in the murders?"

"Not exactly, sir. But he went missing last night before Lady Enright was murdered, and didn't show up again until past midnight at a gaming hell. Suspicious enough, if you ask me."

McHugh nodded agreement. It could have been perfectly innocent, but he was not a man who believed in coincidence. "Keep at it then, until we can eliminate him or catch him in the act. Only time will tell, and I don't fancy another murder in the meanwhile. What about the others?"

"As instructed, my lord, I have looked into everyone who knew about your return when you were still 'in hospital.'"

McHugh winced. He did not like to think of his fortnight interrogation by government officials as being in hospital. True, he had received much-needed rest and medical care for his various wounds, but the ministry's attempt to learn anything useful from his stay at the Dey's palace could hardly be called "in hospital."

He shrugged, letting it pass. "Any likely suspects there?"

"A few. Difficult to backtrack weeks after the events, but my men are on it. The most likely are not easy targets. The first, Mr. Ethan Travis, is a savvy one. We can never tail him longer than a minute or two. He catches on too fast and gives 'em the slip."

"It will not be Travis. He saved my life, and I saved his. I'd trust the man before my mother."

"He knew you were back—"

"Who's next?"

"Lord Kilgrew, of course. He knew before anyone else. And there is something suspicious about him. He comes and goes at odd hours. It appears he knew most of the victims personally.''

Rob contemplated that. It was possible that Kilgrew was the killer, but highly unlikely. What would his motive be? Why would Kilgrew want to discredit him? But men in high places had been known to go balmy under unrelenting pressure. Rob nodded. ''Keep looking into that one.''

''Then there's, ah, your brother, my lord.''

''Doogie?'' Rob nearly laughed outright. ''What possible motive could he have?''

''Well, er, before you returned, my lord, he came to town ready to claim your title and lands. If I understand correctly, there is no little amount of money involved?''

''He thought I'd been executed. That's what our agents were told by the Dey's intelligence network.''

''Aye, but he was preparing to go before the court of—''

''He did not know I was back until the day I was released. The murders started when I was still in hospital.''

Dawson fidgeted, looking uncomfortable. ''There's some speculation that your escape was not as secret as you thought. And with lands, money, title and a new fiancée at risk, a man's apt to do anything.''

That was a sobering thought. But Douglas a murderer? No. It would be easier to believe that Rob himself was the murderer and blanking his memory after the deed. ''Am I to assume that those closest to me are most likely to be incriminating me in these killings? I can trust no one, it seems. Is that all you have in the way of suspects?''

''Aye, sir. At the moment.''

''Do what you must.''

The man nodded and reshuffled his papers.

''Shall we get on with the woman?'' McHugh said, sitting back in his chair, his sense of anticipation heightening. ''Tell me what you've got.''

"'Tis a puzzle, sir. She does daily errands, the same as any lady's companion. On the surface, quite ordinary."

"But—?"

"But how much business can she have at a solicitor's office in a week? Or a dressmaker's shop? Seems she's always one place or the other."

McHugh remembered the time he'd been waiting for Zoe and Afton had left the dressmaker's, the time he'd run into her outside Mr. Evans's office, when she'd told his fortune, the scent of lilies of the valley, and how he'd been inexplicably drawn to her, even shrouded in widow's weeds. God, what a fool he'd been not to suspect her. But she'd seemed so damn innocent. So bloody believable.

"…background is fuzzier, sir," Dawson was saying. "I have not gotten the reports from Wiltshire back yet, but I suspect they will be much the same. The mother died when the boy was still an infant. The father wasn't much of a businessman, and lost what wealth there was. The land was protected, though, and survived the courts. The family has lived in genteel poverty since the father died years ago. They've worked hard to pay their debts and earn their own way, but they managed it. The boy is off at Eton now, and spending the holidays with friends in the country."

"Was there no other family but Mrs. Forbush?"

"None but a maiden aunt by the name of Henrietta who hires out as a ladies' traveling companion and tour guide. She's abroad at the moment. Greece, my sources tell me."

Abroad? Or dead? Which was the truth? "Keep digging, Dawson. There's got to be more. Something there doesn't feel right."

Any more right than the fact that when he'd learned the truth, he had unleashed his frustrations on Miss Lovejoy. That she had been dancing with him as Afton and deceiving him as Madame Zoe infuriated him. The duplicity had been overwhelming—worse than anything Maeve had ever done to him. And when Afton had encouraged him, he'd been only too happy to give in to his baser nature. His self-disgust afterward filled him with remorse. When he'd left her at her aunt's home and gone back to his hotel, he'd roused the staff to bring him a hot bath—as if he could ever wash away the stain of guilt for taking her maidenhead.

He'd taken a virgin like a common prostitute. He had been Maeve's nastiest nightmare, and probably Afton's greatest fear. Hell, he'd been his own worst enemy. And every time he thought of her he grew stiff and ready, desirous of making amends by making love to her the way she deserved.

No, she had lied to him, betrayed him! She didn't deserve any softness from him. And there would never be a repeat of what had happened last night. Never.

Chapter Fifteen

"Meet me at Zoe's salon tonight after eight o'clock. I have information. R.M."

Afton could not doubt the message was from McHugh. Who else could be so imperious when making a request? She would have liked to refuse the summons, but curiosity threatened to eat her alive. Pleading a headache, she had gone up the front stairs to her room and then down the back stairs and out the garden door.

Since Zoe's salon was less than a mile away, Afton did not bother trying to find a coach. In a dark woolen cloak with the hood obscuring her face, she walked the distance, arriving within twenty minutes. She let herself into Madame Marie's salon and used the secret stairs up to Zoe's flat.

Throwing her cloak over a chair, she stooped and struck a tinder to the fire on the hearth, then used a piece of kindling to light the oil lantern and a candle on the mantel. The damp chill of the night had gone bone deep, so she put a kettle on the fire to boil, thinking to make herself a pot of tea.

A single solid thump on the door announced McHugh's arrival, but she had learned nothing the night before if not to be cautious. "Who is it?" she asked.

"McHugh."

Bracing herself to face him for the first time since his—her?—seduction, she undid the latch and opened the door. Something feral flickered in his eyes as his gaze swept up her form. Odd how just his glance could set her nerves to thrumming again.

"None the worse for wear, I see."

"Not where it shows," she replied, strangely relieved that he would not try to ignore what had happened the previous night.

McHugh winced as if her barb had met its mark. "Whiskey?"

She removed a bottle of port from her little cupboard. "This is the strongest I have," she told him. "And the glasses were broken last night."

He shrugged out of his coat and worked the cork from the bottle. With a crooked grin, he accepted the porcelain teacup Afton offered and filled it with port. He raised his glass in a silent toast and then drank deeply. "It's been a hellish day."

Afton sat at the little table and nodded. "A little tedious for me, as well."

McHugh began walking the perimeter of the room. "How do you do it, Miss Lovejoy?"

"What?" she asked.

"How do you simply appear in the flat? I watched you let yourself into the dressmaker's shop downstairs, but I did not see you come out again to access the stairway. So, how do you do it?" He had made his way into the small sleeping alcove, and now looked at the closet door, then back at her with a raised eyebrow.

Afton refused to react. In truth, she simply did not care if he discovered the secret passage. What did that matter when he knew everything else?

He opened the closet. It took him only a moment to push

the few remaining items aside and discover the spring latch that popped the wall open to reveal the dark stairway. He closed the panel and turned back to her.

"Clever. I watched you come and go at La Meilleure Robe. I thought you were inordinately fond of new dresses or simply running errands for Mrs. Forbush, and all the time you were telling fortunes. Where does it exit?"

She hesitated, wondering if her answer would cause problems for Madame Marie.

"Shall I go down and find out?"

"It opens in the closet of the back fitting room, my lord."

"Then Madame Marie is in league with you?"

"No!" Afton could not allow Madame Marie or Mr. Renquist to share the blame McHugh seemed determined to assign. "She has allowed me access due to her friendship with my aunt, but she has nothing to do with my fortune-telling."

He nodded, looking somewhat mollified. "It appears that you have taken every precaution to protect your identity as Madame Zoe. Very clever."

She did not want to encourage conversation about her activities. She tried for a change of subject instead. "You said you had information, my lord?"

"Yes. I have a list, of sorts."

"Of what?"

"Possible suspects for the murders." He strode to the table and dropped a piece of paper in front of her. "Tell me what you think."

She unfolded the sheet and read. Ethan Travis, Lord Kilgrew, Douglas McHugh, Martin Seymour. "These men are your *friends*. I cannot see any of them as a murderer, let alone deliberately trying to implicate you. There must be a mistake."

"I wish there were. Unfortunately, an investigation of those who knew I was back in England, and those who might wish I hadn't returned, have turned up only these names. Nevertheless, I have been unable to determine motives, with the exception of Douglas. He is the logical culprit. With me out of the way, he would inherit the title, estates, money...."

"I cannot believe that. He is so obviously fond of you. Dianthe says he is always singing your praises. Why, he came to blows over an insult to you."

A look of profound relief passed over McHugh's face and Afton realized how heavily that suspicion must have weighed on him. "That was my opinion, also. But I cannot think why any of them would want me dead."

She recalled her earlier interview with Sir Martin. Surely he did not want her enough to go to such lengths...no. No, of course not. The murders had begun long before she had even met Lord Robert McHugh. But some niggling doubt remained. "Sir Martin came to see me yesterday afternoon."

Rob turned back to her, his eyes dark with suspicion. "I have not seen him since the night of your aunt's Christmas soiree."

"He asked me about the events in the closet under the stairs."

McHugh resumed his pacing. "That's none of his business. I hope you did not attempt to explain that madness."

"He thinks it *is* his business, m'lord. He wanted to know if you had despoiled me. And he warned me about you, saying that you had despoiled women before me."

McHugh's upper lip curled in a sneer of self-loathing. "Aye. Martin's got the right of it. I despoil everything I touch, Afton. Too bad he did not warn you sooner."

"I thought you should know what he is saying about you."

"Aye. Underhanded, I'll warrant, but I suspect he has a crush on you. Men in love are apt to do and say stupid things."

"Yes," she sighed. "He did."

McHugh stopped his pacing to look down at her again. "How stupid?"

"He asked me to marry him."

He sat down opposite her, searching her face. "And how did you reply?"

"I begged for time."

He nodded, his features unreadable. "Enough time to make certain you are not carrying my baby?"

That thought had never occurred to her. The shock must have shown on her face because McHugh's expression finally registered a hint of sympathy. "That possibility kept me awake last night. If you are breeding, Afton, I will not abandon you or the bairn. I will set you up with a house in the country—"

A cold feeling settled in the pit of her stomach. Even though her pulse raced when McHugh came near, even though she wanted him anew every time they were together, she could not bear the thought of being secreted in the country to raise his bastard. She wanted all of him or nothing. "I do not want to discuss this."

"You cannot wish it away."

"You are premature. I am likely fine."

He nodded and sat back. "We shall know soon enough."

"I told you about Sir Martin because I wanted to warn you that I think he is not your friend. He slanders you."

"Because he wants to marry you."

"Because he says you are a despoiler of women. He earlier said you were not capable of—that is, that you could not—"

"Underhanded, I will agree. Still, the man's motive was not to slander me, but to protect you. Did his prediction not come true? But I will heed your warning, Afton. All the names on this list will stay there until I can prove them innocent."

She thought of the list of her aunt's last clients. None of McHugh's suspects appeared on it. She reached into the inner folds of the cloak thrown over her chair, withdrew the list she had made of the names from Mr. Evans's appointment book, and handed it to McHugh.

"What is this?" he asked, unfolding the paper.

"My own list, my lord. A list of my aunt's appointments in the weeks before her death."

"*Her* appointments?" McHugh frowned.

"I thought it might be useful. I thought she might have known her killer. That he might have been one of her clients."

"*Her* appointments? Was your aunt Henrietta a fortune-teller, too?"

Afton brushed away his question with a wave of her hand. "But now I see that, by virtue of the raven, her death is tied to the murders implicating you. And, as you can see, there are no names on my list that match the ones on yours."

McHugh tapped the paper with his index finger and narrowed his eyes. "I will grant that the blame for your aunt's death is being laid at my door, but there still must be some connection between her and the others."

"You," Afton said. "You blame her for your wife's death. Some might say that is motive enough. That is why I suspected you. And why the police will, too."

"Why would I blame your aunt for Maeve's death? I blame Madame Zoe."

"Yes. Precisely."

An oppressive silence settled around them as he studied Afton's face. Tension crackled in the air as he began to put the pieces of the puzzle together. He stood so quickly that his chair toppled backward. He did not stop to right it before coming around the table to lift Afton out of her chair and look into her eyes—soulful azure eyes now reddened with lack of sleep and crying over his misdeeds.

"Are you saying you are *not* Madame Zoe?"

She gazed unflinchingly into his eyes. "Madame Zoe is the fortune-teller. I have been her, and so has my aunt."

"Which of you told Maeve's fortune?"

"Does it matter, my lord?"

It shouldn't. Both of them had swindled the ton of their money. Both had duped and deceived innocent people looking for answers. He knew it shouldn't matter. But it did. "Yes," he admitted, his fingers biting into her shoulders. "It matters."

"Auntie Hen," she said simply and without explanation.

Relief mingled with betrayal. "I see." He relaxed his grip and Afton stepped back.

She glanced down at the lists. "So if someone killed Auntie Hen, and wanted to implicate you, it would have to be because of Maeve. That is the only connection between us."

There was common sense to Afton's theory, and a new avenue of investigation. If he could establish a connection between the victims and Maeve, then what? His wife was dead, and he was still the most logical suspect. Then a more frightening thought occurred to him.

He lifted Afton's chin with the crook of his finger. "You set yourself up as bait for the killer, didn't you, Afton? You thought you could catch him by luring him back to the salon."

She shrugged and dropped her gaze. "I did not want to report Auntie Hen's death to the authorities. I could not risk having her identity made public. It would have ruined Dianthe's chance for a good marriage, and Bennett would have been sent down from Eton. But I could not allow the killer to go free. Something had to be done."

"Are you mad?" Rob asked in a hoarse voice. "You were nearly killed."

"I knew the risk, McHugh." She looked up at him again and gave him a little smile, the first since he had arrived. "And I took every reasonable precaution. Someone was always within call." She gestured at the bellpull he had noticed on his first visit. "But last night, only Lady Enright knew I would be here. I did not think I would need help."

"You knew the risk?" he mocked. "Obviously not, Afton. Is there someone waiting at the other end of that bellpull tonight?"

Her silence was answer enough.

"Swear you will not do this again."

"Even if I am meeting you?"

"Especially if you are meeting me," he advised. He couldn't resist any longer. He'd been wanting to hold her, kiss her and feel her pressed against him from the moment he'd walked in the door tonight. Pulling her into his arms, he expected resistance, but she came with a little gasp. When she lifted her arms to fit around his neck, he was amazed. He'd done everything he knew to alienate her and warn her away from him, but she came to him gladly. Almost hungrily.

"Have you no common sense at all?" he sighed, lowering his head to her.

"None," she confessed.

He found himself delaying the moment when their lips would meet, relishing it, anticipating it. How engaging her little moan of impatience was, and when she came up on her toes to make the contact he had denied, he knew she had given him a gift he did not deserve.

Unutterably sweet, her lips softened and parted to accept him. Her heat, her scent, her taste combined to bring his senses to the boiling point. "Afton, do ye not know by now the consequences of tempting me like this?"

"Aye," she answered in his brogue. "Dire consequences."

"Do ye always tease at inappropriate times?"

Her lips moved against his throat, tickling with their soft caress. "The only thing ye did to me last time was leave me wanting more."

Dear Lord, what had he done to deserve this tempting little wanton? "Have a care, or ye'll get it."

"Ah, I was beginning to wonder what it would take."

That breathless challenge was enough to push him over the edge. Twining his fingers through her hair, he pulled her head back to access her mouth. He wanted to be tender, wanted to draw her slowly into his world of desire and need, but she pushed him to the edge of reason with her artless eroticism. She had no idea of her power over him, and thank God for that.

Her tongue slipped sweetly past his lips, taking that initiative for the first time. The action stirred his blood immediately. A part of him couldn't believe she had chosen him—McHugh the Destroyer. McHugh the Despoiler. Another part of him did not care. Whatever her reasons, she was here now. And she might never come to him again. He would not squander the gift this time.

Keeping his mouth on hers, he swept her up in his arms, vowing that this would be no hasty angry coupling against a wall. No, this would be sweet and tender. This time he would have her naked flesh pressed to his. This time he would give her completion.

He sat her on the small bed. Kneeling in front of her, he reached around her, his fingers fumbling with the buttons down her back. He thought himself clumsy and inept until she began working at the knots of his cravat. She seemed almost frantic to have it gone. He took pity on her and left his task long enough to assist with hers. When he'd loosened the knots enough for her to finish, he returned his attention to her buttons. Her little moans were all the encouragement he needed.

She pushed his shirt and jacket off his shoulders in one sweep, her fingers skimming lightly over his skin. He shivered in the cool air, feeling vulnerable with his scars, and thus his past, exposed to her.

"Do they still hurt?" she asked in a faint, trembling voice.

He shook his head, fearing that she would not touch him if she knew the truth. "Only in my mind."

She tilted her head and pressed a fluttering line of kisses down the worst of the striations, amazing him as she said, "They have a terrible beauty. Like you, Robert McHugh. They define you. Strong. Courageous. Enduring."

Chill bumps rose on his arms and the back of his neck. He had hoped someone might be able to ignore the scars, or look past them to the man he was, but that a woman like Afton Lovejoy could find them beautiful and see virtue in them was an unexpected gift.

Need rose in him, white-hot and urgent. With a moan, he lifted her head from his chest and covered her mouth with a bruising kiss. She seemed to understand his need and met his intensity with her own.

He managed to unfasten enough of her buttons to slide the gown down her shoulders and arms to free her breasts. The seductive scent of *Vent de Lis* wafted up to him from the damp heat of her flesh, filling his senses with the awareness of her—as if he needed a reminder that Afton's body was next to his, soft and yielding. Waiting. Urging. He took one firm, rose-tinted tip into his mouth and nibbled with gentle insistence. She cried out, dropping her head back in delight and cupping his with one hand to draw him closer, as he had done the night she had come to search his room.

"Please," she sighed.

The vagueness of her entreaty gave him license to continue. He pressed her down against the pillows, cherishing her other breast until both were puckered and hard with arousal. She was beginning to writhe with pleasure. It would not be long before she would be weeping with the need of him. He wanted that. He wanted her crying his name, begging him to take her, gasping with her orgasm and *still* aching to have him inside her.

He wanted to do all the things that would bring her to that point, and he wanted to make up to her for the quick roughness of their first coupling. But reality was less quixotic. Reality was that he needed her so badly he could not wait.

As he gathered her skirts up, Afton parted her legs to assist him, so caught up in the heat and passion of his ministrations that she was prepared to let instinct override modesty. When he slid one knee between her legs, she spread them to fit him between them. Hoping, praying for what came next, she began to fumble with the fastenings of his trousers. Her fingers brushed his swollen phallus and he jerked and moaned.

"M'God, lass. Leave me an ounce of control, will ye?" he said in a strained voice.

She drew her hand back, afraid she had hurt him somehow. Before she could frame the question, he found and separated the soft folds that shielded her passage, and began a rhythmic stroking that caused her hips to rise to him. She craved the pressure of his hand and the feel of him filling her, touching her where she'd never been touched before. She closed her eyes, imagining him doing those things.

A faint whimpering echoed in the alcove and she realized with some surprise that she was making the sounds. The heat that flickered between her legs ever since that night in McHugh's hotel room was burning out of control. Every inch of her skin tingled and every nerve sang with the tension of being drawn tight.

"Please," she said again.

"Easy, Afton," he whispered, "'twill be worth the wait, I promise ye."

Oh, she prayed so. She could not stand another moment of this ceaseless burning. She needed to find the end of it before it consumed her.

McHugh unfastened his trousers and freed himself with a little moan. He positioned himself above her, his shirt agape to reveal his chest, his trousers down and his member thick, long and erect. The sight of a man in such a state should have shocked her. At the very least, she should have been frightened, but instead a wave of primal need washed over her.

"Hurry," she urged. "Oh, hurry."

With a cough, or a laugh, or both, he obeyed her command. She'd been well prepared this time, and there was no barrier to obstruct the process, but his first tentative probing threatened discomfort. Then, with a sigh, he thrust again and slid downward. The unaccustomed thickness of his shaft filled and stretched her, and she found it profoundly erotic. When he began moving, the friction was like electricity, raising chill bumps all over her body. She arched to him, bringing her knees up, wanting to take him deeper.

McHugh began a Gaelic recitation in a low broken murmur, keeping rhythm with his lovemaking as she spiraled higher and higher. She could feel her destination within reach. She slipped her hands downward to his firm buttocks and pulled him closer as she raised herself up to him.

"Aye. That's it, lass. Let the passion take ye," he muttered with approval. As if he had been waiting for that sign, he quickened the pace, driving her into a frenzy.

She felt the pleasure drawing inward to that center where she and McHugh were joined. Then, in a burst of heat, light and color, long waves of ecstasy washed over her, spreading outward in ever expanding ripples. *Rapture,* she thought. *This is rapture.* She had arrived.

Afton stirred as he fastened his trousers again, tucking in his still-open shirt. Rob smiled, watching her languorous stretch. The force of her orgasm had been so overwhelming that she had fallen into a gentle swoon. And he? When he had spent himself, he'd collapsed to his elbows, trying to spare her the burden of his weight. To his chagrin, he had grown hard again while still inside her, confirming his suspicion that he could not get enough of her. He had withdrawn, eliciting a moan of protest from Afton.

Now her dark lashes fluttered and she sighed deeply. "McHugh, come back here. I need ye."

He laughed and went to pour more port into the little teacup. The delicate piece of china looked absurdly out of place under the circumstances. "Nay, lass. Should I come to ye, I'd stay, and ye canna take much more tonight."

"How kind of you to spare me." She smiled, brushing the tangled copper curls out of her eyes.

"Aye." He grinned. "McHugh the Kind, they call me."

She giggled at the outrageous lie and the sound of her laughter soothed his conscience. His mistreatment did not seem so bad when she laughed and begged for more. Later he would wrestle with his conscience. Later he would find the strength to distance himself from her. Ah, but now he wanted—no, needed—her to take some small pleasure away from this incident. He poured another dram of port for her and took it to the cot.

She sat up, pushing her arms back into the sleeves of her gown. "What were you saying in Gaelic, m'lord?"

"I was quoting a poet. Christopher Marlowe."

"What work?"

"'Come live with me, and be my love, and we will all the pleasures prove....'"

"McHugh." Her voice was soft but had turned serious.

He waved his hand, trying to defuse the mood. He could not bear to hear her rejection. "Words, lass. Words of seduction. No more. But I have better news for you."

"Better news?" She turned her back to him and held her hair out of the way.

He bent to the task of refastening her buttons. "Aye. 'Twill be easier for you in the future. The first time is more difficult, because you don't know where you're going. Now you know."

"That was not the first time," she reminded him.

"Aye, it was. Your first pleasure is the real beginning."

Her breathing became shallow and rapid, and he knew she was remembering the sensations. He left a little kiss on the back of her neck before he stood and moved away. He needed distance or he would ravish her anew.

"We need to come to terms."

"I know, m'lord."

He scratched the back of his neck, trying to choose his words carefully. "I've lost my need to hurt you, but I've warned you countless times that I cannot be responsible for you. I cannot take the risk. There would only be pain at the end of it. I cannot deny the…the attraction between us, and I do not regret it. But nothing can come of it, and it must never happen again. D'you understand?"

She nodded. "It is…impossible."

"Our only business together is in finding the murderer."

"I know." She exhaled a soft sigh.

"You must tell me everything. I need to know all if I am to find out who is killing people."

"I have told you, m'lord. And I will report any new findings. But you must do the same. My aunt is dead, and I will know who killed her. Even…"

"Even if it is me," he finished. He was painfully aware that the evidence alone would convict him of Henrietta

Lovejoy's death, and that Afton had not completely acquitted him.

"Yes."

"And you must stop coming here. You must stop telling fortunes. No more swindling the ton."

She stood and looked up at him, her eyes sparkling with defiance. "I cannot agree to that. I was engaged in this investigation long before I met you. I will not give it up because of your antiquated sense of chivalry."

"Afton—"

She lifted one delicate hand, palm outward, to stop his words. "Do not waste your breath. I am unmovable on this."

"I will not be responsible for—"

"You are not responsible. I make my own decisions, McHugh. I will succeed or fail on my own. You have no part in this."

He did. He would damn well see to it that she did not put herself in danger, and he'd do it any way he had to. He'd follow her, lock her up or drag her along at his side if necessary. "Gi' me a key to this flat, Afton. I want access and I want to meet you here starting tomorrow night. If you do not come, I will hunt you down, no matter where you are." When she looked mulish, he repeated, "A key, Afton. Or I'll tie you up and leave you here."

She went to a peg by the closet door and removed the key hanging there. She tossed it to him, as if she did not want to come too close to him and tempt him to carry out his threat.

"Now get your cloak, and I'll see you home."

"No. If Dianthe should see—"

"Dianthe be damned. I'll not leave you to walk home alone with a murderer on the loose."

Chapter Sixteen

The dim light of a candle in the window of Zoe's salon warned Afton that McHugh had arrived before her—his gambit to make certain she was never in the salon alone. How could the man be so annoying and so endearing at the same time?

She pulled her nondescript black cloak more tightly around herself as she climbed the tenants' staircase, avoiding the entrance through La Meilleure Robe. She would rather not remind McHugh how she had deceived him by arriving through the secret staircase. She had no wish to provoke his ire again.

Their meeting would be brief, since she had nothing to report on the investigation of the names on her list. At least Mr. Renquist had not been discouraged at their meeting earlier. He was certain that, sooner or later, the murderer would give himself away. Afton prayed the rogue would not give himself away by killing again.

Removing the key from her woolen muff, she let herself into the second-floor flat. McHugh was pacing in front of the fireplace. When he turned at the sound of the door opening, his face registered profound relief.

"Where have you been?"

She glanced at the old mantel clock. She was barely ten minutes tardy. "I must have made a late start."

"Good God! Say you're not walking!"

She pushed the hood of her cloak back and dropped her gloves on the little table. "Very well. I will not say it."

"Damn it! Will I have to hire someone to follow you every time you leave the house?"

Her anger at his presumption was softened by the concern in his voice. "If you do that, McHugh, how will I explain it to Aunt Grace or Dianthe?" At his silence, she sighed. "Very well, I will take a coach after dark. But your concern is costing me a pretty penny."

"Then stay at home," he growled. "You're safer there."

"From the murderer? Do you really think he will come here again?"

"He wants you dead, Afton, just as he wants me to hang for it." He picked up her muff and handed it to her. "Come on. We are late."

Was he hoping his formality would help him keep his distance? "Late? Where are we going?"

"You wanted to take part in the investigation, and God knows you've proved I cannot leave you alone. Come on, then. You're suitably dressed, not a single thing to distinguish you when your hood is up. Keep your face in shadow."

She noticed that he, too, wore nondescript clothing, dark colors and a shapeless coat. There would be no way for a casual observer to distinguish if they were heavy or thin, old or young, familiar or strangers. The unexpected adventure filled her with excitement. At last she was doing something to solve the mystery. The greatest risk she had taken before was posing as Madame Zoe, but she feared nothing with McHugh at her side.

"How do you know where to go?"

"As the situation is urgent, I thought it best to hire an

investigator. He keeps me informed of the suspects' comings and goings, their obligations and appointments.''

She thought of Mr. Renquist and how useful he had been to the Wednesday League over the years. Yes, McHugh had been wise to employ an investigator. ''Where are we going tonight?'' she asked. ''Who are we following?''

''Be quiet, Afton, and ready for anything.''

On the street, he hailed a coach and gave an address in St. James Street. McHugh instructed her on the rudiments of what they would be doing, and gave her a long list of cautions if they should be discovered or if anything should go awry.

''If I tell you to do something, do it quickly. I will not have time to coddle you. Do you understand?''

She nodded, annoyed that he would think her in need of coddling. ''You needn't worry about me, McHugh. I can take care of myself,'' she told him as their coach drew up at the corner of St. James Street and Piccadilly.

He helped her down, paid the driver, and took her arm to lead her into the shadows of the buildings. This, she knew, was the bastion of English manhood. St. James Street housed the best of the men's clubs in London, and any man with credentials claimed membership at one of them.

''Which is yours?'' she asked in a whisper.

''White's,'' he answered, following her line of thought.

''And which are we watching?''

''White's.''

She fell silent, discouraged by his obvious reluctance to share information. Clearly, he had taken her along to keep an eye on her, and did not require her help. Looming next to her as he was, silent and steady, his presence was like a cloak around her—protective and all-encompassing. She could feel the warmth of his body at her back and the tickle of his breath on her neck. Her skin tingled with awareness.

She wanted to turn in his arms, press herself against him and lift her mouth for his kiss.

Late traffic was light and the occasional passersby provided a feeling of normalcy. Once, when someone passed near them, McHugh turned and pulled her close, as if they were an amorous couple. She looked up at him and for a moment, the open hunger in his eyes made her think he would kiss her. Then resolve hardened his face and he released her and stepped back.

After a quarter of an hour, a slender figure exited the club and walked briskly toward Pall Mall. McHugh signaled for Afton to follow him. Another right turn led them toward Parliament. Afton was relieved to be moving again. The cold had numbed her feet and hands, and the brisk pace set by their quarry soon warmed her. She wondered if he would hail a coach, but he continued and turned right on Cockspur Street to Charing Cross.

At Downing Street, the man entered a private residence. McHugh pulled her into the shadows again. Minutes passed and Afton shifted her weight from one foot to the other while McHugh betrayed nary a twitch of a muscle. Passersby did not notice them in the deep shadows.

"How do you remain so still?" she whispered.

His head tilted down to her but she could not see his face in the shadows. "Practice," he said. "Months in confinement without enough room to move. My box was roughly the size of an English coffin."

She smothered a gasp. He must have felt as if he'd been buried alive! No wonder he hated small spaces like the closet under the stairs. But if conditions had been so extreme… "McHugh, how did you escape?" she asked.

His fingers bit into her shoulders and he lowered his head to whisper in her ear. "I would have to be very drunk to tell you that story, Miss Lovejoy. Do not ask again."

A chill that had nothing to do with frigid weather seeped

through her. No, she would never ask again. She suspected the answer would terrify her.

She began to understand how deeply he hated Madame Zoe and why he was determined that an incident like the one in her salon could never happen again. By his reckoning, Madame Zoe had sent Maeve on that ill-fated trip and set in motion the chain of events leading to his family's death, his imprisonment and torture, and his inability to love again. It must gall him that he had shared something so intensely personal, so profoundly intimate, with the person he held accountable for that inhuman abuse.

The door to the residence opened and their quarry hurried out with a furtive glance over his shoulder. He looked right and left before entering the street, and then started off at a brisk pace, merging with the foot traffic on Parliament Street. By the time they reached Westminster Bridge, he was moving at a run. He had caught on to their presence.

Afton knew she'd never be able to keep up. "Go," she urged McHugh. "I will follow."

He hesitated and looked as if he would argue, then nodded and pursued the man. Easily outdistanced, Afton was barely able to keep McHugh in sight.

She was halfway across the bridge when the moon revealed the dark shape of their quarry hesitate and throw something into the Thames before starting off again at a sprint. She thought McHugh was gaining on him until she saw him peel off his great coat and hat, and dive headlong into the freezing water.

Her heart leaped to her throat and her shouted, "Mc-Hugh!" came out scarcely louder than a croak for the fear tightening her voice. She lifted her skirts and ran for all she was worth to the spot where he had gone over. She leaned over the stone ledge, searching the black roiling river.

"McHugh!" she shouted again. "Where are you, Mc-Hugh?"

When there was no answer, panic began to build in her chest. Then she thought she saw movement in the murky depths and she wanted to scream with relief.

He had gone over the ledge closer to the south bank, so Afton scooped up his hat and coat, ran to the end of the bridge and onto the embankment, where a wide stone stairway led down to the water. "McHugh! Where are you? Answer me! Rob…please answer me!"

The only reply was the lapping of the river against the stone bank. Tears blurred her vision. How could anyone survive the freezing temperature of the water? She searched frantically for a skiff or rowboat, but none were tied to the iron rings set in the stone stairway. "Help me!" she screamed, but her words were carried off on the wind.

She feared his sodden clothing had dragged him to the bottom of the river. "Oh, Rob…" she wept, sinking to her knees and burying her face in his greatcoat. His scent, masculine and spicy, filled her nostrils and she began sobbing. He couldn't end this way. He just couldn't. He'd survived too much to die at the bottom of the Thames.

"A-Afton…" A faint voice carried to her from the churning water.

"Rob?" she shouted, scrambling to the edge of the stairway.

"Here," he called, not twenty feet away. "I canna see you."

"Rob," she cried again. "Swim toward my voice. This way, McHugh. On the embankment."

She heard the slap of water and a moment later McHugh's dark head bobbed into sight.

"Here, McHugh. Just a little farther."

She reached out to grasp his hand and drag him onto the bottom step the moment he was close enough. He was as cold as ice and his entire body was racked with violent shivering. Great plumes of steam rose in the air from their panting. "I thought you had drowned," she gasped.

He pushed himself into a sitting position and shook the water from his face and hair. "So did I."

She draped his coat around him, knowing that he would freeze unless she could get him dry and warm immediately. She helped him to his feet and supported him so that he could climb the steps to the street level. "Ho! Driver!" she called to a passing coach. She could not take Rob back to his hotel in this condition, nor could she take him home with her. There was only one safe place to go.

McHugh stumbled into the coach while Afton gave the address of La Meilleure Robe and a brief explanation that her brother had slipped and fallen into the river. Then she followed him into the compartment.

When they were underway, he reached across the distance and traced a line down her cheek with one icy finger. "You're crying."

"No," she lied, dashing the tears away with the back of her hand. "It is the cold. And your infernal splashing."

Teeth chattering, he grinned. "Did I hear ye calling me Rob?"

It was all she could do not to throw her arms around him and tell him how desperately afraid she had been that she would never see him again, and how furious she was at him for risking his life for an unknown trinket. "I think I must have called you everything I could think of," she admitted. "Whatever were you thinking, McHugh? Why did you jump in the river?"

"The blackguard threw something over the edge—something he didn't want to be caught with—and I wanted to see what it was."

"Simpleton," she hissed, losing her temper entirely. "You nearly *died.* And what do you have to show for it?

Nothing. You must never, ever do anything so foolish again.''

She stretched out his hand, a wadded object clenched in his left fist. ''Not for nothing, Miss Lovejoy. For this.''

''What is it?'' She squinted, unable to see clearly in the darkness of the coach.

Some piece of evidence. Some incriminating item. Something that would identify the man as the murderer… Rob didn't know. He only knew that if the blackguard wanted to be rid of it, then it would be of interest to Afton and him. He clutched it in his hand and returned it to his pocket.

''Later,'' he said, unable to control shivering so severe that his teeth chattered. Permanent damage from the cold was only moments away.

Afton seemed to realize it, too. She began to chaff his hands between her own, pausing only long enough to breathe heat into the hollow between his palms as he had done that night barely two weeks ago outside the opera. She worked tirelessly as the coach thundered on, the tears still coursing down her cheeks.

Dear Lord, how valiant she was! How steadfast and loyal. He longed to lean forward, just slightly, to kiss the top of her head as she attempted to bring warmth and feeling back to his hands. He longed to tell her that he'd been a fool, and that she'd been right to do whatever it took to keep her family safe and together. And that he was touched how she cared enough about him to be upset that he could have died.

''Afton…'' he breathed.

She looked up at him, her aqua eyes luminous with unshed tears. There was a question in them, and a vulnerability that twisted him inside.

''Th-thank you,'' he said, unable to find words for the jumble of emotions roiling inside him.

The coach drew up outside the dress shop and Afton

stepped down, tossing the driver a coin. The quid was much more than the fare but the driver did not offer change and Afton did not press for it. She was too intent on fitting her shoulder beneath Rob's arm to act as his crutch. They stumbled noisily up the stairway together, and she was able to retrieve her key from whatever hidden pocket she had stowed it in.

Once inside, she left him holding the back of a chair as she piled more wood on the grate and used a bellows to fan it into flames. That done, she helped him to the sleeping alcove and pulled the blanket from the bed.

Understanding the need to shed his freezing garment, he began to unfasten the buttons of his shirt. Numb with cold, his fingers refused to work. He pulled his cravat off and hooked his fingers over his collar, prepared to rip the damn thing off. Afton placed her hand over his and drew it away.

"Let me," she murmured.

He dropped his arms to his sides and she stepped closer. He gazed down at her bowed head as she began to work the buttons, and he felt the first welcome stirring of heat in his middle. If he had not been afraid of leeching her warmth and leaving her chilled, he would have pulled her against him. Her scent, her softness, seeped into his soul but left him hungering for more. "Afton..." he whispered.

She stilled and her hands began to tremble. He willed her to look up but she resisted. After a long agonizing moment, she stepped away and stooped to gather his jacket and cravat. She offered him the fallen blanket with one hand. "Finish and wrap this around you," she instructed, "and I will hang your things on the mantel to dry."

As unaccustomed as he was to taking orders, he was content to let Afton have her way. He could see that she was on edge, ready to snap at the slightest provocation. He had commanded men under stress, and he recognized that her need to be doing something was essential to her sanity.

She pulled the curtain to allow him some measure of modesty. Disrobing was a difficult procedure with his fingers still numb from the cold, but he managed the task in a few minutes, leaving the garments in a sodden heap on the floor.

Afton pulled the only overstuffed chair in front of the fire and gestured to him to sit. He gladly complied and stretched his bare feet out to the hearth. Sensation began to return with a sharp prickling beneath his skin.

He ignored the pain as he watched Afton wring out his clothes and hang them from the mantel to dry. She was so perfectly beautiful with her hair knotted at her nape and long copper tendrils curling around her face that he wanted to touch her again—feel her heat and softness. God, how he wanted all of her and everything she had ever been and would ever be. What a bitter irony it was that love had come to him in the guise of what he most loathed, and he had been too blind, too angry to see it before he had destroyed any chance to win it. He had abused Afton's goodwill beyond enduring.

When she shook out his greatcoat, she removed the wadded cloth from the pocket. As if just now recalling the reason for being here, she held up the white bundle to have a look at it. It appeared to be a man's cravat. As the folds fell out, the triangular shape came into view, complete with deep red stains. Afton held the neck cloth for him to see. "B-blood?" she asked.

He reached for the cloth and turned it over in one hand. "Damn. If this means what I think it does—" He started to rise but Afton pushed him back into the chair.

"If it is, then what, m'lord? Will you put your wet clothes back on and go out on a chase?" She threw her hands up in disgust. "Whatever it means, it is too late to change it. You cannot help anyone if you are on your deathbed with pneumonia."

There was sense in her words, McHugh knew. He could change nothing by putting himself at further risk, but he chaffed to be doing something. Anything. "Afton, I cannot dally here—"

"Dally? This is not a dalliance, Lord Glenross! You were nearly a victim of your own foolishness."

"Fortune favors the bold, Miss Lovejoy," he retorted, a little amused by her assessment.

"Bold?" she repeated. Her face registered confusion and then outrage. Tears sprang to her eyes and she spun away from him. "You may think so, sir, but I think differently. I will grant that you have a reputation for courage. Every single member of the ton says so. They speak of your fearlessness and persistence in the face of defeat. But I think you are one of the greatest cowards I have ever encountered! The very worst kind of all—the kind that hides behind bravery as a ruse to keep others at a distance."

Her denouncement amazed him. He'd been called many things in his life, but never a coward. "I have never run from a fight, Afton. I have never refused a plea for help."

She whirled to look at him again, her face reddened and her lashes spiked with tears. "That is not courage, McHugh. That is despair. You are brave because you have given up on life. You do not care if you live or die, so when you take the ridiculous chance of jumping into an icy river, you are risking *nothing!* You do not need your courage to face death at the end of a sword or pistol—or even a frozen river. Real courage is embracing life—the joy and the pain—and never giving up. You've surrendered, McHugh, and so you have nothing to lose. That is not courage. That is hopelessness."

He stood, forgetting the cold. His blanket slipped and he wrapped it around his waist with a vicious jerk before taking two steps toward her. "What the bloody hell are you talking about?"

"You! You are so devastated by the loss of your wife and son, and so obsessed with avenging them, that you have stopped caring about anything else. You do not care if you live or die, so you court danger so that you can feel something—*any*thing. And I...I..."

The angry words she'd been reluctant to voice had come out in a heated rush. Because they were as true and raw as her wild emotions? "Do not stop now, Afton. Finish it. You *what?*"

She glanced at him, shook her head and sank into a chair to bury her face in her hands. "I cannot bear to watch it any longer."

"Watch what?"

"Rob McHugh destroy himself."

Something fluttered deep in his chest, like the wings of a bird struggling to break free. "Why should that matter to you?"

She looked up, anguish in every line of her face. "I cannot bear to lose anyone else I love. I've lost Mama, Papa, Auntie Hen..."

Was that an admission to loving him? Impossible. He'd done everything imaginable to earn her hatred. But what did she mean? That she cared? Or that she felt responsible for the risks he took? "I know how fond you are of assuming the burden for everyone, Miss Lovejoy, but do not think you are responsible for my actions."

"Where have I heard those words before?" she mocked, brushing at her eyes.

He hadn't realized his words had been an echo of hers from the night before until she posed the question. "I am not alone in losing sight of what is important," he murmured. "You think only of your sister and brother, and how they would perish without you. And of avenging your precious auntie Hen. You are willing to risk scandal, ruin, your future, and even your pretty little neck to accomplish your goals, and devil take the hindmost.''

''Then we are two of a kind,'' she admitted, looking more than a little unsettled with that realization.

He moved closer, intending to comfort her. He wanted to show her the tenderness that always seemed to elude them at such times. He wanted to love her as she should be loved, holding nothing back and asking nothing in return. ''Afton,'' he breathed, reaching out to smooth her wayward tendrils back into place.

She shrank away and stood, a look of misery on her face. Retrieving her cloak and muff, she hurried to the door. ''Stay until morning, m'lord. Your clothes will be dry by then. There is enough wood for the fire.''

''Stay with me, Afton.''

''I cannot, McHugh. You've said so yourself. It would only end badly. We are both too…too damaged.''

''But—''

''I will hire a coach. Do not worry about me.''

The door closed with a soft click and he sank back into the chair in front of the fire.

With Afton gone, the cold returned. Everything inside him rebelled at the thought of losing her. He wrapped himself in the soft wool, searching his heart for answers.

Chapter Seventeen

McHugh took long strides down St. James Street, the early morning sun on the fresh fall of snow dazzling his eyes with its brilliance. He knew where he was going, and he knew what he had to do. Looking neither right nor left, he was so consumed by his thoughts that he scarcely noticed the hubbub of traffic and the noise of street vendors hawking their wares.

He could not rid himself of the memory of Afton's accusation. She had been wrong, though. He was not devastated by Maeve's loss. Saddened, yes. Guilt-ridden because he had not loved her, yes. But it was Hamish who was his true loss. Rob's chest constricted at the memory of the smiling, fair-haired child. The lad had been bright and funny, and they had adored each other. Within a month of his birth, Rob had forgotten that he was not Hamish's father and had accepted him as the McHugh heir. Maeve had been jealous of his relationship with the lad, as if she had only given birth to Hamish to spite him and could not bear that he found any joy in claiming another man's bastard as his heir.

Rob could not remember—if he had ever known—what he had done to earn Maeve's hatred and disgust. Since she had come to him pregnant, he realized now that she must have hated him even before their wedding night. Within a few months of Hamish's birth, she'd ceased her incessant tirades against him and grown cold and distant. It was then that she'd done the real damage, naming him "McHugh the Destroyer," calling him an animal with intemperate, unnatural needs—accusations that had nearly destroyed him. He accepted the blame for the failure of their marriage then, because he had no way to explain how the sweet, joyful lass of his youth had turned into the cold, critical woman in his bed and in his life.

Then he'd met Afton Lovejoy. Afton, with her gentle teasing, her banked passion and her simple wisdom. As Madame Zoe, she had told him, "You 'ave not learned that dreams, no matter 'ow impossible, make dreary lives worth living, and that when 'ope dies, the 'uman spirit dies." My God! She'd been right. He had given up on ever finding any measure of peace or contentment. But had he given up hope? Or was he just afraid to hope—afraid of the risk it implied and of the depth of emotion that might be required of him? Of the pain if he lost it?

But Afton smiled at him, challenged him and matched him measure for measure. Whatever errant spark Maeve had neglected to extinguish leaped to life, and he'd begun to want again. With wanting came desire, and from desire grew affection. He hadn't wanted that; he'd even fought it with anger and guilt. Yes, he'd fled from the return of emotion like a stallion with a wildfire at his heels. Failing that, he'd tried to distance himself from the threat of love. He'd thought, idiot that he was, that he could separate his lust for Afton from his love for her. He'd been wrong.

Because of Afton, he understood that Maeve had been fighting her own demons. Poor Maeve. She had allowed her anger and bitterness to destroy their family. Despite what she had done to him and to Hamish, he could forgive her now, and pity her. She had never known the peace of letting go of old hurts and wrongs.

He halted outside St. James's Palace, staring across the street at Queen's Chapel. It had been Maeve's favorite. She had attended Sunday services there when they'd been in London. The structure was small, built in the classical style, and beautifully elegant. Snow obscured the London grime and lent the chapel a fairy-tale appearance, befitting the occasion.

The time had come to put Maeve and Hamish to rest. He crossed the street, a strange serenity settling over him with the knowledge that he was finally ready to make the memorial arrangements.

Afton was just putting the finishing touches on her toilette when Grace's abigail knocked softly on her door and said that Mrs. Forbush would like to see her in the morning room. Afton glanced at the little clock on her dressing table. It was only half past nine. Grace and Dianthe did not usually rise until noon after they had been out on the endless rounds of receptions, soirees, musicales and the like. Perhaps Grace wanted to discuss her plans for New Year's Day.

Afton was a little disconcerted to find Lord Barrington in the morning room with Grace. His cheeks were still ruddy from the outdoors, and she noted his hat and coat tossed over a chair. Grace gave her a look of profound relief and went to the sideboard to pour her a cup of tea. Afton nodded to Lord Barrington in lieu of a curtsy and sat at the table, noting that Grace looked as if she had dressed quickly. Her sleek, dark hair had not been smoothed into its usual chignon, but tied at her nape with a white ribbon and left to fall to the small of her back. Afton concluded that Lord Barrington had roused Grace from her sleep and now they wanted to talk to her. This could only mean one thing.

"Thank you for joining us, dear," Grace said, placing the cup of tea on the table in front of her.

"Of course, Aunt Grace." She smiled and turned to their guest. "Lord Ronald, how nice to see you so early in the day. Have I forgot some appointment?"

"No, Miss Lovejoy," the man replied. "I, ah, wondered if you might indulge me with the answer to a few questions."

"If I am able," she said, stirring a teaspoon of sugar and a drop of milk into her tea.

"Grace…that is, Mrs. Forbush and I have noted that Lord Glenross has demonstrated an…interest in you."

"Oh, I think you have misunderstood," she demurred, feeling heat rushing to her cheeks. She glanced at Grace and noted the dimple in her cheek had deepened—a sure sign that her aunt was holding back an angry contradiction. Then she had not discussed Afton's connection to McHugh. Afton turned back to Lord Barrington. "The McHugh is still grieving for his wife. If he has shown any favor to me at all, it is because of his friendship with Sir Martin Seymour. And now his brother appears to have focused his attention on my sister. I suppose we could find ourselves in-laws."

"Hmm," Lord Ronald intoned. "Nevertheless, he appears to converse with you quite frequently."

Afton fidgeted with her napkin. It had never occurred to her that anyone might have observed how she spent her time. Or was it McHugh who had been observed? "Yes," she admitted. "He and I have a certain ease in our speech."

"What do you discuss?"

Afton's mind went blank. What was Lord Barrington hinting at? "Many things, Lord Barrington. Could you be more specific?"

Lord Ronald looked uncomfortable. "This is a delicate matter, my dear. Have you ever discussed his association with the military?"

"Military? Ah, yes. He was in the military until very recently, was he not?"

"Actually, Lord Glenross was discharged after the Bombardment of Algiers in 1816. His return there last spring was not official and against advice to the contrary. He was acting without authority."

"To find his wife and son," Afton finished. "Yes, I believe I heard that somewhere. And yet I also heard that the ministry took full advantage of his return to Algiers. Was he not in government custody a full two weeks immediately upon his escape?"

Lord Barrington had the sense to look embarrassed. "Well, I suppose you could say that. Glenross cooperated, and he needed the medical care, you know. Bloody Berbers. And one in Glenross's position is never completely done at the Foreign Office, my dear. One feels an obligation to one's country."

"I have admired that about Lord Glenross. Well, in answer to your question, no. He has never discussed his experiences but to say that he is recently returned from Algiers."

"Yes, poor man," Lord Barrington murmured. "I am surprised he is not quite mad. Of course, if what we suspect is true, he may very well be mad."

Afton's heart stilled and she clasped her hands tightly in her lap, out of Lord Barrington's sight. Had they found out about the ravens and McHugh's connection to the murders? "I have always found him to be in possession of his faculties," she ventured.

Lord Barrington cleared his throat and straightened his cravat. "Yes, well. Has he ever mentioned anyone he held a resentment against?"

Aside from Madame Zoe, he hadn't. But, of course, she would never admit that. She frowned, trying to look thoughtful, and shook her head.

"Perhaps an old commander? Someone who'd stood in his way or stopped him from doing something?"

"Lord Barrington, I do not mean to be rude, but why are you asking me all these questions? Lord Glenross has always been the model of…" not decorum, certainly, and not courtesy, "…civility."

Grace coughed and Lord Barrington thumped her on the back, his attention never leaving Afton's face. "This morning, Glenross's former commander was found in his study by his housekeeper. He'd been murdered."

Afton did not even try to hide her surprise. She thought of the bloody cravat McHugh had fished from the Thames. She would wager everything she had that McHugh's former commander had lived on Downing Street. "Why, that is appalling!" she gasped.

"Did you see Glenross last night?"

God in heaven! If she admitted to being with McHugh, she would open herself to other questions, too. Like a house of cards, everything she and Auntie Hen had constructed so carefully would come tumbling down. Bennett would be sent down from Eton in disgrace, Dianthe would grow old and die a spinster, they would lose the estate in Little Upton.

No, she could not admit to seeing Rob without confessing where they'd been, and why. She needed to talk to him before she admitted anything. Evasion and a quick escape were the only answer. "Are you saying that…you think he had something to do with it?"

"I am only saying that circumstances do not look good for him, Miss Lovejoy. I am certain the officials in charge of the investigation will be asking him a good many questions before long, and I would like to keep this as quiet as possible. Bad press for the Foreign Office, you know, and we have an obligation to protect our operatives, especially if they've been driven mad."

Mad? Was that what the authorities were saying? She did

not want to believe it. She stood, desperate to end the interview before she gave something away. She had to find McHugh and warn him. "Sorry I couldn't be of more help, Lord Barrington. If I should think of anything, I will let you know."

By the time McHugh arrived at his club at noon, the place was humming with gossip. Men huddled in small clusters, speaking in undertones and shaking their heads. The folded square he had fished out of the Thames the night before felt conspicuous in his pocket, and he resisted the urge to pat it and make certain it did not show.

He strolled into the quiet billiards room and glanced around. Ethan Travis nodded to him before he separated himself from his brother-in-law, Lord Lockwood and Lord Auberville. They appeared to have been embroiled in a serious discussion.

"You've heard?" Ethan asked him.

Dreading the answer, McHugh answered, "No, but I can guess."

Ethan raised an eyebrow and waited.

"Kilgrew?"

"Murdered at his home in Downing Street last night."

"How?"

"Appears to have been stabbed. And rumor has it that there was a rope around his neck."

McHugh groaned and shook his head. It was the same method as the others… "Damn. I was afraid of that. I was outside Kilgrew's last night, Ethan. I saw a man run from the house and I gave chase."

"Good God! Do you know who it was?"

He nodded. "Aye."

"Who? Half of London is looking for the bastard."

"I can't be positive he was the murderer. I saw him admitted to the house, and then run out a short time later. He seemed panicked. He crossed Westminster Bridge and threw something off. I had to make a choice—go after him or find what he'd thrown away.''

Ethan's eyes narrowed but he waited until McHugh caught his breath.

''I went in after the article.''

''I always knew you were insane,'' he murmured, shaking his head. ''Well, did you find it?''

McHugh patted his pocket.

''What is it?''

He led Ethan to a private alcove at the far side of the room before he pulled out the cloth. Ethan took it and unfolded the square, turning it over in his hands several times before finding the mark almost obscured by blood, and then looking up. ''Your cravat?''

''It would appear so,'' McHugh said. ''It has my initials, does it not? And this morning I found that one of my cravats is missing.''

''I don't understand, McHugh. Why would the murderer try to frame you, and then carry away the evidence?''

''That has me concerned, as well,'' he admitted. There was always something left at the scene that would point to him. What had been left at the scene of Kilgrew's death if not the cravat?

''Well, tell me, man. Who was it?''

He hesitated. He was not ready to share that information about Martin Seymour. Seymour had no reason to murder Lord Kilgrew. And if he'd been removing McHugh's cravat from a murder scene staged to implicate him, he deserved McHugh's gratitude, not an accusation. But if Seymour had wanted to frame McHugh, why hadn't he left the cravat clutched in Kilgrew's hand? In truth, things were looking worse for Doogie. Who else had access to McHugh's room and personal items? Douglas could have killed Kilgrew and

Seymour could have come along later and tried to remove the planted evidence.

"Tell me, McHugh. You should know the evidence is not favoring you at the moment."

"Why in God's name would I want to kill Lord Kilgrew?"

"It was no secret you were angry with him for not sending troops into Algiers when Maeve was kidnapped."

"That is hardly a motive for murder."

"Men have been murdered for less."

"Do you think I did it?"

"Of course not," Ethan snorted. "We may not have agreed with the man or his methods on occasion, but he always did what was best for England. I'm just warning you that the ministry's upper circle is beginning to piece together the recent rash of deaths. Your name has been mentioned in more than a few."

This was bad. Once the raven connection was made, an arrest warrant would be issued. "I am being framed, Ethan. Someone wants me to hang. Kilgrew was on *my* list of suspects because I went back to Algiers against his orders."

Ethan nodded as if he had deduced as much. "Who hates you enough to see you hanged?"

"Damned if I know," he muttered.

"Is there anything about the victims that could tell us who is doing this?"

"I haven't found a pattern yet. There has to be something that links them together. I cannot believe this is random. Like Kilgrew, I have had disputes with most of the victims, but I haven't even known them all."

"Disputes, eh? So someone is ridding you of your enemies? Does that mean the killer is your friend?"

Ethan smiled at the thought. "A friend who leaves my belongings at the scene of his murders?"

Ethan looked over his shoulder and then gripped Mc-Hugh's arms. "Madame Zoe! Is she safe?"

Rob could not answer that question. The first Madame Zoe had been killed, and the second Zoe was none too safe. "For the moment, yes."

"You would not—"

"No. We have…come to terms. I have warned her to use every caution."

"Who else, McHugh? Who else do you have a grudge against? We must warn them immediately."

"I've racked my brain trying to guess who would be next, but it eludes me. I never suspected Kilgrew would be in the mix at all."

"Is there anything I can do to help?"

McHugh clapped Ethan on the back affectionately. "Keep your eyes and ears open. See if you can discover if anything of mine was found at Kilgrew's house."

"Aye." Ethan nodded. "That should be easy enough."

"Do you know who will be appointed to Kilgrew's post at the ministry?"

"Auberville's name has been mentioned, as well as Lord Barrington's and Lord Lockwood's. They are young for the position, except for Barrington, but entirely competent and qualified."

Good. That would give Ethan easy access to information. "Warn me if you get wind of anything from those 'upper circles.'"

Afton loosened the string at the neck of her cloak and smiled indulgently as Dianthe prattled on about who she would dance with tonight, and if Douglas McHugh would be in attendance. Grace winked at Afton, and she knew her aunt, too, was amused by Dianthe's youthful joie de vivre.

"Do you think he will have that devastating brother with

him?'' Dianthe asked with a sideways glance at Afton. ''You know, the one that seems smitten with you, Binky.''

''They are occasionally together,'' she allowed.

She hoped she would see McHugh at the recital. She had gone to the salon to meet him at the appointed time, but McHugh had not come. She had waited as long as she could but she had promised Aunt Grace and Dianthe that she would accompany them to the private recital of nocturnes performed by Hortense and Harriett Thayer, after which there would be dancing and refreshments. The Thayers were a force to be reckoned with in London money circles, so Afton knew attendance would be excellent exposure for Dianthe.

When they arrived at the Thayer home, she was relieved to see Rob McHugh standing in conversation with their host. He turned slightly, as if sensing her presence, and acknowledged her with a nod. Yes, he would find a moment to speak with her. She nodded back and followed the other guests to the music room, where chairs had been set up facing a small raised dais holding a pianoforte and a violin.

Sir Martin Seymour was engrossed in a conversation with a group of giggling women, and Afton recalled his statement that he was very popular. She found herself wondering what he saw in an impoverished, untitled spinster like herself. He could do much better.

He looked over at her and smiled. With a few words of apology, he disengaged himself and came to join them. ''Ah, Mrs. Forbush and the Misses Lovejoy. How nice to see you. I fear I missed you at your entertainments last night. I hope you were well.''

''Oh, yes,'' Dianthe said. ''Afton did not come out with us, but Grace and I had a very nice time.''

''I am pleased to hear it,'' he replied. He turned to Afton with a look of concern. ''Does London society pall, my dear

Miss Lovejoy, or were you simply indulging your natural reserve?''

''Indulging,'' she laughed.

''And yet you appear to enjoy party games. I suspect you must be very good at them.'' He delivered the line with a smoothness that belied the meaning beneath the words. Was he referring to the game of hide-and-seek at Grace's Christmas gathering?

''Some games, Sir Martin,'' she admitted. ''Others can get out of hand.''

Grace cleared her throat and took Dianthe by the arm. ''We shall leave you to discuss the relative virtue of party games while we go find chairs.''

''Thank you, Aunt Grace,'' Afton said, her gaze never leaving Sir Martin. The moment they were out of hearing, she asked, ''Were you going to give me away, my lord?''

He affected a wounded expression. ''Never! 'Twas my feeble attempt to tease, Miss Lovejoy. You know full well that you have my deepest affection.''

In point of fact, she was beginning to suspect the opposite. A gentleman would not have reminded her of that moment of madness under the stairs, but she did not want to argue the point now.

He took her arm and led her toward a set of French doors leading to the terrace. ''I wondered, Miss Lovejoy, if you have had time to think upon our last conversation.''

''I have been busy,'' she said evasively. How could she reject him in public? She owed him the courtesy of a private interview at the very least.

''May I importune you to consider, Miss Lovejoy? I am eager to know your decision,'' he said. ''My entire future, my very happiness, depends upon your answer.''

What had happened to his vow to give her as much time as she needed? ''I…I promise I will have you an answer

tomorrow, Sir Martin. I shall give the matter my full attention until then. If you would like to call at three o'clock?''

He gave her a satisfied smile. ''Excellent.'' He opened
the French doors and pulled her through to the terrace. ''Until then, a token?''

The rush of cold air startled her and, before she could
react, Sir Martin had tugged her into his arms and pressed
a gentle kiss on her lips. Though it was soft, tender and
almost worshipful, the kiss still felt intrusive. She had not
invited it, nor did she welcome it. Anger flashed through
her and she brought her hands up to push him away.

As quickly as he had grasped her, he let go, regarding
her with a small triumphant smile. ''Think of that whilst
you ponder my proposal, Afton.''

She certainly would. Sir Martin's softness was no match
for McHugh's strength. Could she settle for less than the
ecstasy she'd found in Rob's arms?

She did not answer Sir Martin's challenge. Instead she
whirled and slipped back through the door to go in search
of her aunt and sister.

As she hurried toward the music room, she passed Charles
Fengrove and recalled that his name had appeared on her
aunt's client list. ''Oh, Mr. Fengrove,'' she said, stopping
him in midstride.

''Yes, Miss Lovejoy?''

She drew him aside, thinking quickly how to question
him. ''I…I was chatting with a friend of yours the other
day. He said to give you his regards.''

''Indeed?'' Mr. Fengrove smiled politely, while his gaze
swept her with a look of appreciation. ''Who might that be,
Miss Lovejoy?''

''Lord Glenross.''

''The McHugh?'' Fengrove's expression changed to one
of doubtful skepticism.

''Yes. Your name came up in conversation with…'' she

eached for any possible common name "…with one of the Thayer twins. I have forgotten now whether it was Hortense or Harriett. Then Glenross said he had not seen you since his return. He said he always held you in high regard."

"Did he?" Fengrove's eyebrows raised nearly to his hairline.

She affected a thoughtful expression. "Yes. I believe so."

"I did not know he noticed me. I was actually better acquainted with his wife, Lady Maeve."

"You were friends?"

He laughed. "Not precisely. We did not actually care much for one another. I think she did her best to have me blacklisted from society."

"Heavens." Afton frowned. This was not what she expected, but it was interesting nonetheless. "I cannot imagine why."

"I never speak ill of the dead, Miss Lovejoy, or I would tell you."

Would this make Mr. Fengrove McHugh's enemy? The bell warning the guests to take their seats rang. She glanced toward the music room. "Well, take care, Mr. Fengrove." Perhaps that was not a strong enough warning. "I mean, *do* be careful."

He gave her a puzzled smile. "Thank you, Miss Lovejoy. I shall have to thank Glenross after the recital."

And she would have to remember to warn Glenross about her latest fabrication. She found Grace and Dianthe standing in conversation with Charity Wardlow, Laura Tuxbury and Julius Lingate.

Charity took her hand in greeting. "Heavens, Afton! You are quite chilled. Are you feeling well?"

"I may be coming down with something," she admitted. She drew her aunt away from the group, glancing in McHugh's direction. "I have acquired a little cough," she whispered. "Shall we sit in the back?"

Grace shook her head. "I think there is an advantage in putting Dianthe forward. We do want her to be seen, do we not?"

"Yes, of course," she said. "I forgot myself."

"But a cough could prove disruptive," Grace continued, a twinkle in her dark eyes. "If you do not mind sitting alone, I am certain Dianthe and I could spare you."

Afton shot her a grateful look. Grace was more observant than she had suspected. She took a chair in the back row on the aisle. Within a few minutes, Hortense and Harriet took their places on the dais. Mr. Thayer clapped his hands for attention and asked the remaining guests to be seated.

She noted McHugh's position near the back of the room. He was standing, one shoulder propped against the door-jamb, as if he was not committed to staying. Hortense played a quick riffle on the pianoforte and then began.

Within a few minutes, McHugh moved past Afton's chair and touched her shoulder. A moment later, he was gone. Afton counted slowly to ten, muffled a cough and stood. She coughed again on her way to the music room doors, in the event that someone noticed her exit.

She hurried down the corridor, trying to guess where he would be waiting. "McHugh?" she whispered.

As she passed the parlor, he reached out and seized her arm, dragging her into the room. Excitement bubbled up-ward, and she smiled. He stopped and turned so quickly that Afton landed against his chest. A long moment passed as she gazed into deep green eyes. His pupils dilated, darken-ing his eyes further. Afton knew he was going to kiss her even before he tilted his head toward her. Heedless of the risk of being discovered, she came up on her toes to meet him, fitting herself to his chest, her breasts aching for the contact.

His mouth covered hers, his tongue making an erotic de-mand. Oh! No tender intrusion here! *This* was wild, swee

nd all-consuming. This was fire in her blood. This was the
eason she would never marry Sir Martin.

McHugh groaned and held her away. "Ye canna stay so
lose to me, lass. I have no willpower when it comes to
ou."

Afton sighed, thinking she had no willpower, either. But
he had pride enough to keep from being second best. She
moothed her gown and cleared her throat, trying to com-
ose herself. "You did not come to the salon tonight."

"No. I was looking for Martin Seymour. I've been one
tep behind him all day. I saw him with you moments ago,
ut now he's nowhere to be found. Did he tell you where
e was going?"

Afton shook her head and dismissed the subject of Sir
Martin with an airy wave. "Mr. Fengrove may approach
ou to offer his regards. I told him you were asking after
im."

"Why?"

"It was a pretense to question him. His name was on
Auntie Hen's list."

McHugh looked pensive. "Hmm."

"And that is not all. I must warn you that Lord Barrington
ame to Grace's house this morning. He was asking ques-
ions about you, McHugh. And about our…friendship."

McHugh's expression became veiled, cautious. "Did he,
ow? What did he want to know?"

"He asked if I had seen you last night."

"What did you say?"

"I evaded the question. He told me about Lord Kilgrew
nd I asked if he thought you had something to do with that.
le said that the circumstances did not look good, and that
here was some speculation that you might be…mad."

"Mad McHugh," he repeated. "Is that how this farce is
o be played out?"

"I only know that he wants to talk to you, and he asked me to keep him informed about you."

"Are you going to tell him, Afton?"

"That…that depends upon you, McHugh. Do you want me to?"

"No. I cannot be helped by dragging your name through the mud. If you were called to testify at a trial, you would be censured by society."

Afton was ashamed of the relief that washed over her but her conscience still needled her. "I am your alibi, McHugh. They would have to acquit you if I swore that I was with you and that you did not enter that house."

"If they did not think that you were lying to protect your lover. Either way, Afton, your secret would become public knowledge. There is no way to hide these things in a trial. I won't let you risk that."

"But—"

He laid his finger across her lips. "Shh. No arguments. I haven't been arrested yet."

"What next, McHugh?"

"Guard yourself, Afton. Trust no one. Not even…"

"Yes? Not even who?"

"Not even those you have trusted in the past. And do not allow anyone to draw you away from a crowd."

Had he seen Sir Martin pull her out the French doors? Was Rob warning her not to trust him?

"Never fear. I'll keep ahead of the authorities." He grinned. "It is a job they trained me for."

She smiled at the irony. "And what shall I do?"

"Keep watch. And meet me at the salon by half past nine tomorrow night. I should have news by then."

Chapter Eighteen

Afton's carefully rehearsed words evaporated in an instant when Sir Martin sat down beside her in Grace's small sitting room the next afternoon. Afraid he would try to take her hand, she poured him a cup of tea from the pot on the little tea cart in front of them to keep him occupied.

His hand trembled slightly as he accepted the cup. "Have you made your decision, my dear?" he asked.

She wondered if it was appropriate to smile politely when you were about to refuse someone. *Quick, kind and clean,* her aunt had advised. "I am afraid I—"

Sir Martin sat forward and interrupted. "Before you answer, my dear, may I have a moment to plead my case? I fear I was not very eloquent when I first asked."

"You were very eloquent," she disagreed. "I was touched by your words, and honored. But—"

He laughed and shrugged. "And here I have been thinking what a fool I was that I neglected to mention what I can offer you, apart from my affection.

"You see, I am sensible to the fact that you have taken responsibility for your younger sister and brother. My connections will stand them both in good stead. I know a number of people who could advance young Bennett in whatever endeavor he chooses. Should he wish to continue his education after Eton, I have excellent contacts at Cambridge. After that, I could find sponsors should he wish to stand for Parliament.''

She sat back and studied Sir Martin's face. How had he so unerringly found her weakness? This was a much more seductive argument than his affection. How could she refuse?

''As for your sister…well, I think she will be ready to entertain offers very soon. When that time comes, she will need every advantage and connection at her disposal. I mean no disrespect when I remind you, Miss Lovejoy, that her marriage portion as the younger sister will not be quite up to snuff.''

Afton was about to argue that she had always intended to add her portion to Dianthe's but there seemed little point in that. It would never be Sir Martin's business how large or small Dianthe's settlement would be unless he was the groom.

His expression sobered as he leaned forward with an air of confidentiality. ''I have observed her attention to Douglas McHugh. That might have made a good alliance had it not been for Glenross. Even allowing for the fact that Doogie is the only one capable of fathering the next Lord Glenross—''

Oh, the liar! Was he still trying to frighten her away from the McHugh? She had half a mind to tell him that she had discovered for herself that Rob McHugh was perfectly capable of fathering an heir, but how could she explain her knowledge?

''—the impending scandal would put him quite beyond the pale,'' Sir Martin finished.

''Scandal? What scandal?'' she asked before she could stop herself.

His mouth quirked in an odd manner. "You must have heard, my dear."

"Heard what?"

He met her gaze squarely and announced, "Why, the authorities are looking for McHugh. They wish to question him in regard to Charles Fengrove's death late last night. Quite tragic. And then, of course, about Lord Kilgrew's death and the grudge McHugh held against Kilgrew for refusing to launch a rescue mission to find Maeve."

Fengrove! Oh, dear Lord! What could have happened? "They cannot be serious!"

"I assure you, they are." Sir Martin cocked his head to one side and regarded her through narrowed eyes. "I hope you have not already consented to an alliance between Miss Dianthe and Douglas."

"No," she admitted. "No, but...I—"

"Yes, 'tis a very sad case, is it not? But not surprising it has come to this in view of McHugh's ungovernable passions."

Afton felt the heat creep into her cheeks. Any sensible woman would not rise to that bait, but she was not sensible when it came to McHugh. She could not prevent the chill in her voice when she said, "Not surprising, Sir Martin? Why is that?"

"McHugh's volatile temper coupled with his undying devotion to the lady Maeve was bound to crush him. 'Twas just a matter of time."

Afton picked up her teacup again and took a sip. "Men have loved deeply before without doing violence, Sir Martin."

"Your compassion does you credit, Miss Lovejoy. I shall pray you are right. McHugh and I have been friends for a very long time, and I would be distraught indeed if he has done something ill-advised. Meantime, of course, it would be prudent to avoid him whenever possible."

"You think he loved Maeve so deeply that he would kill for her, even after she was gone?" she asked.

Sir Martin's face took on a distant look, as if he were focusing on some long-ago time. "When we were younger, he was always playing the knight-errant. Maeve thought him quite dashing. We all did. But he never grew out of that passion for fighting lost causes, whether for a peasant's rights or the king's rights. McHugh has never known when to give up. Maeve grew bitter because he had more time for his causes than he had for her." His voice broke and he stopped to clear his throat. "And when he had time for her, he claimed her body and soul."

Afton studied Sir Martin's face, startled to see the raw emotion there, and suddenly, the subtle clues fell into place. "You loved her, too."

Sir Martin blinked and a guilty flush tinged his cheeks. "Everyone loved her. And Hamish. Such a fine young lad. Sharp as a tack and filled with promise."

"How sad," she mused.

"Aye," Sir Martin agreed. "And now McHugh's remorse drives him to another sort of excess."

"What sort?" Afton asked, caught up in Sir Martin's story.

"Revenge."

No. McHugh might devote himself to Maeve's memory until the day he died, but he would not begin killing people against whom he held a grudge. Held a grudge? But there were some victims that McHugh hadn't even known.

Some detail called to her. Something just out of reach. Some piece of the puzzle teasing her.

"But how have we digressed?" Sir Martin asked, shaking off his brooding. "Ah, yes. Miss Dianthe. Well, I am glad to hear that you have not agreed to any alliance, at least for the time being. And, you see, here is another instance of what a great help I can be to you."

"No," Afton murmured, lost in her own thoughts, trying to grasp the elusive connection between the murders.

"No? I cannot be of help to you?"

"No, I cannot marry you," she said.

Sir Martin put his cup down and stood. He straightened his jacket, almost as if he were gathering the remnants of his pride, and she regretted blurting her answer in such a way.

"Ah, well." He sighed. "I was afraid that might be the case, Miss Lovejoy, but I had to give you one last chance to come to your senses."

Afton was still mulling over that statement when she heard the front door close behind him.

A cold wind whipped up St. Martin's Street from the Thames. Somewhere nearby the watch called the hour of eight. The street was still crowded with vendors and people hurrying about their business, and the closer the chase led her to Seven Dials, the more crowded the streets became and the more difficult it was to keep her target in sight.

She did not know if she would glean any information from following Douglas McHugh, but she had to try. There was only tonight and tomorrow left before the New Year and the end of her investigation. After Sir Martin had departed, she'd spent the remaining afternoon trying to grasp the clue that kept eluding her. At last she thought she might have identified the missing piece. It was so simple, really, and yet quite complicated.

McHugh swore he did not even know all the victims and that he might not have liked the ones he did know, but he hadn't disliked them enough to kill them. Perhaps, then, the murders and McHugh were separate items connected only by a single common link—the murderer. Someone who was killing for his own reasons but could gain something if McHugh was made to take the blame.

When she had finished her shopping and had seen Douglas McHugh on the street, the temptation to follow him had been too great to resist. Though she'd defended Douglas to Sir Martin, there was a tiny part of her that acknowledged how much he had to gain if Rob was out of the way.

She shifted the parcel she carried to her other arm and slipped around the corner. Douglas was just disappearing into a tavern. She would have to look for a darkened mew or doorway to hide in until he came out. She stepped sideways into the stairwell of a tenement building, spurred on by the sound of footsteps behind her.

"'Ere now," a rough voice growled. "Where d'ye think ye're goin'?"

Afton did not respond, certain the stranger could not be talking to her until he stepped into the shadows beside her and seized her right arm, dragging her backward, deeper into the stairwell.

"Stop!" she squeaked. "Let loose of me!"

Instead, the stranger lifted his free arm, wielding a cudgel. He brought it down toward her head. She deflected it with her raised forearm and a sharp pain raced down her arm, causing her fingers and wrist to tingle.

"Thought ye were goin' t' gi' me the slip, I did." His grip tightened, cutting off her circulation. He raised the cudgel and aimed for her head again. "Won't get me pay if you gets away," he explained, as if speaking to a simple child.

"H-help!" she shrieked, flailing her other arm and kicking out, hoping to make contact. The occupants of the tenement would not come to her rescue—they were too accustomed to being deaf and blind to their neighbors' quarrels. *"Help!"*

Voices grew louder and Afton realized the occupants of the pub must have heard her calls for help and come to see what was transpiring. She threw her entire weight toward the street. "Please! Someone, help me!"

Douglas McHugh's horrified face was the first she noted, and then Rob directly behind him. "Get her, Doogie," Rob called as he reached over her to grab her attacker by the neck.

As the man released her, Douglas caught her before she could slam against the wall. "Steady, Miss Lovejoy," he cautioned, cushioning her from the scuffle.

"Mind ye're own business, ye bloody bastard!" the man croaked. McHugh had him by the neck and was squeezing tighter.

"She is my business," he snarled.

"She's me wife," the man lied. "I ain't doin' nothin' wrong."

The crowd hooted and catcalled. Judging by their cries of encouragement to McHugh, the man—called "Dirty Eddie" by the crowd—was not popular with them. Afton could guess why.

McHugh's backhand caught the man across the face and split his lip. Blood spurted from his nose, crooked now and broken. "Who the hell are you?" McHugh demanded.

"Er 'usband!" He flinched and brought his hands up in a defensive gesture when Rob raised his arm again. "Wait! Wait!" he begged. "I don't even know 'er. Take 'er, gov'nor. She's yours."

The crowd lost interest now that the scuffle was over. They dispersed back to the pub, calling advice for the disposal of the villain, while coins changed hands from the quick bets that had been made. McHugh waited until they were quite alone before continuing his questions.

"Who are you?" he asked again. "And who sent you?"

"I don't know what ye mean," the man whimpered, wiping at his nose with the back of one sleeve.

McHugh's remorseless hands tightened around the man's throat. "Think harder."

"I just thought I'd get me a piece o' arse, gov'nor. No 'arm in that, is there?"

McHugh slammed the man against the tenement wall so hard that Afton thought he would lose consciousness. "Gi' me the truth or I'll tear your lying tongue out wi' my bare hands and feed it to the dogs." The pause drew out a fraction too long and McHugh drew his arm back to deliver another punishing blow.

"Wait! Wait," the man squealed. "I ain't nobody. I don't even know 'er, gov'nor. Take 'er. She's nothin' to me."

The savage blow opening a cut on the man's cheekbone caught Afton by surprise. Now she understood what Grace had meant when she'd warned that McHugh was completely ruthless when pursuing a goal. "Who sent you? And why?"

Blood and mucus oozed down the man's chin and cheek and over his jacket. "I was supposed to put 'er out of the way, gov'nor. Quiet and cleanlike," he whined. "'E said I was to use a knife an' leave a rope around 'er neck."

Her? Afton's head swam. Someone had hired this man to *kill* her? The knowledge turned her knees to water and she tightened her grip on Douglas's arm to support herself.

"Son of a bitch," Douglas murmured, staring at the man.

A muscle tensed in McHugh's jaw and Afton knew the questions were not over. He was so fierce, so determined, that she could easily see why he had gained his ruthless reputation.

"You were supposed to leave something when you were done with the job," McHugh said. "Give it to me."

The man's eyes rounded with fear. He fumbled for his jacket pocket and brought forth a small white linen square embroidered in white with a G and a small raven. Glenross.

"Who hired you?"

The man whimpered and shook his head. "Don't know. I never saw 'im."

"You are stretching my patience," McHugh snarled. "Do not ask me to believe you took this on without pay. Unless—" his hand around the man's throat tightened "—you love your work."

The man's words tumbled out in a rush. "I didn't see 'im, gov'nor. Never seen 'im before an' never since. I swear it. 'E 'ad his collar up an' 'is 'at pulled low. 'Twas dark. 'E gave me five quid an' said there'd be five more when I finished the job."

"How were you to be paid?"

"'E said 'e'd leave the money at the Crown and Anchor when 'e knew the job was done."

McHugh's hands relaxed and he dropped them to his sides. He stared at the man for a long moment, as if trying to decide whether to believe him or not. "I know who you are, Dirty Eddie, and do not doubt I will find you if a single word of your story proves false."

"She's just a skirt, gov'nor," the man wheedled. "Nobody'll miss 'er. 'Ow about we share 'er? You c'n 'ave 'er first."

Afton tensed. McHugh had been turning, ready to accept the man's story, but those words brought him around, fists doubled, to lay the ruffian out unconscious with blinding speed.

"Jaysus," Douglas breathed. He let go of Afton and knelt by the man to feel for a pulse. "He'll live, but he's going to look like hell tomorrow. And he'll have a headache to end all headaches."

McHugh turned and met her gaze. "Get a coach, Doogie," he said.

Afton's knees wobbled, more from the look on Rob's face than from the attack. What was he thinking?

* * *

McHugh did not trust himself to touch Afton or speak during the coach ride to Zoe's salon. He honestly didn't know if he would rail at her for being alone, ask her what the hell she thought she was doing, or grab her and hold her close.

Instead, he retrieved her parcel and led her back to the street corner where Douglas waited with a coach. He handed her up, then followed, taking a place on the facing seat.

"Tomorrow, Doogie. You know where," he said as the coach pulled away from the curb.

The silence between Afton and him was unnatural and awkward. It did not escape him that her hands trembled and tears shimmered in her eyes. He suspected that she was holding herself together with every scrap of strength she could find, but he could not comfort her. Their physical passion was too volatile, too explosive. If he started, he would not stop until he had possessed her completely. And he'd promised that would never happen again.

He still needed her, needed to confirm that she was safe and unharmed. With a slowly rising intensity, he wanted to pull her against him and absorb her into his being. But she needed his reassurance more than his passion, his gentleness more than his strength.

Twice now, Afton had been the target of murder, yet she swore she had no enemy but him. He was no longer her enemy. Far from it. But she was in danger because of him, and he did not know how to protect her.

Marry her. The surprising notion came to him with heartstopping clarity. If he married her, he could take her home to Scotland and keep her safe from the insanity of London and the Foreign Office. If they were married, he would never have to leave her side, never risk losing her to the vagaries of fate. The institution he had sworn he would never enter into again suddenly seemed the most blissful solution to his dilemma.

She sighed deeply and shifted in her seat. Again his desire stirred, and he realized that if he married Afton, he would lose her to his own intemperance. If he had been too demanding of Maeve, whom he hadn't loved, what might he demand of Afton, whom he did love?

Yes, he loved her. He loved her independence, her courage, her determination, her gentle teasing, and the fire of passion that burned as deep as his own. But she'd made it clear she would no longer welcome his attention when she'd admitted that they were both too damaged to love one another.

The coach pulled up at La Meilleure Robe, and he let her go ahead to unlock the door while he grabbed her parcel and paid the driver. By the time he joined her, she was kneeling in front of the hearth, laying kindling on the banked embers and fanning them to life. He locked the door behind him and set the parcel on the little table. Afton had shed her cloak and hung it on a peg by the door, and he did the same.

When flames crackled brightly, she stood and held her hands out to the warmth. "I am so cold," she confessed, breaking their silence.

He had a hundred questions. A thousand. But they would wait. He went to her and wrapped his arms around her, drawing her into his warmth. She melted against him with a little sigh.

"Thank God you're safe, Afton. If he had hurt you…"

"He did not," she mumbled against his shirtfront. Long overdue sobs shook her slight frame and she clung to him as if to a lifeline in a stormy sea.

"There, there," he soothed, feeling clumsy in his attempt to comfort her. "You're safe. No one will hurt you now."

"I cannot help wondering…" Her voice trailed off.

"What?" he prompted.

"Who hates me enough to want me dead?"

He shook his head, drawing her closer. "It is not you, Afton. It is me. If you had been found dead, you'd have had my handkerchief in your hand."

"Yes," she sighed. She tilted her head back to look into his face, and smiled. "But you'd have an alibi. You were in the pub across the street with Doogie."

"Yes…Doogie." And the questions came crowding forward again. Mustering every ounce of strength he could, Rob held her away at arm's length. "We have to talk, Afton." He led her to a chair and sat her down. "I warned you not to go out alone. What were you doing outside the tavern tonight?"

"Following your brother."

"Why? Did you hope he would lead you to me?"

"I thought he might be the murderer."

Rob sighed, exasperated at her disregard for her own safety. "Did I not tell you to leave that to me?"

"Yes, but I had a new theory about the murders. I wondered why you knew only some of the victims. If you did not know them all, then there could only be one common link."

"And that would be?"

"The killer. He would have to be someone who knew most of the same people as you, but was killing for his own reasons. And you are one of his victims, because you are being set up to hang for his crimes. Therefore, the killer must have something to gain if you should die."

"Christ! And that led you to Douglas," he said, finishing her line of reasoning. "There is a certain logic there, but I would stake my life that Douglas is not the murderer."

"He came to town barely a month before the murders began. Who else has so much to gain if you are dead?"

"There are other motives than physical gain," he allowed. *L'amour ou l'argent, monsieur,* she had told him the first time he had seen her as Madame Zoe. Love or money. If it was not money, then—

Love? Who had he spurned? He'd sown his wild oats long before he and Maeve had said their vows. And after Hamish was born and Maeve had locked her boudoir door, she'd given him her blessing to find comfort elsewhere. He'd had other women since, all of them meaningless, and none who expected more from him than a night's pleasure. Certainly none that were pledged to or belonged to another man.

Rob tugged at the hair on the back of his neck. There was something to Afton's theory that rang true, though, but he couldn't think with her sitting within reach. Every time he looked at her, she was studying him with those deep azure eyes that revealed her soul. His arms ached to hold her. He wanted to feel her heart beating next to his. Once, just once, before he let her go, he wanted to make love to her as she deserved. Not angrily, not like a schoolboy who could not wait, but softly, sweetly, deeply, as lovers do, thinking only of her, bringing her the best instead of the worst of him.

She stood and touched his arm. ''I am sorry, Rob. I should not have doubted Douglas.''

He lifted his gaze from her hand to her eyes. She'd called him Rob. He could not even remember Maeve calling him that. The unexpected intimacy sent a tingle of pleasure up his spine and made him smile. ''Ye called me Rob, lass. For real this time.''

She smiled back. ''You must be mistaken. I would never do that. It wouldn't be proper.''

''Are ye sure? I could have sworn I heard it.''

Her lips twitched and she turned away, busying herself with the string securing the parcel. She removed a loaf of bread, a large wedge of cheese, a bundle of candles, a bottle of wine and four apples. "I thought you might need these," she said over her shoulder.

"Why?" he asked.

"Because you cannot go back to your hotel. The authorities will be waiting to arrest you. Aunt Grace told me that Lord Barrington authorized the warrant late this afternoon."

He fought the urge to grin. *She* was protecting *him*. When had that ever happened before? "I am not surprised," he said. "I have been expecting it. What surprises me, Afton, is that you are willing to shelter me. That is a considerable risk if you are discovered."

"I feel somehow responsible for this mess. If you hadn't come looking for Madame Zoe—"

"I'd still be in this tangle. The killings started before I found you, Afton."

"I know." She sighed.

He touched her arm. "I do not want you taking the blame for any of this. Whatever set the wheel in motion, it was not you. You were merely a means to an end."

"I should have told the authorities about Auntie Hen," she said, looking up into his eyes. "If they had known..."

"God, no," he whispered. "If I had known she was dead, I wouldn't have come looking for her. I'd never have known you, Afton. And I wouldn't have missed that for any price. Even hanging."

She moaned, recognizing the truth in his words, the deep emotion, and she wanted him more in that moment than she ever had before. She lifted her mouth to his. "This is madness."

"I know," he answered, his lips moving against hers. He pulled her against him and stroked the length of her spine. "We cannot do this."

By the time his hand reached the nape of her neck and fondled the curls there, she was trembling. "No. We mustn't."

"It would only end badly," he murmured against her throat.

"Horribly," she agreed, reaching up to cup his head and hold it to her. She would *die* if he stopped now.

"And God knows, I've been less than considerate."

"Much less," she gasped when he nibbled delicately on one earlobe. Her breasts began to tingle and ache for his touch.

"Nothing can come of it," he warned.

She bit gently at his lower lip until he opened his mouth to let her tongue in. "Nothing," she said, savoring the sweetness of his kiss.

His voice betrayed incredible strain when he lifted his head to look into her eyes. "I swore I would never do this again."

"I swear I will not tell."

He chuckled, squeezing her closer. "I should stop now."

"A pity," she answered, coming up on her toes to fit her hips to his, "since I would kill you if you stopped now."

"So my choice is—"

"Face me or the hangman's noose."

"You, Afton. It will always be you." He lifted her and carried her to the little bed at the back of the room.

Instead of falling on her like a starving wolf, he placed her carefully against the pillows. When he straightened, she was afraid he intended to leave her, but he pulled off his jacket and unknotted his cravat. His slow smile told her all she needed to know. This was going to be different than what they'd shared before. Their passion was not mixed with anger this time, or urgency. This was something deeper, more significant. That realization made her breathing quicken. She pushed herself up and began fumbling with her buttons.

"Leave that to me."

Settling against the pillows again, she watched in fascination as his chest came into view. Though she'd seen the scars before, she had never fully appreciated how the muscles beneath his skin were firm and defined. She was reminded again how strong this man was, how brave and determined. He sat on the edge of the bed to remove his boots.

She traced one livid scar with her fingertip, marveling that anyone had survived such savage treatment, and he shivered, whether from her touch or the cool air in the salon, she did not know. She only knew she wanted to possess McHugh for as long as he would let her.

He did not flinch from her touch when she began stroking his chest and back. She was dimly aware that he was unfastening the buttons down her back, but that had less importance than what she was doing. She was intent upon exploring McHugh, learning the secrets of making love to a man.

Would they like much the same things as a woman? she wondered. Beginning at the hollow of his throat, she traced a line of kisses down his chest to the light matting of dark hair. Curious, she shifted her attention to his nipple, kissing and nibbling until he groaned and wove his fingers through her tresses.

"Afton, you're the devil. How can you make me want ye so? I'd forsake everything for your touch."

"Magic, McHugh. The same magic you work on me."

"Aye," he growled between clenched teeth, "and I've no right to ask ye, lass, in view of m' past behavior, but could ye leave me wi' a shred of self-control?" He held her away and groaned. "I need to feel your skin against mine," he said, fumbling to free her from her dress.

His gentleness was a stark contrast to his rage at the stranger who had tried to kill her. To know that he had that power and fury within him, and was still capable of such tenderness, was incredibly arousing. His touch made her feel cherished and…and loved.

Discarding her gown, McHugh turned his attention to her shoes and stockings. He pushed her chemise up to find the bare flesh at the top of her hose. As his hand skimmed up her leg, she bent her knee and he kissed it. "Gi' me the other knee, and I'll kiss that, too."

Unable to resist his playful teasing, she obeyed. He gave her the kiss, then lowered himself between her knees to remove her garters and stockings. Before she could demure, he untied the ribbon of her chemise and pulled it over her head.

He gazed down at her, a strange light in his eyes, and she shivered with pleasure from his praise and felt her breasts grow taut in response to the heat of that look. "I've never seen you naked, Afton. You are magnificent."

Warmth washed through her, heightening her desire. "Return the favor, please," she asked, groping for his waistband.

He groaned but let her have her way. When she had unfastened it, he helped her push his trousers down his hips. His shaft sprang free, swollen and fully erect, and she moaned. "Hurry, Rob. I need you."

"Nay, lass. No hurrying this time." He covered her mouth with his, breathing life and heat into her, then trailed kisses down her throat to one aching breast. He took the sensitive tip into his mouth and traced the perimeter with his tongue. She arched, writhing with pleasure as he drew her into his mouth, nibbling, licking and sucking.

She reached for him, intending to drag him into her, her hand closing around his velvet heat. He seemed to grow in her hand, and he twitched and groaned as if in agony. "Let loose, lass, or pay the consequences."

Oh, she *wanted* to pay the consequences! But McHugh was in distress. She released him.

He was breathing hard. "Ye're on the edge," he told her, making it sound like high praise. "I've been there, Afton.

I know how ye feel. But I'm not ready to finish this. Let me ease ye."

He lifted her hips and his dark head moved lower. Parting the narrow folds protecting the very center of her, he found her with his tongue. She gasped! The sensation was so intensely intimate, so deeply erotic, that she closed her eyes, savoring the wild stroking that threatened her sanity.

Grasping tight to the shreds of her self-control, she held back. He was prolonging her agony, denying her what she wanted most—him, inside her. Every muscle she possessed grew taut and quivered with expectancy, then, when she was no longer able to resist, heat and light burst over her in a shimmering wave. She wept with the sheer miracle of it, and wondered dimly why McHugh was praising her.

"That's it, lass. That will keep ye until ye're ready for more."

More? What more could there be? And yet for all the lovely heat and radiance washing over her, there was something missing. Something beckoning just out of reach. But she would trust McHugh to take her there. He had not disappointed her yet.

He began his rhythmic stroking again, building the heat until she was moaning. Desperate to please him as he'd pleased her, she laced her fingers through his hair and tightened them, pulling him upward. She kissed him, his cheeks, his chin, his throat, before trying to roll over him to the supine position.

"What are ye doing?" he asked in a startled voice.

"What you did to me," she said between kisses.

He made a choked sound, close to a laugh, before pulling her back up. "Good God, but I love you, lass," he groaned. "Not this time, eh? I want to please you. Tell me what you want."

"You," she demanded, all coyness gone. "Inside me."

He sighed. "Sweet words, Afton. Ask me again."

"I don't want this to end, but I *need* it to," she said.

"I know," he admitted. "I know. We shall end it, then."

And with that, he rolled over her again and fitted himself to her. His penetration was painless this time, eased by his patient preparation, but he slid into her slowly, lacing his fingers through hers and holding them against the pillow, clearly relishing every sensation. Feeling wonderfully wanton exposed to his view, she smiled up at him.

Her skin tingled and burned. The throbbing inside her intensified. When McHugh began moving, she matched his strokes, increasing in tempo until a blinding, shimmering heat burst over her. Then she was floating, drifting, powerless to fight the onrushing darkness.

Chapter Nineteen

Rob propped himself on one elbow and looked down at Afton. She was so bloody beautiful that it made his heart ache. Dark lashes fanned out over flushed cheeks in perfect little crescents. Her coral lips, still swollen from his kisses, were slightly parted, as if waiting for his return, and the glorious copper tangles, still damp from the physical demands of their lovemaking, framed her face.

Afton was no Maeve, so refined that she could not bear the smallest display of need from her partner. Afton invited it. Provoked it. Her passions ran as deep and strong as his. He wondered if she'd been aware that she had wept when he'd come into her. She'd wrapped her legs around him and chanted the sweetest tune he'd ever heard. *Yes, Rob, yes, yes...*

He wanted to remember her this way. He would save this image to call forth on those distant lonely nights in the Highlands, when he needed to chase the desolation away. This one perfect moment was all he would have of her then. That, and a lifetime of regret that he could not offer what Afton Lovejoy deserved.

She stirred and murmured something that sounded like his name. Her lashes fluttered, then opened, the sensual lethargy still simmering in her eyes. She smiled up at him, touchingly vulnerable.

"Ah, there you are." He grinned.

She smiled back and reached up to run her finger along his cheek. "Here I am. How long have I been asleep?"

"An hour or two." He smoothed her hair back and pressed a kiss to her forehead.

She stretched and pulled the blanket a little higher. "Why did you not wake me?"

"I was watching you. Did you know you make little sighs when you turn over? Or that you say words in your sleep? Not sentences, just single words. Like *Rob* and *please,* and *want.*"

A deep pink washed her cheeks. "I cannot imagine—"

"From that pretty blush, I'd have sworn there was nothing wrong with your imagination. Or your memory."

The mantel clock chimed twice and then fell silent. "Two o'clock?" She struggled to sit up. "I've been gone too long. I must get back before Aunt Grace comes looking for me." She pushed the blanket away and began groping for her clothes. "I hate to leave you this way, McHugh, but there is food and wood enough to last you the day. I will come back tonight."

"I can't stay here, Afton. I'll see you home and then find Douglas. He was going to rent a room for me at an inn down by the river."

"But the salon would be more private," she argued. "Who would think to look for you here?"

He shook his head. "If I am found here, Afton, it would not go well for you or your family. There would be no keeping your secret then." He sat up and retrieved her chemise from the tangle of clothes on the bare wooden floor.

She took the soft white lawn and dropped it over her head before shaking the wrinkles from her deep blue gown. "How will I find you?" she asked over her shoulder.

"You won't." He pulled his trousers on, steeling himself against the pain. "You know this—" he gestured at the bed "—was the last of it, do you not?"

She turned to face him, her expression unguarded and raw with pain. "Aye."

He prayed she was not remorseful for letting him make love to her. "About tonight…"

She turned away from him, busying herself with her buttons.

"Afton, it was the most amazing gift anyone has ever given me," he said. "But it only makes the inevitable end more difficult."

She nodded, scooping up her stockings and garters.

"I'd only make you miserable. In a very short time, you'd come to resent me."

"Yes, I know," she said. She turned to him, her face composed now, and her eyes reddened but dry. "I've always known I could never measure up to Maeve. And I could never bear living in her shadow. It would break my heart to wake up each day, knowing you will always love someone else."

"What?" He could not comprehend her words. Was she saying that she could not be with him because of his love for *Maeve?*

She pushed her bare feet into her shoes and shrugged into her cloak. "Your undying love for your wife is legendary."

"Maeve? No, Afton. You do not understand. It is my fault. I thought—"

"No," she interrupted, waving him to silence before stuffing her stockings and garters into the inside pocket of her cloak and heading for the door. "Do not pity me, McHugh. I do not regret any of this. How could I have loved you and not given myself to you?"

Loved him. Afton loved him? A bittersweet joy washed over him. He wished he had not wasted so much time fighting his feelings for her. Holding the blanket clenched around him, he stumbled after her. "Afton, listen to me. You were right. I was the worst kind of coward. I was afraid to love you—afraid of failing you, too. Of losing you. I never loved Maeve."

But she was gone before he could finish. Cursing, he dressed hurriedly and went to the window to look out at the street. There was no sign of Afton. He would have to follow and make certain she arrived safely back at Mrs. Forbush's house. But first, he needed to make certain that she knew where to find him if he could not come to her.

He opened the small letter box on the shabby escritoire and removed a paper, pen and the little ink bottle. "My dearest Afton," he wrote, "Please come to me at the White Lion in Holburn. We must talk. R.M."

He propped the note against the crystal orb in the center of the table. If he did not catch her tonight, she would find his note tomorrow.

Afton slept badly, and came down to breakfast midmorning with a headache. Her memory was saturated with McHugh—his slow touch, his deep sigh, his sure knowledge of her body. His firm answer to her question.

How will I find you?

You won't.

Her wistful sigh drew a curious glance from Aunt Grace, and a look that said they would talk later.

When Dianthe excused herself to write a letter to her friends in Wiltshire, Afton pushed her teacup aside and went to look out the window at the gently falling snow and the icicles forming on the eaves. Oh, how she missed Auntie Hen and their home in Wiltshire. How she wished life were as simple again as it had been when she was small.

How she wished McHugh had never married Maeve or set foot in Algiers.

A slender arm went around her shoulders and Grace gave her a warm squeeze. "Afton, is something amiss?"

"Hen…"

Grace nodded, her smoky eyes glistening. "I miss her, too. And today is the final day. December 31. Tomorrow we shall have to go to the authorities and tell them about Henrietta. But, Afton, she will still rest in peace. She would not want you to put yourself in danger. And tomorrow you will have to go to the authorities. I can arrange for you to speak with Lord Barrington, if you prefer."

Afton dashed her tears away with the back of her hand. "I am in so deep now that I am afraid I will not be able to stop."

"Whatever do you mean? How deep are you, Afton?"

"Over my head. I have learned things I do not wish to know, and I am afraid of what it will bring. And I have done things.…" She sighed and turned away from the window. "But never mind. I will find a way out."

"Afton? Where were you so late last night?"

She waved away her aunt's concern. "At Auntie Hen's salon. With…" She sighed and shook her head. Aunt Grace would have to know. "With Rob McHugh."

Grace touched her forehead thoughtfully. "I see," she said. "Do you love him?"

She nodded and tears filled her eyes. "But last night he said that nothing could come of it."

Frown lines appeared at the corners of Grace's mouth. "That does not sound like McHugh. I find it difficult to believe that he would…and then turn his back on you. Is he still angry over Zoe's fortune-telling?"

"It was not like that, Aunt Grace. He has known for several days now who I am. At first he was angry, and I was afraid he would expose me, and then we agreed to help one another. We…I hoped I could take whatever he could give, but I find I cannot bear to be his second choice to Maeve.''

Grace began to pace, her head down and her finger still pressed to the center of her forehead. ''I do not care what the ton says, Afton. From my observations, I do not think McHugh adored his wife. I knew the lady Maeve, invited her to one of my Friday salons and did not find much admirable about her. She had a vile temper and an overdeveloped sense of refinement. She was a parvenue, you see, by virtue of her marriage to McHugh. And 'twas common knowledge that she had a lover, though she had sense enough to be discreet and keep the man's identity a secret. No one could ever guess who had the courage to wrong McHugh.''

Maeve? The legendary Maeve? Afton thought back to her conversations with McHugh. She could not recall him ever declaring his love or devotion, but neither could she recall him denying it. Was Aunt Grace right? And if so, why was McHugh so determined to keep her out of his life? Ah, yes. Madame Zoe. The cause of his family's deaths and of his imprisonment.

''Have you asked him if he is pining for Maeve? You are superior to her in every way, Afton. If Glenross cannot see that, he is blind.''

She nearly smiled at the sight of her aunt trying to look stern when she was not much older than Afton herself. ''I believe you might have a prejudice in my favor.''

Grace's housekeeper knocked politely on the open door. ''Beggin' your pardon, Mrs. Forbush, but this has just arrived for you. The lad said it was urgent.'' She placed an envelope on the breakfast table and left the room.

''It is from Barrington,'' Grace said as she broke the seal and opened the envelope. She scanned the lines and then sat heavily. ''Oh, Afton!''

She hurried to Grace's side and took the envelope from her hand. "What is it?" she asked.

"McHugh."

Heart racing, Afton unfolded the paper and read the few lines.

My dear Mrs. Forbush,

Please be advised that Robert McHugh, Lord Glenross, was arrested this morning for a series of murders, most recently that of Lord Kilgrew. He has been taken to Newgate to await trial.

If your niece was hoping to make an alliance with the McHughs, either with Glenross or his brother, I would advise against it. Please give her my condolences. I will come by later this afternoon to give you the details.

Yrs., Barrington

Afton refolded the paper and gave it back to her aunt, a plan forming in her mind. "Do you know Lord Auberville well enough to request him a favor, Aunt Grace?"

"Yes."

"Please ask him to arrange for me to visit McHugh at once," she said over her shoulder, already heading to her room to change. "It is urgent, and McHugh's future depends upon it. My future, as well."

The instructions for Afton's visit arrived within the hour. Since McHugh was considered extremely dangerous, he was being held in a private cell in the hold for the condemned below ground level. She had not been granted an interview in a visitor's room and Auberville had not been able to intervene. If she wanted to see McHugh, she was told, she would have to go to his cell. Auberville sent a small vial of strong scent and a list of items she would be able to take inside.

She was grateful she had begged Grace to wait in the coach. Afton hadn't been prepared for the search of her person by a prison matron. As humiliating as that had been, the vulgar comments about her being McHugh's high-priced "flash girl" were even worse. She was asked for money at every turn, but denied her request to buy McHugh better accommodations. She was told that he was considered the most dangerous prisoner in Newgate, and he was not to be allowed outside his cell, even if the prison was on fire.

Accompanied by two burly guards, she was led through a series of corridors and down a flight of stairs underground, the odors growing more vile with each step. Daylight never penetrated this part of the prison and darkness settled in on her despite the lanterns hung on hooks at intervals. She was guided through two locked doors into a large central room where the smell of excrement, unwashed bodies and fetid straw assailed her. Through the gloom, she could make out a row of cells lining the walls. The chill here went straight to the bone and she noted that vapor rose in the air from every breath. Bile rose to her throat and she quickly uncorked the vial Auberville had sent her. She held it beneath her nose while one of the guards used a long stick to drive the prisoners away from a row of cells.

"You! Stand back," the other guard ordered Afton. He went to the cell farthest from the door and banged on the iron bars. "Stand away, face against the wall," the man shouted over the howling of the prisoners, "or this'll be the last o' yer visitors." A minute later, he signaled Afton forward.

He unlocked the cell, pushed her through the door and locked it again so fast that she had no time to accustom herself to the gloom. There was no light in the cell, and now Afton understood why Lord Auberville had told her to bring candles and a tinderbox. "McHugh? Rob?" she called, her heart pounding so hard she could scarcely breathe. Silence stretched out for a long moment, then a slight scraping sound carried to her from an unseen corner. Dear Lord! Had they put her in the wrong cell? "Rob?" Her voice wavered. "Are you here?"

My God! Was that Afton's voice in this god-forsaken hellhole? He turned and stepped out of the corner and peered into the dimness of the cell. "Afton?"

He heard her quickly stifled gasp when he moved into the light. He must look like hell. He hadn't gone with the constables easily. It had taken six of them to subdue him, and he was certain he bore the marks. When they'd thrown him in the cell, they'd stripped him of everything but his shirt and trousers. Coat, jacket, vest and boots—all gone now, along with his watch and chain. He did not want her to see him this way. "Get out, Afton. *Guard!*"

"No," she exclaimed. She turned to Rob, with tears in her eyes. "I hate seeing you here, but not enough to go." She pulled her cloak off and draped it around his shoulders. "Where are your clothes? Your coat and boots?"

"Guards took them," he told her. "I am lucky to have been stripped of nothing more."

"I shall make them give them back," she said indignantly.

He could not withhold a cynical laugh. "They will demand money, and then steal them again tomorrow. Do not waste your time, Afton."

She reached up and touched his forehead. "How can anyone sweat in this frigid cesspit? Are you ill?"

"It's this place," he admitted, stepping back from her touch. He couldn't deal with that now. Maybe never. "I cannot tolerate confinement."

Her face paled and he knew she was remembering his

reaction to the closet beneath the stairs. She reached out again but he stepped away. Slowly, she held out the smaller of the two paper-wrapped bundles she had brought. "Lord Auberville said you would need these things."

He pulled the paper away. Candles. Flint. Light. "Thank God." He hated the dark almost as much as he hated confinement. He squatted near the wall and struck a tinder to the wick of one candle. The flame wavered, then burned brightly.

As the dark corners of the cell came into focus, Afton gasped. He glanced around, seeing his surroundings through her eyes.

Not much to see, he thought, only a pile of putrid straw in one corner, a slop bucket in another and something foul growing on the stone walls. The cell was long and narrow, no more than five feet wide and nine feet deep, meant to contain four or five men. Ah, but as a dangerous prisoner with a record of daring escapes, he ranked a private cell. Luxurious accommodations indeed, when compared to the Dey's dungeon.

Rob turned to look at her—so beautiful, so fresh and clean, so treacherous. His betrayer. At this moment, he didn't care if she'd told the authorities where to find him. He would face the hangman with a smile if he could have her just once more, hear her sighing his name. But not here. He could not defile her with this filth and corruption, and with the guard looking on.

She clutched her skirts away from the slime on the stone floor and asked, "How did they find you? You did not go back to your hotel, did you? Oh, I knew I should have stayed!"

Was she playing coy? "I left you a note, Afton."

She frowned. "I have not been back to the salon since last night."

"How did you learn I had been arrested?"

"Lord Barrington has been appointed to Lord Kilgrew's post. He sent a message to Aunt Grace this morning. But how did they know where to find you? Who knew where you were?"

He hesitated, then stated, "Doogie knew. And you."

"Me? I did not know where you were, McHugh. You would not tell me."

"It was in the note," he said.

She shook her head as if to deny his silent accusation.

Did she expect him to believe her? *Could* he believe her? God in heaven! He did not want to believe either alternative. "It was not my own brother, Afton," he said. "I've told you before that Doogie is not capable of murder. He would not set me up to hang."

"Nor would I! There must be someone else." She looked so wide-eyed and earnest that he wanted to believe her. But who else had known where to find him? She was his betrayer, or Doogie was.

"Then why did you come?"

She stepped toward him as if closing the distance between them would make him believe her. "Lord Barrington is calling on Grace later this afternoon. I wanted you to know that there is no need to protect me. I am going to tell him—"

"No." Rob coughed, the damp and chill slowly, insidiously, taking their toll. "Tell him nothing, Afton."

"But I was with you when Lord Kilgrew was murdered. I will tell them that we watched someone go in and out of Lord Kilgrew's home, and that he threw a bloody cravat off Westminster Bridge. When I testify to that, they will have to release you."

"A bloody cravat with my initials on it?" He laughed. He was not about to let her sacrifice herself for nothing. "They'd never believe it. No, Afton. I forbid it! It isn't just Kilgrew. They've charged me with the other murders, too. Most recently, Fengrove's."

"But they do not have evidence."

He pulled her cloak off and returned it to her before it became as lice infested as the straw in the corner. "The raven buttons, Afton. Livingston, Fengrove, the others. The only murder they don't know about is Madame Zoe, because you found her and covered it up. I took the button away from Eloise's house, but they still charged me with her death."

"You cannot expect me to do nothing while you sit in here! Even if I didn't know what this does to you, Rob. Even if I couldn't see it in your eyes."

He needed to make her understand what she was risking. "I see. Then you will tell him that Madame Zoe was your aunt, and that she was murdered, too, and you have been hiding that from the authorities for your own purposes? And that after Eloise Enright was murdered, you surrendered your virginity to me? And that when Kilgrew was murdered, we were cavorting through London, and later I was naked in your salon? None of it can remain confidential, Afton. If you are able to secure my release with this information, it will be discussed over brandy and cigars in every club in London. If I am held for trial, you will be called to testify, and all of London will become privy to your deepest secrets through the *Times*. How will that affect Dianthe and Bennett? Is that what you want for them?"

She shook her head, looking up at him in desperation.

Those startling aqua eyes swam with tears and he understood the depth of her dilemma. Her duty to her family was all she had lived for these past years, but her tender conscience balked at remaining silent when he was accused of crimes she knew he had not committed. He would not have his freedom at the cost of her pride and the future of her family. "I forbid it, Afton. Promise me."

She looked away, and something in the shift of her shoulders told him she had abandoned the fight. She held out the other package.

He took it, removed the paper and looked reverently at the bread and cheese. "Food fit for the gods," he sighed.

Two luminous tears rolled down her cheeks. God, for one last embrace! How he longed to make love to her and tell her how deeply he loved her. Had she been guilty of it, he'd have forgiven her anything—from Zoe's fortune to giving away his whereabouts. But it was the future that mattered now. He was a realist, and he knew that he was as good as convicted. He would probably hang, and he did not want her wasting her life mourning him. He would give her the only gift he could, though it tore at his heart.

"Go, Afton," he said, holding his hands at his sides so he would not pull her into his arms. "And do not come here again. I do not want to see you." He banged on the iron bars and signaled to the waiting guard that the visit was over.

Afton paced the small parlor worrying her dilemma from every direction while she waited for Dianthe and Grace to come down to tea. Honor McHugh's demand to keep her silence? Or expose everything—all the details of Auntie Hen's murder, her masquerading as a fortune-teller, her indiscretion with the McHugh? And he was right—there would be no way to keep it secret. They would become fodder for London gossipmongers. Dianthe would be anathema to the ton, and Bennett would be shunned by the same people who had hosted him for the holiday and played cricket with him at school.

She did not mind losing everything, but to watch Dianthe and Bennett suffer for her actions was intolerable. They would be worse off than if she and Auntie Hen had stayed in the country doing needlepoint while taxes and runaway expenses ate what was left. Her choices, then, were between her duty to her family and all she and Aunt Henrietta had worked so hard to achieve, honoring McHugh's request, or laying bare her sins in exchange for McHugh's freedom. Perhaps his life.

She pictured him again as he'd been in that tiny cell, shivering with the cold and the demons of his past, and she knew she could not leave him there. Though everything in her screamed to protect her family, she said a silent prayer and set her course.

"I am so excited about the masquerade ball tonight. What a delightful way to greet the New Year," Dianthe chattered as she and Grace entered the room.

Afton turned from the window and committed her sister's happy face to memory. She would not be seeing much happiness in the near future.

"Have you seen my costume, Binky? I am going to be Queen Elizabeth, complete with ruffled collar and coronet. What are you going to dress as?"

"I...I forgot the masquerade was tonight, Dianthe. I have a headache. I do not think I'll go."

"You must! Sir Martin vowed he would not leave until you dance with him."

How surprising, in view of her rejection. "When did he say that?"

"This morning when Grace and I took a turn about Hyde Park. He stopped us and we had a nice little chat. I think he is still sweet on you."

"That will end soon enough," she said. "When he finds out what I've done...."

"Oh, I am certain it is nothing he would not forgive you for, Binky. He has always been most attentive...well, mostly since Lord Glenross began paying attention to you."

Grace sighed and began pouring tea into three cups. "That's enough teasing, Dianthe. Afton? Is there something you wanted to say?"

The words had been building inside her since Dianthe had arrived in London, and they spilled out now in a rush. "Auntie Hen is dead."

Dianthe's cup rattled in the saucer when Grace handed it to her, and she placed it carefully on the tea table. She composed herself admirably and folded her hands in her lap. "Pardon me?"

"Auntie Hen was killed the day before you arrived in London."

"In Greece, or on her way home?"

"In London. In her fortune-telling salon. She was never a tour guide, Dianthe. We only told you that to spare your pride. We did not want you to know how we were able to afford all the extras so that you could have a London season, nor did we want Bennett to know where his tuition at Eton came from."

There was a long silence and Afton could see that Dianthe was attempting to take a firm grip on her grief. What mettle the girl had! Afton had not given her sister enough credit.

"I recall the gypsy who taught us all to read the cards, Binky. She used to laugh as if she knew something we didn't. When you told her you didn't believe in magic, she promised you would one day. I always thought it great fun when Auntie Hen read my cards. I am not surprised that she could make a living at it. And, Binky, I understand why you might not want me to know, but I wish I had. I could have helped. And I would never have spent as much on gowns and such. What puzzles me is why you did not tell me she was dead."

"There are a dozen reasons. We had worked so hard to get to this point, and I knew you would go into mourning and withdraw from the season if you learned that she had been murdered."

"*M-murdered?*" Dianthe's hand went to her throat.

"When you said 'killed' I thought you meant in an accident. But murdered? Oh! Who would do such a thing?"

"We do not know. That is why I have been posing as her. To find out."

"Posing? Posing as Auntie Hen?" Dianthe blinked.

"As Madame Zoe," Afton confessed.

"*You* are Madame Zoe? The infamous fortune-teller?" She nodded. "And Auntie Hen before me."

"Heavens above! You must tell the authorities at once," she said.

"I intend to—within the hour, beginning with Lord Barrington. But I wanted to tell you first." She glanced at Grace for support, and she was not disappointed. Their aunt gave her a gentle nod of approval and encouragement.

"Poor Auntie Hen." Lacking a handkerchief, Dianthe wept into her napkin. "Oh, Binky, my heart is breaking."

"I know, Dianthe. I am sorry for it, but there is worse to come."

"Bennett? Oh! Say it is not Bennett!"

"No, Bennett truly is in Devonshire for the holidays. It is me, Di. I have...done things that will cause the family shame. There is scandal in the offing. You and Bennett and—" she met Grace's patient gaze "—and Aunt Grace will suffer for my bad behavior."

"I am certain you overexaggerate, Binky. I know you. I know you could never have done anything—"

"I have been intimate with Robert McHugh."

Dianthe's mouth dropped open and she sat back in her chair as if she'd been slapped. "He...he will marry you, of course?"

Afton shook her head. "He has been arrested for murder."

That left Dianthe speechless. Her mouth opened and closed several times, but she did not frame words.

"He did not murder anyone, Di, but he will hang if I do

not come forward. I was with him at Madame Zoe's salon when Lord Kilgrew was murdered. So, of course, I must tell the authorities, regardless of the personal consequences.''

Grace smiled. ''You are very brave, Afton. I admire your integrity.''

''The Lovejoys will be a laughingstock,'' Dianthe whispered, more to herself than to anyone else. She looked up at Afton, her china-blue eyes round with wonder. ''Well, at least the ton will not soon forget us.''

Absurdly, Afton gave a choked laugh and then Dianthe began giggling through her tears.

''Is this a joke you can share?'' Lord Barrington asked from the doorway.

Within three minutes, Afton had told him the details of Auntie Hen's death and the full sum of her indiscretions with McHugh.

''And he forbade you to tell me, eh?'' he asked. ''Just like him. I vow, the man is suicidal.'' He heaved a deep sigh and slapped his thighs as he made to stand. ''Still, Miss Lovejoy, this changes nothing. You were not with him at the time of every murder, were you? I shall keep your little secret. No sense in disgracing the family for no reason. There is more than enough evidence that he committed the others.''

''Fabricated evidence, sir. Does it not seem odd to you that a man with McHugh's experience would be careless enough to leave a button or some other personal item at every scene?''

''Could be his signature. Like a calling card. When we find a multiple murderer, we often find similar details at all the scenes. What was left at the scene of your aunt's murder?''

''His raven stickpin,'' she admitted. Then she recalled that McHugh had come to the salon after Lady Enright's murder, and he had shown her the button he had found there.

He had removed the evidence. If the authorities had charged him with her death, they must have another reason, "What did you find at Lady Enright's house that implicated McHugh?"

"He let himself into her house with his lock picks. Left them on the foyer table and must have forgot them there when the deed was done."

"What are lock picks?" Afton asked. Sir Martin had once told her that McHugh could pick any lock known to man.

"Angled implements you insert in a lock and manipulate to open doors, padlocks and the like. McHugh was expert at it."

"Lock picks?" Dianthe asked. She frowned as if trying to remember something. "Ah, then that is what they were."

"What were, m'dear?" Lord Barrington asked.

"Sir Martin had some," she said, sipping her tea. "They must not be uncommon."

Afton's heart stilled to a slow thump. "Sir Martin?"

"We were at Tansy Welch's party the other night, and he dropped them from his jacket pocket when he checked his watch for the time. He had an appointment, he said."

"What night?" Afton and Lord Barrington asked at once. Dianthe turned to their aunt. "Aunt Grace?"

"Tansy's party was Saturday. The day after Christmas."

Lord Barrington glanced at Afton. They both knew what that meant. It was the day Lady Enright was killed. Afton pressed the momentary advantage. "There, you see. Lock picks are not McHugh's exclusive provenance. Sir Martin could just as easily have been the killer. I think, my lord, that McHugh is being framed for murders he did not commit."

"Why?"

God forgive her, she would not mention Douglas. McHugh was so certain his brother could not have done it that she had to believe him. "I do not know. Perhaps a better question would be 'why would McHugh murder people he did not know, or those against whom he bore no ill will?'"

"Madness. The Dey's torture unhinged him—"

"Nonsense! He is as sane as you, my lord. You must realize that some of the murders occurred while he was still in government custody. Are you charging him with those murders as well?"

Lord Barrington flushed. "He was not locked in, and he was allowed to sleep with his window open. Helped with the nightmares, he said."

"Was he well enough to go about London committing murders?"

He narrowed his eyes. "What are you saying?"

"That if he did not murder Lord Kilgrew or even one other person where a raven button was found, then it stands to reason that he did not kill any of them. Perhaps you should look elsewhere. Other men had means. Look at the lock picks. Sir Martin also had some."

"Christ's blood!" Lord Barrington cursed.

"Release him, my lord. I am prepared to testify on his behalf in any court, in front of any assemblage."

"I shall see what I can do," he conceded.

"Today," she insisted.

"Here, now! That's a bit presumptuous."

"Ronald," Grace purred, "as a favor to me?"

The man sighed in defeat but his eyes held a new respect. "You're a brave young woman, my dear, as well as a stubborn one," he said to Afton. "For you, and for your aunt—" his gaze lingered on Grace "—I'll move mountains."

Chapter Twenty

After warning Dianthe to stay in plain view of Grace and the ballroom and to be especially careful of Douglas McHugh and Sir Martin Seymour, Afton sent her off to the masquerade ball at Reginald Hunter's manor house. Lord Barrington had promised to send word as soon as McHugh was released, and Afton decided to wait at home for the news. McHugh wouldn't come to her. He'd said he did not want to see her again.

She paced near the front window, waiting for a messenger or Lord Barrington himself. Finally frustrated, she wrote a quick letter to Bennett, warning him of the impeding scandal, then to his headmaster at Eton withdrawing him from classes and arranging to collect his trappings before the term reconvened. Bennett's pride would suffer greatly if he had to face his friends once they knew that his sister had…

Afton addressed the letters and resumed her pacing. The thought of Dianthe and Bennett suffering for her heedless actions, facing ridicule and ostracism on her account, brought tears to her eyes. How, in trying to protect and preserve the family, had she gone so terribly wrong? By this time next week, the Lovejoys would be back in Little Upton with their tails between their legs, returning to London only if Afton was called upon to testify as to McHugh's whereabouts. The future was too dismal to contemplate.

Her stomach knotted when she thought of Rob spending the night in that squalid cell in Newgate, but she abandoned hope that he would be released tonight. Surely word would have come by now. She needed to know he was free and safe, even though he would be angry with her for ignoring his demand that she keep her silence. And that was likely the least of it.

His faith in his brother was such that he believed she herself had betrayed his whereabouts to Lord Barrington. And why not? Was she not the conniving fraud he accused her of being—bilking the ton of their money? How would he punish her for *that?* she wondered.

A clock in some distant room chimed the hour of nine. Heavens! Dianthe and Grace had been gone only half an hour and it felt like half a day. Afton threw her hands up in disgust and headed for the door. There was no profit to be had from berating herself or pacing a path in Grace's expensive Turkish carpet. She may as well go to Zoe's salon and destroy the little appointment book and all the notes she had made in order to insure her clients' confidentiality. Then she would finish packing up. Between Auntie Hen's effects and Bennett's things, they would have a full coach back to Wiltshire.

McHugh strode toward Bloomsbury and Grace Forbush's home wondering how he could want to damn Afton and bless her at the same time. Amazingly, she had managed to secure his release, but at her own expense, though Barrington had been clear that he was being released only—not exonerated. If one more piece of evidence against him surfaced, he would be back in Newgate by dawn. Barrington had also told him who had informed the watch where to find him. Rob hadn't been surprised.

After telling Barrington that he would inform Afton of his release, he'd gone to his hotel, tossed his clothes in the fireplace, bathed with a strong lye soap and shaved. Decently dressed again, he found his old clan dirk and slipped it in his boot. His midshipman's dagger would turn up eventually, probably in someone's back.

He stopped to gaze up at the stars and breathe deeply of the warm wind blowing in from the southwest, turning the snow to slush. For one brief moment, everything was clear and uncomplicated. He was free again. Afton would be waiting.

Then reality returned. There was still much to be done—a killer to be caught and a woman to be wed.

If there was any advantage to his imprisonment in Newgate, it was that he'd had no distractions and an excess of time to think. He knew now, with unshakable certainty, that what Afton guessed had been right. He hadn't known all the other victims. He was just another link in that chain, the same as Afton's Aunt Henrietta was. He hadn't known *her*—as Henrietta Lovejoy *or* Madame Zoe—and the only thing they'd had in common was Maeve.

So there was the common denominator! Maeve. Rob had asked himself whom he'd spurned, when he should have asked himself who had spurned *him*. Maeve. She was the connection. Once he'd realized that, everything else fell into place. But Maeve was dead. He'd stood at her grave, and Hamish's, in a small village outside Algiers just before the Dey's men had caught up to him. Ah, but there was someone else. Maeve's lover—Hamish's father. That hadn't been so difficult to figure out, after all.

Afton looked for the note Rob said he'd left, but it wasn't on the table. Her gaze swept the room, stopping on the floor near the fireplace. Had an errant draft from beneath the door blown the missive there? The troubling thought of who could have betrayed McHugh's whereabouts teased the back of her mind as she picked it up and glanced at the steady handwriting. If Douglas had hired the room and Rob had told only her, via this note, then who could have given him away?

With a sigh, she wrapped Auntie Hen's crystal orb in tissue paper and placed it in the wooden trunk at the foot of the bed. The small mantel clock was next, and she had to still the pendulum before wrapping it, too, in tissue. Eleven o'clock. Another hour and it would be the New Year. She prayed 1819 would bring better things than this year.

With a touch of melancholy she stripped the bedding, folded it and placed it on top of the breakable items as padding. The blanket still smelled of Rob, and would until she took it home and washed it. Or perhaps she would never wash it. She'd sleep with it every night, burying her face in his scent, remembering.

She shook off her brooding and returned to her task. Just a few items left and she'd be done—tarot cards, teacups and then the little client book waiting on the bare tabletop to be burned.

She heard footsteps on the stairs and her heart beat faster. The McHugh! She spun toward the door and crossed the room, expecting it to open. When a knock came instead, she realized that the guards must have taken his key along with his coat and jacket. "McHugh," she said as she threw the bolt and opened the door.

But it was not him.

"Sorry to disappoint you, Miss Lovejoy. Wish I *were* the McHugh. He seems to have all the luck with beautiful women. But then...I'd be a murdering bastard, wouldn't I?"

She did her best to hide her confusion. "Sir Martin. I thought...that is, I expected—" She shut her mouth before she could get into more trouble.

"Quite all right, dear girl. I've known for some time. Mind if I come in?"

Yes, she did, but he was already in, doffing his hat and pulling off his gloves.

"I couldn't let the year end without bidding adieu to you as well, my dear. When I saw Miss Dianthe and your aunt arrive at the masquerade without you, I suspected where you would be. Thought I'd come and share a 'cup o' kindness for auld lang syne,' as Robert Burns says. Have any whiskey?"

"I—"

"Of course you do. Must keep it on hand for the McHugh, eh?"

He knew? To hide her confusion, she turned toward the cupboard, trying to think if she had any whiskey. She knew that was a mistake when she heard the door close and a little click as the bolt was thrown. An icy chill crept up her spine.

When she turned again, he was standing by the table, lifting the tarot deck. "Ever read your own cards, m'dear?"

"No, Sir Martin. 'Tis all nonsense, you know."

"Aye, I know." He dropped the cards on the table and looked up at her, a relaxed smile on his face. "But damn amusing nonsense. I was laughing so hard over the Bebe Barlow affair, I thought I'd have a stroke. McHugh was fit to be tied."

"You knew…back then?"

"I've known for months."

"Months?" *Then he'd known even before Auntie Hen was killed?* "How did you find out?"

"Simple, really. 'Twasn't too difficult to discover Madame Zoe's salon. I only had to find someone who had an appointment with her, then follow them."

"But why?"

The frozen smile on Sir Martin's face was all the more

frightening for its lack of sincerity, as if he were only maintaining it for the sake of civility. Instinct warned her not to provoke him. If what she had begun to suspect was true, she would need her wits about her. "Where's that whiskey, Miss Lovejoy?"

She opened the small cupboard, removed the bottle of port she'd brought for McHugh and poured two teacups half-full. Taking one to Sir Martin, along with the bottle, she affected an air of relaxed unconcern.

"If you knew, Sir Martin, why did you not tell me sooner?"

"Because, Miss Lovejoy, I still hoped your good sense would overrule your passions. I thought I could win the whole thing if you just married me."

"Whole thing?" she queried, making a pretense of drinking.

"McHugh," he replied, as if that explained everything.

"You wanted me because the McHugh wanted me?"

"He always took what I wanted. Why shouldn't I take something he wanted?"

"What did you want, Sir Martin?"

"Maeve. Little Maeve MacGuire. From the time she'd kick up her skirts to come running after us, she held my heart."

"But she loved Rob McHugh," Afton finished. She could easily understand the appeal a dark-haired, larger-than-life adventurer would hold for an impressionable young girl. Hadn't she herself fallen victim to it?

"Loved him? Nay. She loved me. But the old Lord Glenross and Liam MacGuire formed a betrothal before their bairns were out of the cradle. Despite that she was untitled and he could have looked higher, their lands adjoined, you see," he snarled, "and their fathers were comrades from the Colonial War. Liam saved the old lord's life, and this was old McHugh's way of paying the debt."

Afton frowned. Maeve had loved Sir Martin? No, he must have imagined it. Was he delusional? "But you said theirs was a love match. That McHugh was devoted to her."

Sir Martin laughed and lifted his teacup. After a deep drink, he refilled his cup and looked up at her. "Aye, that's what I said. I was rather proud of that fabrication. I thought it would discourage you from growing closer to him."

She recalled the veiled conversations and shook her head. "And his inability to…"

He laughed. "Nice touch, eh? That was before I found you in the closet together and realized that you must know the truth. I tried to warn you away, though."

"He was not devoted to Maeve?"

Sir Martin shook his head. "He was not cruel, unless indifference is cruelty, but he did not love her. Even when she bore another man's bairn as the Glenross heir, he did not divorce her. He accepted the fault as his for not winning her loyalty. And all she could see was that he did not care enough to avenge his honor."

Afton was astonished. "Hamish was not…"

"Not McHugh's," Sir Martin confirmed. "He was a Seymour."

Her knees went weak and she sat in the chair opposite Sir Martin. Grace was right. Rob hadn't loved Maeve.

"I wanted to tell him, but Maeve would have none of it. She loved me, you see, and she was afraid McHugh would kill me. She did not want Hamish to go through life labeled a bastard. We prayed McHugh would not return from the first Algerian assignment, but he lived and came back to claim her and Hamish. Then Maeve got it into her head that if she went to her sister in Italy, I could follow and we could be together. Rent a villa in Tuscany and live as husband and wife."

"This…this is appalling," Afton whispered. And yet a part of her could understand. She could live with McHugh's love, or even his hatred, but she was not certain she could bear his indifference.

"Appalling? We loved each other, Miss Lovejoy. Do you not know what that is like?"

She did. It was exalting and painful at the same time. It was soaring joy and plummeting depths. It was both irrational and the only thing that made sense in this world. Yes, she had an inkling what that was like.

"But she and Hamish never arrived in Rome. The damn Barbary pirates boarded her ship and took everyone hostage. McHugh raised heaven and hell to get them back, but when the Dey found out they were his, there was no ransom high enough. And now…" Sir Martin paused to finish the contents of his cup and pour another "…now they are dead. And someone has to pay for that, Miss Lovejoy."

"It was you. You found the note he left me last night. You told the constable where to find him."

He nodded. "Easy enough, and even got Barrington's thanks."

"How did you get in here?" But she already knew the answer to that question.

"McHugh is not the only one who knows how to pick locks, Miss Lovejoy. I've come and gone here as I pleased. But after tonight, I will be finished."

"W-with what?"

"Anyone who had a part in it."

"But it was Maeve who demanded to go. Rob tried to dissuade her. He—"

Sir Martin's fist came down on the table with a bang and his eyes narrowed dangerously. "'Twas more than that, you silly little twit. She wouldn't have gone if it hadn't been for the others."

"What others?"

"The ones who made her feel like she didn't belong. The ones who hurt her feelings or wounded her pride. If not for them, she'd have been content to stay in London. Fengrove found out about us and insulted her, said she was a slut, and threatened to tell McHugh. Livingston tried to seduce her, caught her in a garden and claimed a kiss. He wanted more, but McHugh sent him packing when he came across them. Lady Enright, well, she encouraged Maeve to consult with Madame Zoe. And Madame Zoe told her that her destiny awaited her—but the blasted bitch didn't tell her that her destiny was death.''

Dear God! Afton had been fighting the reality, but it was true. Sir Martin *had* to be the man who had murdered so many innocent people. That he was admitting it to her now could only mean one thing—she was next. She glanced quickly at the bellpull beside the fireplace. Was there anyone in the dress shop to hear? If she could distract him, keep him talking, perhaps she could reach it, or the little knife in the pocket of her cloak by the door.

She stood and moved toward the fireplace as if she were going to put more wood on the hearth. ''But you haven't explained Lord Kilgrew. What did he do to Maeve?''

''Refused to send another mission into Algiers. Worse, when McHugh tried to go himself, Kilgrew stalled him. In the end, McHugh went without sanction. I was glad when I heard he'd been captured. Who knew the Dey wanted to play with him? He should have killed McHugh on the spot. But never mind. It all works out better this way.''

She had to stall him, keep him talking. ''What way?''

''Why, with him taking the blame. He murdered Maeve the day he put her on that ship bound for Italy. And now he'll hang for killing you, too.''

Afton struggled to keep her voice steady. She was almost to the bellpull. ''Me? What have I done, Sir Martin? I did not even know Maeve.''

''Aye, but you chose the McHugh. I gave you every reason not to. I even asked you to marry me. That would have been sweet, having you to myself. How fitting that I would have the only thing McHugh ever cared about, when he took the only thing I ever wanted.''

One too many mistakes, Zoe. You could have had it all. Fear raised chill bumps on Afton's arms. He meant to kill her, and she knew it was not the first time he had attempted it. Standing to the side of the fireplace, she turned to face him, her hands clasped behind her. She groped for the bell rope, praying he would not notice.

''You assume the McHugh wants me, Sir Martin. I have seen no evidence that he would have a moment's discomfort if I should live or die.''

Seymour laughed, and for the first time, Afton noted an edge of dementia in the sound. ''Really, Miss Lovejoy, you are not a very good liar. Did you think I didn't notice the way he watches you when you aren't looking? The way he smiles when you smile? He's smitten. Anyone with eyes would agree.''

''If that were true, Sir Martin, he would not have told me he never wanted to see me again.''

''Hmm. Very well. At the risk of vulgarity, I stood outside the door last night. I heard you moaning and urging him on. You were so engrossed in what you were doing that neither of you noticed when I picked the lock to see for myself.''

Afton burned with outrage. He had violated her privacy and sullied the beauty of that moment. How dare he intrude?

''You were wrapped around him like some wanton hussy from the docks. Not a lady at all. No, just a common whore.''

Her fingers found the cord behind her. She pulled once, then twice. A faint tinkle sounded below them and Afton prayed he would not notice. Alas, he cocked his head to one side.

''What was that?''

"What?" she replied, hoping he would keep talking rather than focus on her.

He shrugged and then returned to his denunciation. "But after seeing you like that, I decided to change my plans. Aye. Instead of merely killing you, I would have you first. That would be fitting payment for his taking Maeve."

"But it is too late for that, Sir Martin. Rob is in gaol. He cannot be blamed for my death, because he is locked up and under guard." She tugged the little cord behind her again as he began his reply, hoping his voice would mask the sound.

"Then you haven't heard? No, of course not. The McHugh was released more than an hour ago. When they find your body, m'dear…" He stood and slipped his hand into his jacket to withdraw a wicked-looking dagger already stained with blood. Firelight glinted off the edge of the blade. "McHugh's midshipman's dagger will be artfully displayed. Haven't decided just how, yet, but I trust it will come to me in the process." With a demented smile, he started for her.

How could things have gone so wrong so quickly? Rob cursed under his breath and called to the driver. "Faster!"

The black coach skidded on the ice as it rounded the narrow corner, the rear wheel slamming against the bricks of the opposite building.

"He's bloody well going as fast as he can," Lord Barrington shouted over the clatter of the wheels. "Any faster and we'll be smeared on the cobbles."

Rob didn't bother with a reply. He knew Barrington thought he was crazed, but that didn't matter now. Nothing mattered but finding Afton.

Upon his arrival at the Forbush mansion, Grace's man-servant had told him the ladies had gone to the masquerade ball hosted by Reginald Hunter, Lady Sarah's brother. But when he'd arrived at the masquerade, he'd found only Grace and Dianthe. They swore they had left Afton at home, waiting for word from Lord Barrington.

She could only have gone one place—the fortune-telling salon. He'd seized Lord Barrington's arm on the way out Hunter's door and pressed him into service. Once they found Afton and Rob was satisfied that she was safe, they would go after Seymour. And Rob needed a witness so he could not be charged with murdering the son of a bitch when they found him.

His heart grew cold at the thought. He wished now that he had gone to Afton directly from Newgate, but he hadn't wanted her to see him filthy and torn again. He'd wasted precious time making himself presentable and walking to Bloomsbury to clear his head and form his declaration. The thought of his missing dagger caused a churning in his gut. What mayhem might be planned for that? If his delay cost Afton her life, how would he ever forgive himself?

He had spent years torturing himself because he hadn't loved Maeve, and feared that lack was some deficiency in him. And now he loved Afton with every breath he took and still tortured himself over the tears he had caused her, the fear he had deliberately inspired, and the threats he'd made when he'd still thought she was Madame Zoe. He wanted to make it up to her. Please, God, let him make it up to her.

The coach drew up in front of La Meilleure Robe and Rob jumped down. Barrington followed, grumbling under his breath. As Rob paid the driver, he caught the sound of a bell ringing and then falling silent from the depths of the dress shop. His pulse raced and apprehension spurred him up the stairs, with Barrington catching his urgency.

He tried the door but it was locked. The crash of a chair overturning and the thumping of a scuffle drove him wild with anxiety. "Afton?"

The key! He didn't have the damn key! A muffled screech cut short drove him to throw his shoulder into the door. "Afton!" he shouted, banging on the solid panel. "Afton, answer me!"

Barrington arrived in turn and shouted imperiously, "Open up, in the name of the king!"

Rob would have laughed if the situation had not been so dire. He was afraid to waste precious time breaking into the dress shop downstairs and searching for the hidden door. If he couldn't find it—if he could not get to Afton... Instead, he applied his shoulder to the portal again and was rewarded with the creak of stressed wood. Again and again he pounded the door, shouting all the while.

The struggle inside grew louder as if edging closer. He could hear Afton gasping and Sir Martin's cursing. "Give it up, Seymour. It's too late. You can't get away with it," he shouted.

There was a clatter, a pause and then a high-pitched scream. Desperation took hold and Rob renewed his attack on the door. Wood splintered and the hinges gave way enough to free the bolt from its catch. The door swung inward two feet before landing against something solid. He pushed again and forced enough of an opening to fit his shoulder through and gain entry.

He stumbled over a broken chair blocking the door and took in the torn bellpull lying uselessly, and then Afton, crumpled against the wall, unconscious, her stomach stained with fresh blood. Seymour stood over her, panting, one hand concealed by his jacket.

Broken china ground under Rob's feet as he started for them. Heart in his throat, he hurried to her side, yelling at Barrington to secure Seymour.

Barrington crashed through the door after him and shouted a warning just as Seymour slashed downward with

Rob's midshipman's dagger. Rob threw himself over Afton, exposing his back to the blade.

The thunder of a pistol shot rang out and Seymour screamed, clutching his left shoulder as the dagger clattered to the floor. Rob looked up, still gripping Afton to his chest. A stranger wearing a dressing gown stood framed by the closet door, a smoking pistol in his hand.

Barrington cursed. "Who the hell are you?" he asked the stranger.

"Francis Renquist," the man replied, tucking the pistol into the sash of his robe.

"Where did you come from?" Barrington asked.

"I heard the bell." Renquist crossed the room in long strides and twisted Seymour's hands behind his back, ignoring his cries of pain. "Came up the back stairs. Anyone have some rope?"

Rob nodded toward the now useless bellpull on the hearth. Afton moaned and stirred in his arms, disorientation showing in her eyes as she glanced at the chaos around them.

Renquist grinned. "Good use for it, eh? You all right, Miss Lovejoy?" he asked as he tightened the bell rope around Seymour's hands.

Afton hesitated and then nodded. Rob looked down at her midriff and his anxiety grew again. "Let me see, Afton."

"Er, well, I ought to get Seymour to a surgeon, eh? You'll see to Miss Lovejoy, McHugh?"

"Do you need a doctor, Miss Lovejoy?" Renquist asked.

She glanced down at her gown and shook her head. "It is Sir Martin's blood. If he had not meant to rape me first, I would not have been able to reach it." She unclenched her fist and dropped her little knife into Rob's hand.

His concern eased and a blinding fury replaced it. He turned to Barrington over his shoulder. "Get him out of my sight before I kill the bastard."

Seymour was muttering incomprehensively, his bound hands behind him. "All done...all gone...you can rest now, Maeve...."

Barrington spun him around and pushed him toward the door. "Come to my office tomorrow, McHugh, and we'll wrap this up. Good God, the man's quite mad."

"Miss Lovejoy?" Mr. Renquist asked, kneeling beside her with a wary glance at Rob. "Shall I take you home?"

Afton shook her head. "Thank you, Mr. Renquist, but McHugh will see me home. Marie will be waiting for you."

He nodded. "I am surprised she did not come running when she heard the shot. I had better go tell her you are safe. We'll talk tomorrow." He stood again and returned to the secret staircase. The closet door closed behind him with a soft click.

Rob brushed Afton's hair back from her cheeks and studied her face, searching for any sign that she was injured. When he'd seen the blood on her dress, he'd thought Seymour had stabbed her. He'd felt the sharp pain in his own stomach and a part of him dying with her. He couldn't lose her. He couldn't let her out of his sight again.

"Rob." She sighed and lifted her face toward his, closing her eyes, inviting a kiss.

Anger, frustration, anxiety and love churned in a confusing mixture. He knew he didn't dare accept that invitation or he'd take her here, on the floor in the midst of the wreckage, with the door hanging off its hinges. It was always that way with Afton—urgent, intense and uncontrolled. He needed a moment—time to compose himself and master his hunger for her.

Rob stood and lifted her to her feet. He turned the table and unbroken chair upright and retrieved the tarot deck and a small bound volume with handwritten notes. He placed them on the table and glanced up at her.

Afton seized the book and tossed it into the fire. "Auntie

Hen's notes," she explained, watching the pages curl and blacken. "Now everyone is safe."

Everyone but her. Scandal loomed on the horizon. Within two days there would not be a single resident of London who did not know the whole sordid story. Ah, but it was worth it. The killer had been caught, the McHugh had been acquitted and Aunt Henrietta had been avenged.

She heard shuffling and turned back to the table. Rob held the tarot deck and began turning cards up in a nonsensical pattern. "I see changes in your future, Miss Lovejoy," he said.

Thinking of the last time he had told her fortune, she nodded. She could only pray this one would not be so grim. "So do I, Lord Glenross."

"I see a change of residence," he continued.

"Little Upton," she agreed.

"No. No, it looks to be farther north. Heather. Mountains covered in pine and heather. Yes, I believe it is Scotland."

Scotland. Her heartbeat tripped over that word. "What am I doing there?"

He turned over three more cards. "Naked in bed, most times. Then…governess? Nanny? I see you surrounded by children."

She held back her smile, afraid she might be wrong. "How many?"

He turned over three more cards, then another three. He glanced up at her, his green eyes no longer icy, but sparkling with humor. "An even dozen?"

She went to the table and spread the cards apart, pretending to see what he saw. "Ah, then I'm opening a school for wayward Scots?"

"The most wayward Scots of all. McHughs, every one."

"Am I equal to the task, my lord?"

"You will have to be. Without you there would be no little McHughs. And no future for me."

She stepped closer, fitting easily within the circle of his arms. "The least you could do, my lord, is say it plainly."

"Damn it, Afton, I rehearsed a tender speech. But the truth is that I'm drowning in you. My every pore is saturated with you. My blood speeds you through my veins. I cannot draw breath without you. I cannot see a future without you in it. I...I love you. Marry me?"

She tilted her head back to look into his eyes, dark now with passion. Finally she recognized what it was that she had seen in his gaze that night in Aunt Grace's closet when the world had faded and she'd floated among stars, moons and suns. She'd seen *forever.* She'd been frightened of it then, shaken by the intensity, but now she welcomed it. She smiled. "If it is in the cards, how can I deny my destiny?"

He bowed the deck and sent the cards spraying upward. As they fell in a shower around them, he tightened his embrace and kissed her with a tender passion.

Epilogue

January 5, 1819

Sunlight filtered through the barren trees, spreading a timid warmth over the intimate scene as the minister read the funeral service from the *Book of Common Prayer*. Afton smiled, feeling Auntie Hen's presence. Dianthe and Bennett flanked her, holding her hands. The Wednesday League— Lady Annica, Charity, Lady Sarah and Aunt Grace—stood on the opposite side of the newly dug grave, reciting the prayers with the minister. Masses of pristine white roses covered the narrow coffin, which had been lowered into the grave.

At last Aunt Henrietta would rest in peace, mourned by those who loved her. Afton sighed deeply, a feeling of completion sweeping away the last of her anger and fear. Only love remained, because only love endured.

''Amen,'' they intoned as the minister finished the last prayer, commending Henrietta Lovejoy to her maker.

''Thank you,'' Afton whispered to the woman who had been more than a mother to them.

They turned to leave the cemetery and she caught a

glimpse of Rob McHugh, standing by the stone arch at the entry. She excused herself from the group and went to him.

"Why did you not join us?" she asked, taking his arm and falling into step behind the others.

"I couldn't be certain I'd be welcome. I said some harsh things about your aunt." His large warm hand covered hers where it rested on his sleeve. "Are you all right?"

She looked up at him and smiled. "Just curious. Where did you find so many roses in January?"

He grinned. "How do you know it was me?" Faced with her stern expression, he capitulated. "Several greenhouses, and I imposed upon a few friends with conservatories."

"It was the perfect gesture. Aunt Henrietta would have loved them."

"I hope you will not be mad at me for the next gesture."

She furrowed her brow. "What have you done?"

"I have written the headmaster at Eton, canceling Bennett's withdrawal. I paid his tuition through the end of his term."

Now she *was* annoyed. "McHugh, I will gladly face any scandal with you by my side, but my siblings are not so pragmatic. They will be humiliated when the uproar occurs. Bennett would rather be home in Little Upton where he will not be the object of jokes and taunts."

"I spoke with Barrington earlier this morning. He does not see why anyone has to know about Madame Zoe or your…little indiscretions."

She smiled. McHugh's uncharacteristic sensibility was really quite charming. "But I will have to testify—"

"Martin Seymour has been judged insane and committed to Bethlehem Hospital. There will be no trial, just a private hearing in chambers. Since he was caught red-handed, there is enough testimony to keep him locked up for the rest of his life without dragging Madame Zoe into it."

"Then there will be no scandal?"

"None." He grinned, clearly expecting her gratitude. "No trial, no gossip."

"Drats!"

"I beg your pardon?"

"I was hoping to become your wife in true McHugh fashion—high passions and low expectations."

He threw his head back and laughed heartily, startling the crows in the trees overhead and sending them skyward. It was a sound she had heard precious little of when he'd first come back from Algiers, but one growing daily dearer to her heart.

"Ye've a wicked sense of humor, Miss Lovejoy. That just might be my favorite thing about ye." He kissed the top of her head. "And you were right about magic, Afton—it does exist."

Happiness filled her heart. "How do you know?"

"Because you redeemed me from a life without laughter or passion. Because I found my own very real magic. You, Afton."

And when his mouth covered hers, Afton would have sworn that she could hear the laughter of that ancient gypsy from that distant summer. Oh, yes. She finally believed in magic.

* * * * *

Be sure to watch for Grace's romance,
coming only to Harlequin Historicals in 2005.